EVIDENCE

OF

MURDER

KnightGuard
Security
BOOK 2

Lila Ferrari

ACKNOWLEDGMENTS

A great big thank you to everyone who read my words, made suggestions, and gave me encouragement.

Special thanks go to the members of Space Coast Authors of Romance. The enthusiasm and knowledge this group has shared has been invaluable and an inspiration to me.

Extra special thanks goes to Ray Ferrari. You have been my rock and best friend. Your suggestions have made this book even better.

And thanks to Chris Kridler for editing my rough drafts and keeping my story on track.

Any errors, blunders, or inaccuracies made are all mine.

EVIDENCE OF MURDER

Courage, justice and redemption

A CURIOUS ACCOUNTANT,
A SELF-DOUBTING PROTECTOR,
A MURDERER WHO HAS NO PROBLEMS KILLING AGAIN.
CURIOSITY CAN KILL—SO THEY SAY.

Accountant Marlee Burns is curious and gutsy, qualities that lead her right into trouble. After accusing her CEO of embezzlement and witnessing him shoot her boss, she has no choice but to run. She wants to clear her name and get justice, but her troubled past and the killer's machinations mean the police won't be inclined to believe her. And before she can prove her innocence, she must avoid a ruthless murderer who is intent upon silencing her.

Wounded detective Ben Green couldn't save his girlfriend from getting killed. His confidence in his ability to protect is shot. He's heading to his friend's fishing camp to contemplate his next move—stay on the force, join KnightGuard Security or get out altogether. His peace of mind is shattered when sassy accountant Marlee stumbles into camp, invading his space and then his heart.

Will he, can he, protect Marlee from the monster intent upon killing her?

KNIGHT**GUARD** SECURITY

BOOK 3 OF KNIGHTGUARD SECURITY, *Evidence of Lies,* tells Pete and Julie's story. Look for a preview at the end of this book.

As always, reviews are nice. If you enjoy the book, please leave a review.

Follow me on:
  Twitter: @lsferrariwrites
  Facebook: @lilaferrariauthor
  Instagram: @lsferrariwrites
  Pinterest: @lsferrariwrites
  Goodreads: @lilaferrariwrites
  Bookbub: @lilaferrariwrites

For more information on books by Lila Ferrari, visit her website at www.lilaferrariwrites.com, where you can subscribe to her newsletter to get updates on releases, fun facts and enter giveaways.

KNIGHTGUARD SECURITY SERIES

EACH BOOK IN THE SERIES is a stand-alone and can be read in any order.

Evidence of Betrayal — Book 1 (Luke and Grace's story)

Evidence of Murder — Book 2 (Ben and Marlee's story)

Evidence of Lies — Book 3 (Pete and Julie's story)

Evidence of Deceit — Book 4 (Joe and Claire's story)

Evidence of Revenge — Book 5 (Sam and Mark's story)

Evidence of Secrets — Book 6 (Hank and Laura's story) - available soon

Evidence of Evil — Book 7 (Logan and Maddie's story) — available in 2022

For Ray,
Always

CHAPTER ONE

Robert Gilligan hummed along with the car radio after a long night and day of crazy, fantastic sex with the love of his life, Amber. They fucked like bunnies in heat on every surface of the fancy hotel room overlooking the ocean. He would have liked to continue all weekend, but Amber had to leave early to go home to change for "a thing." He hated "things," and women seemed to have a lot of those. However, it was a shower for her best friend, so here he was—satiated but frustrated. He could never get enough of Amber.

As he headed home, an accident on the highway detoured him through downtown Lakedale. Plenty of time to rehash the best weekend of his life so far.

Thinking about Amber got him hard again. *Damn.* Another cold shower and a date with his hand. Not the first time, not the last.

A honking horn brought him back to reality and the realization he was driving past the commercial area where his accounting firm, which was providing him with the lifestyle he always wanted, was located. So different from his childhood where new clothes and food were in short supply Not that anyone would ever know that part of his history.

His money now was all in offshore accounts. Knowing how to manipulate the books was the gift that kept on giving —to him. He'd planned ten years for this moment, and in a few more years, it would be him and Amber on an island wearing nothing at all unless they wanted to.

He saw lights on in the front office and frowned. The office was closed on the weekend. Did the cleaning people forget to turn them off?

The blinds were half-open, and someone was walking around. Robert slowed down for a closer look. Was that Jim? What the hell was Jim doing here on a Saturday night during their slow season when there was no reason for anyone to be here?

He turned his headlights off and pulled around to the backside of the building where security cameras didn't have a good angle. He parked here when he didn't want people to know when he came into the office to monitor accounts. Even though he could work at home, the office was more accessible. Just couldn't be too careful. How fortunate it was that his building was in a nearly deserted office park.

Now that he thought about it, Jim and that bitch Marlee Burns had been acting somewhat squirrelly lately.

Marlee asked him something about one of his accounts a while ago—the one from which he made personal withdrawals. What a laugh—personal withdrawals. She shouldn't know anything about that account, except she took a call from someone at their firm questioning a withdrawal when he was away from the office. She asked him about it. Him. As if he would ever tell her anything.

Would she have talked to Jim about it? He knew she didn't mention it to Amber or she would have told him, but then Marlee didn't tell Amber everything. Marlee was outspoken and nosy, and she wasn't one to let things go, even though he told her a couple of times that he would look into it. Furthermore, Jim was her boss, and rumor was they were dating, so maybe she did tell him. Stupid move. His future happiness was not going to be derailed by those two.

He got his gun from the glove box and tucked it behind his back. Gently closing his car door, he swiped at the sweat dripping down his forehead. The heat and humidity of Florida were a constant, even in the fall. He let himself in the back door and stopped when he heard murmuring. He inched closer. Jim was talking to a woman.

"Marlee, I think I found some discrepancies in this account. Figuring it out will take a minute. Would you mind getting us some coffee?"

"Sure thing."

Marlee. Of course, it was her. In his business, as always. Robert couldn't believe his ears. Damn if she wasn't the bane of his existence.

Footsteps moved away and toward the kitchen. Time to find out what the hell was going on. He snuck up behind Jim, who was looking intently at his computer and writing something down.

"What the hell are you doing?" Robert kept his voice low.

Jim jumped and turned, his eyes wide and afraid. He tried to cover up what he was looking at, but Robert saw one of his client accounts open, exposing all his little secrets.

Again, he asked, "What are you doing?"

"N-noth-nothing." Jim's eyes darted over to the computer. "Just had some work to catch up on."

"Liar." Robert pushed him aside and looked at the computer screen. "You have no right to look into any of my accounts."

Jim's eyes narrowed, and his chin came up defiantly. "I have every right if you're embezzling."

"You need to prove that."

"Oh, but I can." Jim got cocky. "I've been following the breadcrumbs for a while, and I'm going to the police with my evidence." He leaned back in his chair, folded his arms and smirked.

The blood rushed to Robert's face. "Calling the police isn't happening. I've worked too hard to get where I am. My future isn't going to be ruined by shit like you."

He grabbed Jim by the collar. "You son of a bitch, what do you have?"

Jim's body twitched as he struggled to get away. He gagged. "I have everything I need on a thumb drive that will send you to jail," he spat out.

"Not happening." Robert held on to Jim's collar and reached behind his back to pull out his gun.

Jim's eyes widened in disbelief. He twisted to get out of Robert's hold, but Robert held on tight. Jim gulped. It was the last thing he did before Robert pulled the trigger. Jim went down. Robert hadn't killed him. Yet. He needed that thumb drive.

A high-pitched scream assaulted his eardrums. Damn, he'd forgotten about Marlee.

He turned and saw her running out of the break room, throwing the coffee cups she was holding onto the floor, coffee splashing everywhere.

"Marlee," he yelled. "Come back here. It isn't what you think."

But she didn't turn back, just kept running. Robert started after her but tripped over Jim's prone body. Marlee was too fast. She got to her car and fishtailed out of the parking lot before he could get out the front door.

Damn it all to hell. What a way to finish a weekend of fucking. Getting fucked.

What to do? The better question was, what would that

stupid bitch do? Go to the police. Riiight. Like he hadn't mentioned so many times that his cousin was chief of police. Go home? Hopefully. Marlee rented the small renovated garage behind Amber's house. She also confided in Amber quite frequently. A bonus for him. Maybe tonight he would get lucky again.

He dialed Amber on the off chance she was still at home. She was and agreed to what he asked.

He hung up and walked back to deal with Jim and decide what to tell the police, if anything. He needed to be smart and think this through.

CHAPTER TWO

Marlee Burns couldn't believe the bad luck she was having. It started with her hearing Robert Gilligan, the CEO of her accounting firm, shoot Jim, her friend and boss. She wondered if Jim was dead but didn't stay around to check after she heard their angry voices and then the shot.

Robert chased her out of the building, yelling, "Come back. It isn't what you think!" and brandishing a gun. How stupid did Robert think she was? It was exactly what she thought.

She couldn't stop her body from trembling. Seeing Robert holding the gun was disturbing enough. Hearing the shot and seeing Jim on the floor—oh God. She ran and didn't even check to see if Jim was alive or dead. Not that she could have done anything to help.

This nightmare couldn't be real. On the drive over to her house, her thoughts were jumbled, but she had little time to think about what to do. Should she call the police? Yes. No. Yes. She pulled up her phone. Gah. No juice. No calling the police.

Calling the Lakedale police was dicey at best. Robert was always bragging about his cousin, who was the police chief. Would they believe her over Robert? Where could she go? She couldn't drive to her dad's. Robert knew where he and her grandma lived, and she could be putting them in danger. Staying at her house wasn't an option until this mess was sorted out. Robert could find her there, plus she didn't want to put her friend Amber in danger.

Finally, she reached her driveway. She glanced at Amber's house. Good, no lights. Amber wasn't home. She'd hurriedly thrown some clothes and food in her suitcase and ran out. Then the coup de grâce—as she drove out, someone shot out the side window of her car. She didn't think Robert could get there that fast, but apparently, she'd been wrong. Bad luck all the way.

She drove for two hours in the dark, nervously looking over her shoulder for blue and red flashing lights. She was relieved when she found the remote fishing camp with the "closed for renovations" sign. She drove down the gravel path lined with small cabins, their porch lights on, and stopped when she saw this cabin set back in the trees.

Pulling her car behind the cabin into some bushes, she had a devil of a time opening the car door. Being a city girl didn't help. The branches reached out like talons, snagged her hair and cut her arms and legs. And the bugs. She didn't want to think about what was lurking in the bushes. *And please, don't get me started on snakes.* Ugh.

She snuck up to the cabin's front door and tried to open it. Locked. Shit. Peeking in a window, she didn't see anyone or anything that showed signs of life. The cabin was empty. Good. First thing that went right for her tonight.

She walked around to the side of the cabin and attempted to push open a bedroom window. No dice. Stuck shut. Next? She was in luck. The kitchen window was unlocked and opened easily. She was able to pull herself up and over the sill, landing in the sink, the faucet poking in her stomach, making her gag—just great, a fitting end to the day. After disentangling herself from the faucet and climbing out of the sink, she unlocked the front door.

The trip back to find her car took a little time. She hadn't followed a path to the cabin, and now all the trees and bushes looked the same. But time was all she had at this point. After brushing every thorny shrub in the woods away from her body and missing her car once, she finally found it, got her suitcase, and plowed back through the bushes again. There was a lot of croaking from the frogs. The thought they were laughing at her crossed her mind. She shook her head. There were other more important things to think about than frogs laughing.

She walked into the bedroom and tried the bed. It was comfortable, and there were sheets on it. Score. She tried the electric switch but turned it off quickly. There was no way of knowing if there were people in the other cabins. It was better to stay in the dark. The little porch light gave her enough light to move around the cabin without tripping over anything. She undressed and lay down. Sleep evaded her for a long time. When she finally fell asleep, her dreams turned into nightmares— Robert waving the gun, Jim lying on the ground, lots of blood, death, gore. Ugh.

Shafts of sunlight through the window woke her early. Birds were chirping outside. She got up and walked into the kitchen, desperately needing caffeine. She unpacked the food she brought with her and placed it on the counter. No coffee. Damn. Nothing to do about it now. Peeking outside the front door, she didn't see anyone around. Maybe Sunday was a quiet day here in the country.

She hoped to relax and collect her thoughts. She spotted a lake in the distance and thought a walk down to the peaceful lake would distract her. She pulled out the one item her dad insisted she carry for self-defense, put on her sunglasses, and strolled down to the dock.

Sitting by the water lulled her into a nap. When she awoke, the sun was high in the sky. Yikes. It had to be around noon. Her stomach rumbled. When was the last time she'd eaten? Was it lunch yesterday? She couldn't remember. Jumping up, she walked back to the cabin and noticed a black truck parked in front. Robert? The owner? What to do?

She couldn't run because her things were strewn around in the bedroom, including her purse and her phone. And the car keys. The clothes she could leave and replace. Her life, she couldn't.

BEN GREEN ARRIVED at the fishing camp Sunday around noon and got out of his car. He stretched, trying hard not to pull any more stitches from the wound in his arm. Getting shot on the job was an inconvenient bitch. But not being able to save his date, Kimmie, was making him wonder where he was going with his life. That sniveling drug-addicted idiot grabbed Kimmie as she paid for her headache medicine and then used her as a hostage before shooting her dead for no reason and then injuring Ben.

He couldn't get Kimmie's pleading eyes out of his mind. Her surprise turned to terror as the asshole held a gun to her head while she was clutching the medicine box. That picture would never leave his mind. He couldn't draw a bead on the addict. His right arm was useless, and the gun shook in his left hand.

Kimmie was the same height as the asshole, and she froze. He tried to tell her to drop down to the floor with his eyes so he could take a shot at the junkie. But she didn't understand. He couldn't save her. Fortunately, the cashier pressed the alarm button, and the police arrived. Unfortunately, the scumbag shot Kimmie before an officer killed him.

Ben questioned his job choices. What could he have done differently? The guy didn't have to kill Kimmie. She was no threat to him. All she wanted was something for a headache, but the druggie was trying to rob the store. Drugs had addled his brain, and Kimmie was dead. Ben was so tired of liars, junkies, rapes, and crime in general.

His captain insisted he take time off to heal. It was a relief to get away from Black Pointe. Kimmie's death and his getting shot again took so much out of him—mentally and physically. At least, his job on the police force would be waiting unless he decided to hang up his badge and work for Samantha "Sam" Knight, who owned KnightGuard Security. The time off gave him time to think over his career choices.

At the moment, he was leaning toward going to work for her. Sam promised to go easy on him until he felt he was ready to take on more responsibility. There would be less stress and less shooting—at him.

Ben wiped his face with his hand. The sweat streaming down his neck was itchy. The exertion of driving was taking its toll. His shoulder ached, and he was tired. While it was cooler at the lake, the weather in Florida was still warm and humid.

Looking around the quiet fishing camp, Ben was glad he came. His friend and owner of the camp, Seth Bowman, told him it would be closed for two weeks. No one would be around except for some workers updating the lodge and a few cabins. Fine by him. He had enough to deal with right now without other people around. If he went to the coast, which was certainly closer, he would have to fight the hordes of people wanting to be by the water. Here he could unwind. Relax. Fish a little—no, a lot. Sounded good to him.

As he glanced at the gravel path leading to the cabin, Ben was overcome by a sense of calmness, something that he'd been missing in his life. The small, rustic cabin nestled in the trees, overlooking the serene lake he'd fished so many times, was just what he needed. A warm, soft wind was blowing, and Ben heard frogs croaking to their neighbors.

He ducked as a flash of black flew close to his head and into a tree screaming *caw, caw, caw*. Crows? No. Grackles. They were pests and everywhere in Florida. He remembered asking Seth about them. Even though Ben was a city boy, he loved nature.

It was a typical wood-shingled cabin. Ben stayed at the camp a couple of times with friends and knew the cabins included the basics—a screened front porch with rocking chairs, one bedroom, bath, a living room with a fireplace and a small kitchen.

Ben left his duffle bag and food in the truck and walked up the few wooden stairs to check it out. When he reached for the door to insert the key, he found it was slightly ajar.

Did Seth forget he was coming? Did he rent the cabin to someone else? Did the workmen forget to lock the door? Most importantly, did he need his gun? He'd left it under the seat in the truck, not expecting trouble. Better to have it than not.

He went back to his truck to retrieve it, clicked off the safety. Walking back to the cabin, he got into position and pushed the door open. "Hello?"

No answer.

He glanced around the living room—empty. Walked into the kitchen and saw an assortment of food spilling from a bag on the counter. Maybe Seth stopped by and dropped off the food? If so, he would have to thank him. Ben brought what he considered essential—cans of beans and some meat to grill, on the off chance he didn't catch any fish. He had coffee and of course, beer—everything he would need for the week. However, the counter held some cheese, snacks, peanut butter, yogurt, and bread. They were all things he would eat except for the yogurt.

He checked the bathroom. Empty.

He peered into the bedroom. It contained a comfy-looking chair, a small dresser, a side table, and a queen-size bed covered with a blue and white quilt. In the middle of the bed was an open suitcase with clothes strewn around. Whose clothes? He questioned again if he was in the wrong cabin. Weird.

He called out, "Hello? Anyone here?" No answer.

He walked out to check the number on the door. Yep. It was the right cabin. So, who was here? Seth did tell him he would be the only guest in the camp. Had whoever been here made a mistake, or had Seth? He stuffed his gun in the small of his back and strode back to the bedroom. He peered down at the mess on the bed. His mind went blank for a second before processing that he was looking at women's clothes, bras, and panties. Ben glanced around the small room. Nope, there wasn't another suitcase nor any men's clothes. He carefully pushed the clothes around, didn't see a purse or any identifying information, and started to stand up.

He sensed eyes on him—a whiff of perfume. A slight wind whispered behind his back. What was it?

He started to turn around. Then intense pain. His muscles tightened up. He fell face-down on the bed, unable to move. He heard another whoosh. More pain and then darkness.

WITH HER HEART in her throat and sweating profusely, Marlee quietly pushed open the front door and tiptoed in. A tall, very muscular man was in the bedroom going through her things. Yep. Bad luck.

Marlee didn't think twice about tasering the guy, then clunking him on the side of his head with a piece of wood from the fireplace for good measure while he was immobile. He went down like a cut tree in the forest. She hoped she only knocked him out and not killed him. She felt for a pulse. Faint but beating. Good.

She couldn't take any chances that Robert had him follow her. But she needed to find out who he was.

After finding some rope in the kitchen, Marlee struggled to get the big guy tied up to the chair. It was always good to know your enemy, Grandma once said. She hoped to get more information from him or at least let Robert know she wasn't going to say anything.

Then she panicked. The list of things she'd never done, let alone thought about, was growing longer.

Witnessing a shooting. Check.

Getting shot at. Check

Tasering someone. Check.

Hitting someone over the head to knock him out and tying him up. Check.

Running from a killer. Check, check, check.

Crap, what was next? Strip the guy naked? Well, that was an awkward thought. Although, if she had to strip someone naked, he would be the one. *Stop! What am I thinking? I'm in deep doodoo and ogling someone who might want to hurt me.*

But what a hunk! At least from where she sat. Even with the blood dripping down his forehead, it didn't detract from what looked like a mighty fine body.

The guy appeared to be about six feet tall. It was hard to judge his weight because he felt like five hundred pounds of dead weight when she tried to get him into the chair.

As she was tying his arms behind the chair, she stared at

the multi-colored snake tattoo running down his right arm. It was an intriguing design, and if she had more time, she would have liked to explore it closer. Inch by inch. *Dear Lord in heaven, what am I thinking?*

———————

BEN TRIED to open his eyes, but his lids were heavy. What the hell? It felt like there was a sticky substance on them. He attempted to brush away whatever was on his eyelids, but as he tried to lift his hands, he couldn't. A wet cloth was passed over his eyes, clearing away the goo—no, blood. His blood. He finally focused. *What the fuck was going on?*

Completely awake now, he realized he was still in the bedroom. His hands were numb and, goddamn it, tied behind his back. His gun? Not at his back. He prayed it fell on the floor when he was hit and not into the hands of whoever hit him.

An angry wood sprite sat in front of him, holding the bloody wet cloth and glaring into his eyes. He shook his head. Gah! That hurt.

He looked again. No. It wasn't a sprite but rather a small, slender woman who was staring at him with terrified blue eyes. Something funky was going on with her hair until he realized it was full of leaves and twigs. He noticed the smudges on her face and lots of scratches on her arms.

What the hell happened to her?

She was trembling and licking her lips. Was that a gun in her pocket? His gun? A gun aimed right at the family jewels.

"Did Robert send you?" Her voice quaked and would have sounded gruff if it wasn't so high-pitched. Her eyes were blinking rapidly now. The woman was scared to death. Of him? Christ, he didn't even know her.

OK, he could play this game with her for the moment. "I don't know Robert, and no one sent me."

She leaned a little closer, although not too close, or he would have been able to pull her down with his legs. Or maybe not. Damn. His legs were tied to the chair too. He must have been really knocked out not to notice that.

"Then who sent you?"

"Lady, no one sent me. I'm on vacation. My friend offered me this cabin for a week."

Ben kept his voice calm. He didn't want to frighten her more, and he didn't want the gun to discharge accidentally.

She seemed to be getting more agitated, her voice shriller. "I don't know who sent you. But I'm not going back. I've done nothing wrong. I didn't see anything. Tell Robert I promise I won't say anything to the police. To anybody."

This situation was crazy. What the hell was she talking about?

"Lady, Nobody. Sent. Me. I don't know what the hell you're talking about."

Introduce yourself. Make it personal. Isn't that what they were taught to do at the academy in situations like this? "Look, my name is Ben Green. I'm up here to enjoy my vacation."

The woman stared daggers at him.

Okay, so much for personal and bonding.

Blood was dripping into his eyes. He shook his head, sending blood drops flying. He blinked. His head hurt like a bitch. Trying again to connect with the crazy woman, he said, "Look, I'm bleeding here. Can you wipe my face.?"

"Ha. Don't think I don't know you're trying to trick me into getting me closer." She kept her hand on the gun in her pocket and placed the bloody cloth on the floor.

Enough already. Ben was hurt and he needed to take a piss.

"Sweetheart, I don't know what is going on here, but you

just assaulted a police officer." *Hope that put the fear of God in her.*

The woman stared at him. "Riiight. And I'm the Easter bunny."

Sarcasm. Just great. "Look, my badge is in my wallet, left pocket of my pants. You can check."

"So not happening. I don't trust you."

"You don't have to trust me, but when I get loose ... " Ben hesitated. "And I will. Not only will I prove it to you, but I'm going to arrest you." *There, that should spark some interest.*

She sat there for a minute processing what he told her. Opened her mouth, gulped air and closed it. Nothing came out for a second, then she pulled her hand out of her pocket and covered her face and squeaked. "Oh, God! Oh, my God. How would I know that you were a police officer? Why didn't you say something?"

Oh, Sweet Jesus. "You could have asked before you tasered me and knocked me out."

Ben was still angry that she was able to sneak up on him and tie him to the chair. He took a deep breath. "And how the hell did you get me into this chair? I have at least a hundred pounds on you."

The woman still had the gun, but at least she wasn't pointing it at him anymore. Come to think of it, where was his? Did it fall on the bed when he fell? If not, could it be his gun that she was hiding in her pocket? Jesus, he hoped not.

She had the audacity to smirk. "I'm stronger than I look. I work out. A lot."

Ben snorted. "Great. I've been taken down by a fit sprite."

She glared at him. "Laugh all you want. But you're tied to the chair, and I'm not."

Cheeky bitch. Ben had to give her that. He began working the knots. His hands were too numb to wiggle the ropes, but he could feel the rope getting looser on his legs. A start, at least. He still felt drained, and what the hell was going on with his head?

He needed more time to loosen the ties, so he said, "I have ID in my glovebox. Go to my truck and look for yourself. I'm not going anywhere."

Ben could see her thinking it over. Finally, she nodded. Decision made.

When she came back a minute later, her hand was back on the gun in her pocket.

"Well." She huffed. "You're telling the truth." She cocked her head and stared at him like he had two heads. "But I'm still not untying you."

Ben's head throbbed, and he was still bleeding. His hands and feet were numb. He was not above pleading. "Please, untie me. I promise not to arrest you."

She processed that for a moment. "Riiight. Not going to happen. You could still be lying and working with Robert's cousin. What I'm going to do right now is pack my suitcase and bring it to my car." She glanced at the door, nodded to Ben and said, "You should be able to untie yourself. By then, I'll be long gone, and you can pretend this never happened."

Oh, sweet Jesus, did she really think she could trust him not to go after her, especially after knocking him out and tying him up?

Not expecting an answer, she walked around him as far away as possible and bent over to pick up her clothes that were strewn on the bed, packed, and carried her suitcase out.

Ben couldn't get his head around what just happened. Bizarre. That's the only way he could describe the situation. He dealt with all sorts of weird scenarios, but this one was right up there.

He struggled with the ties, slightly loosening them more until he heard the woman's footsteps coming back, then stopped.

She walked back into the bedroom, still holding the gun in her pocket.

"Take your time getting loose. By the way, in case you were thinking of following me ... " She smirked. "You won't be able to. I slashed your tires."

Ben groaned. Could this get any worse? The woman was seriously fucked up. He started thrashing about, trying to loosen the ties.

Realizing he might get loose before she could leave, she turned and ran out of the cabin.

YES! The last tie came undone. Ben whipped the loosened ties off his hands and then untied his feet. He had seconds to stand up, shake the sleep from his hands and legs, stop the dizziness, and catch up to the crazy woman.

He saw red. The woman was not getting away from him, especially not without giving him answers. He ran out the door and realized she was only about ten feet in front of him, thrashing through the brush and heading toward a tree stand. The top of a red car was barely visible in a clump of bushes. His head felt like a basketball, and blood was dripping into his eyes again.

Hopefully, he wouldn't pass out before he caught up to her.

MARLEE CLOSED HER EYES. She feared being accused of shooting Jim, and all she could think about were hunks and tattoos? *Get a grip.* But Ben did have that streaked blond hair and scruffy beard she liked. She wondered what color his eyes were. It was hard to tell with them closed and blood dripping over them. *Stop thinking. Jesus. What is wrong with me?*

Enough already. She was running in fear for her life—not on a date.

The fishing camp was a great find and a small respite. But here she was again, plunging into bushes, fighting thorns, bugs, and whatever creepy, crawly creatures were hiding, ready to pounce on her. She shuddered. Ick.

Marlee finally found her car and reached to open the door. Whoosh. She fell to the ground. The breath knocked out of her. Her eyes mesmerized by ... legs. Creepy, crawly BUGS. *Oh God!* Her mouth was open just enough to inhale musty pine needles.

Did Robert finally find me? Or is it Ben? He shouldn't have been able to untie himself so quickly.

She spit out the needles and screamed, then tried to squirm away but was unceremoniously turned over. Just as quickly, her hands were tied. She looked up into furious baby-blue eyes. Crap. It was Ben. An angry Ben, with blood dripping down his face, fury radiating from his eyes.

BEN WAS sure the sprite was going to get into her car and take off before he could get to her. Fortunately for him, she didn't appear to have any professional evasion skills and was a little slow. She also didn't seem to have a plan A or plan B. Just plowed through the bushes, leaving a trail a mile wide, making enough noise to scare a herd of elephants. She wasn't even aware of how quickly he got rid of his ties. And he wasn't letting her go. He needed answers.

He quickly tackled her and tied her hands. Picking her up popped more stitches in his arm, which he ignored. At this rate, he was concerned his arm would never heal. He threw her over his good shoulder while she squealed and wiggled and tried to kick him. She swore at him, using language he hadn't heard in a while. He plodded back to the cabin, which did little to ease the pain and blood flowing down his face. Ben took a second to catch his breath and then set the squirming, potty-mouthed woman down none too gently in the same chair she tied him to . He sat on the bed and happened to glance down at the floor.

Peeking from under the nightstand on the floor was his gun. Lady luck was finally smiling on him. He held on to the little witch while he bent down to pick it up.

"Oh my God, are you going to shoot me?" Marlee screeched. The color bleached from her face.

"What in God's name are you talking about, woman? I'm not going to shoot you. Although if you run again and I have to chase you, I might be tempted."

He tucked the gun behind his back and looked at her again. He hadn't paid much attention to the woman before, as he had been a little concerned about the gun in her pocket. She still looked a bit worn around the edges, with branches sticking out of her hair, a dirtied, torn white blouse, gray pencil skirt and, damn, heels? What were they called? Kitty? No, kitten heels. His sister informed him of that factoid last time he saw her.

The clothing threw him for a loop. She certainly wasn't hiking or fishing in those clothes. "What the hell are you doing out here and in that getup?"

The woman shook her head, brought her hands up, and zipped her lips with her finger. *Zipped her lips? What was she? Five years old?*

"What the hell?"

She was trying Ben's patience.

He cracked his knuckles. She gasped. That got her attention. Her eyes widened in fear. *What? Did she think he was going to torture her?*

"Now, missy. You're going to answer some questions for me. First and most importantly, where's the gun?"

She had the nerve to look puzzled. "Gun? I don't have one."

"You had one in your pocket before." *Would this woman ever stop lying to him?*

"Oh. That wasn't a gun." She shrugged her shoulders. "That was my finger. You know ... " She brought her hands up and cocked her fingers. "I've never owned, let alone shot a gun."

Ben closed his eyes and shook his head. The knock on the head must have affected him more than he knew if he couldn't recognize a finger pointing at him.

How could a small woman make him feel so foolish, and how did a hundred-pound-plus woman get the jump on him, taser him, tie him up, and then try to run? He seriously needed to turn in his man card.

"Okay, chickee, let's start with your name."

The woman licked her lips. *Oh, please don't do that.* Ben was a sucker when it came to women licking their lips.

"Name?" he demanded.

She hemmed and hawed and finally spit out, "Fine. My name is Marlee Burns."

"Marlee?"

She nodded.

"So, Marlee, want to tell me your story?"

She opened her mouth to speak, but he held up a finger. "First, though, I'm curious about how you were able to taser me and tie me in the chair." He knew in the scheme of things that this wasn't important. But his pride was at stake here, and he sure as hell wasn't letting that go. Even hardened criminals were never able to take him down so quickly.

"Well, for your information, I do work out. First, when I tasered you, you fell on the bed, and I hit you with a piece of wood. Then I pushed a chair over and hauled you onto it." She glared at him. "You're a little heavy, you know."

Ben shook his head. Christ, she was reciting how she took him down like a grocery list. *Amateur.*

"Finally, I tied your hands and feet to the chair." Then she smirked. "Lucky for me, you were close to the edge of the bed. Otherwise, I couldn't have done it."

Lucky for her? Marlee had an attitude in spades.
Well, one mystery solved. Embarrassing as hell but solved.
"Story."

Marlee sighed. "Fine. I work, worked at a small accounting office in Lakedale. A few days ago, I got a call from one of our clients about some funny transactions. When I mentioned it to my CEO Robert Gilligan, he shrugged it off, said he would look into it. I checked again, and nothing was done about it, so I told my boss, Jim, about it. He was looking into Robert's accounts and found some discrepancies and called me in. We were working late last night. I went to get coffee, and I heard Jim and Robert yelling at each other. Next thing I know, there was a shot, a crash, and silence."

She brought her hands up and wiped away a tear. "If I just let things go and kept my mouth shut, none of that would have happened." She sniffed. "I think I'm in trouble."

That was the understatement of the year. Ben felt like a heel, he hated when women cried. He reached over for a tissue on the end table and handed it to her.

"Thank you. Anyhow," Marlee continued as she dabbed her eyes with her tied hands. "I peeked around the corner, and there was my boss. Lying on the floor. Blood was dripping from his body, I couldn't tell if he was dead or alive and Robert was holding a gun. I screamed, and he saw me, yelled at me to stop. Thankfully, I had my purse and keys with me. I ran out to the parking lot and got in my car before Robert could reach it. I didn't know what to do, so I raced home, packed a bag, some food, and here I am." She looked at him with wide, innocent eyes. "Stupid, huh?"

Obviously not expecting an answer from him, Marlee took a deep breath and continued, "Anyhoo, I still haven't figured out why I went home. I don't know how he did it, but I think Robert got there before me. Because as I was leaving, my car's rear side window was shot out. I think he was aiming for me." She sighed, wiping away more tears. "I drove on back roads for miles until I saw the closed sign for the camp and thought it might be a safe place to collect my thoughts."

The story didn't make sense to Ben. If someone was shot, why didn't she call the police?

As if she could read his mind, Marlee said, "I was going to call the police, but my phone was dead. Then I remembered that Robert's cousin is the police chief in Lakedale. I was afraid they would blame me for shooting Jim."

He thought about what Marlee said. "Why would the police think you shot Jim?" He narrowed his eyes. "Unless you did."

Marlee squinted her eyes at him and pursed her lips. "No, I didn't shoot him. I panicked. So, sue me."

The woman had attitude, for sure. "I can understand panic, but if you didn't do it, why were you concerned about calling the police?"

She huffed. "I told you that Robert's cousin is the police chief. I believe Robert is stealing. While I didn't witness Robert shooting Jim, I figured Robert would lie about what happened and frame me?" She shrugged. "Not calling them was probably not my best move."

Ya think? Ben didn't know how to process this. He was a sucker for a woman in need. Actually, he was a sucker for all women. And Marlee looked so forlorn and vulnerable, especially with the forest in her hair and all the smudges on her body.

He leaned over and untied her hands. Marlee shook out the numbness and blew her nose in the tissue, then sat back and closed her eyes, giving Ben time to deal with what she'd told him.

How big a hotshot was this cousin? Would this Robert be able to influence the case if he had pull with the police chief, as Marlee suggested? He'd like to think not, but stranger things like this happened. If he called this into his captain, she would want more information and be curious as to how he knew what happened. Would he then be placing Marlee in more danger? Or himself by association, if Robert was a killer?

Why did he care? He didn't know Marlee from Adam. So, what was it about this sprite that made him feel like he needed to protect her? The kicker was that he was on leave and should be relaxing. Not getting involved in a supposed shooting in another town and certainly not going around slinging women over his shoulder and popping stitches.

Tinkerbell fascinated him. She was fearless and adorable. *Adorable?* He sighed—time to think about that later.

Her story was a little farfetched, but in his line of work, not out of the ordinary. He needed another opinion. He did the next best thing he could think of. He called Samantha Knight.

SAM ANSWERED on the first ring. "Ben, I hope you're calling to accept my offer."

"Seriously considering it. I'm tired of getting shot at." Ben's ex-partner, Luke McBride, started at KnightGuard a few months earlier and was working hard on convincing Ben to come work there. Ben knew KnightGuard and Sam enjoyed a good reputation in the area, and he also knew many of Sam's employees from hanging out with Luke.

Sam laughed. "I heard about that. I hope you're doing okay."

"Well, the arm is better, but I have a little problem, and I need your help," Ben told her the basics and where he was. Sam promised to be there within the hour.

True to her word, Sam drove up an hour later. Marlee was now sitting calmly on the couch, sipping a glass of water, still looking like something the cat dragged in.

Sam looked curiously at both and asked Ben, who was still bleeding, "What happened to your head?"

Ben replied quickly. "Hit it accidentally."

Marlee piped in at the same time and said, "I tasered him, knocked him out with a piece of wood, and tied him to a chair before I found out he was a cop."

Sam closed her eyes. Shook her head. Her lips curled upward. She looked again at Ben, her brown eyes twinkling. "Oh, this is sweet. I am so taking pictures later."

DAMN. There went his reputation. Ben sat there, fuming. Could things get any worse?

He glanced at Sam and Marlee. They were both small, slender women. *Balls of steel meet balls of steel.* Sam was the most determined, fearless woman he knew. Considering this mini version of Sam took him down so easily, he was in awe of both women.

Turning toward Marlee, Sam reached over and rubbed her shoulder. "Please tell me what happened."

Marlee repeated her story to Sam.

Ben heard her story, but it pissed him off to listen to it

again. Innocent women shouldn't have to go through something like this. That is if she was innocent. The jury was still out on that. There were still too many unanswered questions. Was the CEO embezzling? Maybe Marlee was embezzling. Why did this Robert shoot Marlee's boss? Was Jim dead? Did anyone call the police? Was Marlee involved? Most importantly, was Marlee lying?

He needed to know more before he called his partner at the station to ask if he heard anything.

He hoped Sam had some suggestions.

―――――

AFTER MARLEE FINISHED HER STORY, she took a deep breath and looked over at Sam. Whatever Marlee visualized Sam looking like was not the woman sitting in front of her. When Ben said he was calling Sam, Marlee at first thought he was calling a man. When Sam walked in, the slender woman, maybe an inch taller than her own five foot two, was as far from her vision of a security guard as could be.

Sam had pulled her long, reddish-brown hair into a ponytail. She wore a white wrap blouse, skinny jeans, flats, and carried an oversized purse. Not at all what Marlee envisioned a guard looking like—no butch haircut, combat boots, camo pants, black tee, or machine gun. And what was with small women who carried big purses? She glanced over at hers. Yep, big purse.

Sam looked like an ordinary woman except for the intensity she brought into the room and a very fit body.

"You don't look like a security guard," Marlee blurted out. She clamped her hands over her mouth. Would she ever stop being so blunt? Hadn't her mouth gotten her into enough trouble?

Sam looked at her and frowned. "Well, I left my interrogation clothes and cattle prod at home today."

Marlee gulped. She thought Sam was kidding ... but.

"All righty then. Sorry I asked." Her heart was thumping. If she were ever interrogated, everything she knew would be given up in seconds.

"It's all right. I've always wanted to say that." Sam chuckled. "We try not to scare potential clients."

"Well, I'm glad. I do have a habit of just saying what's on my mind." Sam must think she was a complete idiot. Why did she ever ask?

Ben snorted. She gave him a dirty look.

Sam asked her a few more questions. Finally, Sam nodded. "Let me think about this for a few minutes. I have to say, this is a bizarre story, and I definitely think not calling the police is a big mistake even if, as you say, they're crooked." Sam sat there for a few minutes, lost in thought, not moving a muscle.

Marlee was getting nervous. Would they turn her in to the Lakedale police? Contact Robert for more information? He would kill her for sure. She would bet her life on that.

CHAPTER THREE

I t was late. The sun had disappeared in a salmon and gray sky over the lake a while ago. They moved to the porch, and a gentle breeze cooled them as they talked.

Now Sam needed to get back to the city. Ben didn't know where this situation was heading. He and Sam agreed that he would call the Black Pointe police and nose around. She would put out feelers in Lakedale.

"So, Ben, this is a sticky one. What is your gut feeling?" Sam asked. She looked at him expectantly.

Gut feeling? My gut feeling is that I wish I stayed in Black Pointe.

"I think it would be a good idea to have Marlee stay at the camp with me until we know more," he blurted out. *Why did that come out?* It was a stupid idea, but for some reason he didn't want to let the clueless woman leave yet.

"Huh, Ben. Remember, you still work for the police. If they find out you're harboring a potential fugitive, you'll be in a lot of trouble with both precincts. Don't forget, the Lakedale Police will oversee this case," Sam said.

Sam was right. This case would be out of his hands

regardless. Plus, his job would be in jeopardy for harboring a potential criminal, and that sure as heck wouldn't look good on a resumé.

"You're right. I'm on a month's leave right now. The captain knows I want to resign. Tomorrow I'll give my notice, then I can start working for you immediately if that's okay. That way, Marlee will have the protection she needs until we sort this out."

Ben had no idea why he wanted to help Marlee, a woman he barely knew. He also couldn't believe what was coming out of his mouth. Must be the head injury. And he sure didn't understand why he volunteered to help Marlee, since he still felt guilty about not saving Kimmie. It was all confusing as hell. *Was he ready for this?*

Sam smirked. "I see how it is." She looked thoughtfully at him. "Look, that's fine by me. But are you ready to do this? I need your mind to be fully wrapped around this."

Ben thought about it. He was a good cop; he knew that. On one level he knew that there wasn't anything he could have done differently to help Kimmie. There was no dealing with dopeheads. On the other, his confidence in his ability to keep anyone safe was at an all-time low. Could he do this without screwing up? Had to try, right? Like falling off a horse and getting right back on again, wasn't it?

"I'm fine. I can handle this."

Sam lifted one eyebrow and stared him in the eyes. "After everything that has gone on with you lately, are you sure? I don't want this fucked up."

He thought about it for a minute and nodded.

"Okay then," said Sam. "This might be a safe place for her to stay while you're here."

"Excuuuse me." They both glanced over at Marlee. With her brows pulled down, eyes glaring, she spat out, "Maybe it isn't fine by me. It's my life. I get to decide what is going to happen to me, not you two."

Whoa! Ninja sprite! Ben shook his head. This small woman was spunky and courageous, for sure. *Oh yeah. Spunky.* Damn, this little slip of a thing who didn't know shit about him was calling him out. Plus, she wasn't afraid to stand up to Sam. Christ, even he was afraid to stand up to Sam.

He liked her attitude more and more.

Ben smiled.

"Did I say something funny?" Marlee looked at him, hands on her hips, indignant as all get-out.

"Aaah. No?"

Shit, he needed to watch his step with this she-devil. He loved it. After years of just looking for women who wanted a good time for a night or two and didn't challenge him, here he was in the middle of nowhere with a force to be reckoned with.

"You're right, Marlee," said Sam, placing her hand on Marlee's arm. "It is your life, but if what you're saying is true..."

Marlee opened her mouth to reply.

Sam put up a finger. "And I'm not saying it isn't, this man already knows where you live, has shot at your car, and let's not forget he may have killed a man. KnightGuard can help protect you until we get more information about Jim's shooting and not get you killed in the process."

Thankfully, Marlee responded to Sam better than she did to him. After a small "humph," she nodded to Sam. Although he and Marlee got off on the wrong foot, Ben thought he could gain her trust and convince Sam he was the right man for the job.

"We need to have KnightGuard look more deeply into this Robert Gilligan. Is that possible?" he asked.

Sam smirked. "More than possible."

THIS WHOLE INCIDENT WAS EXHAUSTING. Marlee just wanted to get a good night's sleep and to forget everything that occurred in the past twenty-four hours. Well, there wasn't a fat chance in hell that was going to happen.

She didn't know what to expect when Sam walked into the cabin, but the slender woman who showed up wasn't it. Sure, Sam seemed nice, but her eyes were wary. Constantly moving and watching—for what? Danger? Processing what she and Ben told her. Observing every move they made. Sam was just the person to help her. Ben too.

Sam and Ben appeared to believe her—for now. She felt safe with them. Although she felt safe at the office too until Robert shot Jim—go figure.

Sam was very intense and a little scary. Ben was just plain scary but seemed to be nice underneath all the muscles and tattoos, even with the blood still dripping down his head. Good lord, why did she keep thinking about all those muscles? Gah. Had to be the shock of seeing Jim shot. Ben was a mighty fine specimen of a man.

The question was, could she trust them? Marlee thought maybe so since they didn't call the police and volunteered to protect her. However, she also believed Robert, and look how that turned out. She always seemed to trust the wrong person.

This situation was going to take some thinking. She needed sleep. Tomorrow she would decide if Ben and Sam could keep her safe. For sure, she wasn't going to sit back and let others take control of her life. She'd been on her own too long for that to happen. Grandma Burns always said, "God helps those who help themselves." Grandma Burns was the smartest woman she knew.

THEY ALL AGREED that staying at the fishing camp for the week was a smart move. No one knew Marlee was there, and only Sam knew Ben was staying here.

After Sam left, Ben and Marlee stared at each other. He wanted to say more but didn't know what at this point. It was late, his head hurt, and his shoulder ached. He felt old.

"So. Ben. Sam seems really nice," Marlee said and added, "and a little scary."

Ben grunted. "Yeah, she's very competent. KnightGuard Security has an excellent reputation, which is why I want to work for her."

"How did she get into the security business? I usually think of men running that type of business." Marlee thought for a moment. "I don't mean that women can't do it. It just seems out of the ordinary."

"I only know what my friend, who is married to Sam's best friend told me. Seems like when Sam was little, her parents were murdered in a home invasion gone wrong."

"Oh my God," Marlee exclaimed. "How awful for anyone, let alone a small child."

"Yeah. Then there was another incident after high school graduation when her best friend was murdered. She took all kinds of self-protection classes through the years and majored in criminal justice in college. Then she started KnightGuard Security, investigated the murder, and finally put the friend's boyfriend in jail. Her mission for the company is to get justice for and protect the innocent."

Marlee swallowed hard. "Does that mean she thinks I'm innocent?"

"Well," he hesitated. *What did it mean?* They hadn't proved one way or the other Marlee wasn't involved, but it did seem as if Sam believed her story. "I guess it means she doesn't think you're guilty." He paused. "Right now."

Marlee sagged back in the chair and let out a deep breath.

"Listen, it's late. How about we turn in for the night?" asked Ben.

He was exhausted and judging by the huge yawn she tried to suppress and the dark circles under her eyes so was Marlee. Although it was a little hard to tell with the sticks in her hair and the smudges on her face. Ben thought she had the "at one with nature" look going, and that suited her prickly personality just fine.

Ben offered Marlee the bedroom, and he told her he would take the sofa bed. Marlee gladly accepted. He liked that she didn't try to get him to change his mind and insist that she would sleep in the living room. Besides, if Ben slept on the sofa bed, anyone trying to get in would have to go through him first. He felt she would be safer in the bedroom.

He sure wasn't going to tell her that. Marlee would probably insist on taking the sofa bed out of spite.

Knowing Sam would investigate, and she would call the next day reassured him. The decision to work for Knight-Guard was the right call, even though he made it rather abruptly. Tomorrow he would call the station, snoop around to see if they heard anything, talk to his captain, and give his notice.

Sleep. Ben desperately needed sleep. He could hear Marlee settling in the bedroom. The sofa bed was lumpy and small, but he would make do.

Tomorrow, he and Marlee would talk more.

CHAPTER FOUR

Tossing drawers from Jim Matthews's desk wasn't tamping down the fury Robert Gilligan felt. Stupid man. Why did Jim have to get curious now?

Why did he and that nosy Marlee Burns have to investigate the discrepancies she found in the accounting system? And why did she take a call meant for him? He could have resolved that question the nonprofit had in a matter of minutes if he had been there, and no one would have been wiser. Discussing the mistakes that Marlee found in the books only made her more curious after bringing it to his attention a couple of weeks ago. He told her he would look into it. He was the CEO, after all. But did she listen? *No.* He wished he could have fired her, but her father still controlled a stake in the company—his bad luck.

He should have known the bitch wasn't going to let it go. For that matter, why was Marlee looking into accounts she wasn't supposed to? Did Jim help her? Jim shouldn't have known about them either. Probably a fluke in the system and one of them found it. Jim should have ignored it. He had a good job here.

So, she discussed it with Jim. Dumbass move. Marlee was too conscientious, too inquisitive. But not so lucky. Now, she was on the run. Stupid woman even rushed home to pack. Fortunate for him, Amber was home. Unfortunate for him, Amber missed and only shot out Marlee's car window.

Robert was sure Marlee had the thumb drive that could put him in jail. Christ, Jim even divulged he gave it to her as he was begging for his life. Robert had to admit to himself that he got a rush killing Jim. Actually, he had gotten a rush as Jim was begging for his life. But that didn't change the fact that he should have gotten the thumb drive from Marlee before he shot Jim the second time. He wasn't thinking straight when she ran out of the office.

So where would she go? Black Pointe, where her invalid father and grandmother were living? Would she be dumb enough to bring her troubles to them? He didn't think so. He hoped she would call Amber and tell her where she was hiding out. He could take care of her then.

But first, he needed to make it look like Marlee shot Jim. Or maybe not.

The police would look for a reason for Jim's death and maybe discover the missing funds. He needed to be smart about this. He'd hyped up his cousin's indiscretions enough that he didn't think she would go to the police. Besides, his cousin could only help so much. He didn't pay him enough to overlook everything. If they found Marlee, she would tell the police what she saw. What would they do? Would they believe her? He didn't think she actually saw him shoot Jim, and she definitely didn't see him kill Jim.

Perhaps he should report finding Jim's body? Maybe suggest Jim had a gambling problem? No, that wouldn't work. Again, someone might look at the books.

Or maybe let someone else in the office find Jim's body on Monday. Maybe drop the gun by Jim's body or desk so it would be easy to find. It wasn't registered—thank you, cousin Ray. Perhaps the police would think Jim struggled and knocked the gun out of the assailant's hand. That might work. Fortunately, there were many avenues to consider that wouldn't lead back to him.

Think. Think.

Shit, he needed to consider all options before Monday morning. By then, he needed to come up with a plan on how to deal with Marlee. Jim's death was a particularly gnarly problem because he didn't want to involve his cousin. He owed him too much as it was. He also needed to talk to Amber. He needed to find the thumb drive. He needed to erase some security camera footage—so many things he needed to do.

First, though, he had work to do. Robert sat at Marlee's desk and logged in. An hour later he closed the computer and smiled to himself. Done. A few keystrokes here, a few there. Bingo. Marlee now had a good amount of money in her account. Even if she told the police about Jim's death, she couldn't explain the money transfer. Without the security tapes, she couldn't prove he killed Jim or was even there that night.

Was he smart or what? Timing the transfer of money from the office. Insurance just in case things went south. Marlee would be accused of lying and stealing. *Try to worm your way out of that, bitch.*

Bye, bye, sweetheart. Enjoy jail. He and Amber would be enjoying life on a beach.

CHAPTER FIVE

Marlee woke up slowly. Birds were chirping, and the sun was peeking around the drawn shade. She stretched, unkinking some of the knots in her neck and back. She felt peaceful but not for long.

Gruesome scenes of Saturday night assaulted her mind. Jim lying in a pool of blood. Her running through the parking lot and Robert chasing her with a gun.

It took her a minute to remember what happened and then another minute to realize she was still living the nightmare. She was trembling. Her skin felt sticky. She groaned. Shit. The shooting was still too fresh in her mind, and the fact she was on someone's—well, Robert's—hit list made her ill.

She eyed each corner of the bedroom, not wanting to get out of bed. The small, no-frills, rustic room appeared more masculine than feminine with wood-paneling on the walls, one comfy upholstered chair in the corner, and a plain wooden chest and mirror on the other wall. The room was nothing special, but she felt safe for the time being.

Remembering that Ben slept in the other room, she

wondered if he was up yet. How early was it? She brought her wrist up. The gold watch her father gave her for her twenty-first birthday read 9 a.m. She hadn't slept in that long in a while. Last night she was relieved when Ben told her he would sleep in the living room in case someone tried to get in, but she would never tell him that.

Right now, she desperately needed a shower and coffee. God, she would sell her soul for a cup of that sweet elixir.

Marlee looked around for her robe. Did she even pack one? She barely had time to process what she brought or where she put anything after arriving yesterday. There had been no time after she tasered Ben, struck him with a piece of wood, then tied him up. *Ugh*. Not good memories. Her body resisted leaving the warm, comfortable bed, but her mind needed coffee. Marlee got up, scrounged around and found her robe, opened the door and peeked around the corner.

She saw that Ben was up already and standing in the small kitchenette. "Coffee?" he asked.

It was a sin for a man to look that good in the morning. Marlee remembered thinking he was yummy-looking last night, but this morning—*oh, my God!* Ben was barefoot, wearing jeans and a black T-shirt that stretched from shoulder to shoulder, covering too many muscles to count. Something about a muscular, barefoot man turned her on. One of her many fantasies, because sex was all in her imagination. She never experienced mind-blowing, earth-shattering sex, or any sex for that matter, but she could fantasize with the best of them.

Marlee nodded her head. "I'll take it to go. I need to take a shower."

Ben smiled and handed her a mug.

"There's no milk or sugar."

"None needed." She looked away fast. Did he know she

was drooling over him? Marlee hoped not but thought a man like Ben could definitely read a woman's mind.

"I brought a couple of towels. They're in my bag, but I don't have any shampoo or body wash, only soap," he said.

"No problem. I have everything I need. I think." She thought for a moment. "Actually, I packed so fast. I'm not sure what I have, but I'll figure it out."

She walked into the tiny bathroom and looked in the mirror. Wow, scary didn't cover it.

Why didn't Ben tell her she was harboring all sorts of flora and fauna in her hair? Kind of him not to, but she looked ridiculous with the sticks and leaves in her hair, dirt smudges on her face, and her eye makeup smeared so she looked like a raccoon. Last night she was too tired to worry about what she looked like. Maybe she should have been. Oh well. She turned on the shower, let the water get as hot as possible, and jumped in.

Half an hour later, hair washed, body washed, and with clean clothes on, Marlee felt like new again. Ben was sitting at the kitchen table still looking sexy as hell. He looked up when she walked in.

"I'll take a refill if there's enough."

Ben got up and refilled her cup.

"Is Sam coming back?"

"Not today. She'll call when she has more information. I want to go over what happened again. I need to get a clearer picture of what you saw or think you saw."

Ugh, not what she wanted to do. She'd given them the basics last night but still hadn't decided how much more to tell Ben. She hoped she could trust him and Sam. But then she trusted Robert too. Look where that got her. The past couple of days was a jumble of thoughts.

"Um, OK. But can we do this a little later? I want to take a walk down to the lake."

He nodded and reminded Marlee to walk straight down to the lake and not stray too far.

The bright blue sky hosted a few white, lazy clouds. The lake was serene, the water barely rippling—no sounds except for a few birds cawing overhead. No one else was around. Marlee sat on a worn, wooden bench overlooking the docks and a couple of small boats bobbing in the water. It was both relaxing and calming. The temperature was rising, and it was going to be another hot Florida day.

Marlee's eyelids started to droop. Open and close. She shook her head. This was stupid. It seemed like she just got up, and now she was tired again. She didn't want to fall asleep out in the open. The stress was getting to her. She needed a nap in the safety of her bedroom.

Marlee walked back to the cabin and announced to Ben, who was working on his computer, that she was taking a nap. Being chased by a killer, getting shot at, and staying up till the early hours had taken its toll.

VOICES WOKE MARLEE UP. Not a woman's voice. So, it wasn't Sam. It sounded like two men. She lay in bed, pulse racing. Did Ben call the cops? Or worse, did Robert find her? Hearing men's voices was not the way she envisioned waking up from her nap. Marlee didn't dare open the door. The cabin was too small for them not to hear. What to do? Ben promised to protect her until they figured out what to do. Marlee thought she could trust him. But she'd only met him yesterday and not under the best of circumstances.

The hell with Ben. If he thought she would go quietly to her slaughter, he could guess again. Marlee swiped at the sweat racing down her face. She scrounged around on the floor and found her purse, keys, and phone. The dead phone.

She hadn't charged it. *Damn*. But then who would she call? Not the police. Not her father and have him worry. Maybe Amber? No, she didn't want to involve her friend, who might get hurt, plus they weren't that close. Sure, they shared some good times, a few drinks and some confidences but not really serious stuff.

She had to keep Ben and whoever he was talking to out of the room. She spotted the chair in the corner. Yes! That would work. She moved it inch by inch so as not to make any noise and placed it under the doorknob. There, that should stop whoever was in the living room from getting in.

Tiptoeing over to the window, she unlatched it and pushed up. There was slight resistance. She pushed again, then heard a small whoosh as it opened. She stopped and listened. Had Ben heard? She held her breath. Nope, no noise or movement coming from the living room toward the bedroom. The men were still talking. She gently removed the screen and dropped it to the ground. Her hands were trembling. Escaping was never going to work if she couldn't get herself under control.

Thankfully, the window was just a few feet above the ground. Taking another deep breath, Marlee pulled herself up and over the sill. Out the window. Landing in bushes again. Ooopf. *What the hell was up with all this flora and fauna?* She disentangled herself from one aggressive branch that tore her shirt, got up, and raced toward her car.

At least she thought she was running toward her car. Where the hell was it? Everything looked different in the daylight.

Marlee's stomach clenched. Sweat poured down her face. She swiped the drops blurring her eyes. Her heart was pounding so loud, she hoped Ben and whoever else was at the cabin couldn't hear it. Life wasn't fair. None of this was fair. She was just an accountant living a normal life. At least trying to live a normal life. Marlee stopped and bent over to catch her breath.

"THANKS FOR COMING, bro. Did you have any trouble finding the tire size?" Ben looked over at his ex-partner Luke, who'd just arrived.

"Nah, glad to help. What the hell happened? A wood fairy get upset with you and slash your tires?"

Ben grunted. "Something like that." God, if Luke only knew how close he was to the truth. He definitely wasn't offering up any more information than Luke needed. This whole incident was embarrassing enough.

"Need to use the john, and then I'll help you change the tires," Luke said.

Knowing he could trust Luke to help him and not ask too many questions, Ben had called him first thing this morning and gave him the tire size. Ben was grateful Luke didn't ask why he needed two new tires for the truck.

Ben shuffled around the kitchen. He desperately needed more coffee and hoped the noise wouldn't disturb Marlee. She had enough excitement yesterday and looked ready to drop when they finally said goodnight early this morning.

Then, after her walk, she dragged herself back to the cabin and announced she was taking a nap. Ben wanted to question her more about the shooting, her job, why she ran, but that would have to wait. She looked drained. They would talk after her nap when she had more energy, but before Luke left.

"Hmmm. Something you want to share?" Luke asked as he walked out of the bathroom, twirling a red thong in his hand.

"Shit, give me that." Ben reached out to grab it out of Luke's hand. Could his life get any more bizarre or complicated? He was never going to hear the end of this. Luke had the memory of an elephant.

"Oh no, you don't. I swear you're the only man I know who could pick up a woman in the middle of nowhere."

"It's not what you think."

Luke swung around, keeping the thong out of Ben's grasp. "Give first."

Ben punched him in the arm and then heard a crash coming from Marlee's room. "What the hell?"

Rushing to the bedroom, Ben opened the door and almost fell over a chair. A chair in front of the door? What on earth was Marlee thinking? The woman continued to confound him. He looked over and saw the open window. *Damn. Not again.*

Charging out the front door and around the side of the cabin, he spotted a pink shirt loping into the trees. *Deja vu!* Marlee was thrashing through the bushes, sounding like a rampaging herd of wildebeests. Again, making so much noise that it was easy to follow her.

Ben finally caught up to her and grabbed her around the waist. Vines and thorns ripped at his skin. This woman was going to be the death of him.

Arms flailing, Marlee tried to kick him. "Let me go, you bastard. I won't go easily."

What the hell? Won't go easily? The woman was a little off-center. "Marlee. It's Ben. What are you talking about? Why are you running through the bushes? Where do you think you're going?" he shouted.

Marlee continued to struggle. Ben finally turned her around and threw her over his shoulder. No surprise—more stitches popped. He prayed this wouldn't be a regular occurrence. At this rate, his wound would never heal.

Luke was standing in the open door when he got back, grinning like a goddamned Cheshire cat. "Would this be the wood fairy who owns the thong?" Luke couldn't stop laughing. Ben was sure he was going to have to pummel Luke before this was over.

Placing Marlee on her feet, Ben kept her at arm's length while she continued to try to kick him.

"Enough," he roared.

Marlee stopped moving. Eyes wide, she glared at him and then pointed at Luke. "Who's he?"

"I'll tell you if you stop kicking me. Sit down." Marlee started to argue but thankfully closed her mouth and plopped down in the chair with a grunt.

"Coffee?" Anything to distract her.

Marlee nodded.

Ben got a mug, and he and Luke sat across from her. "This is my ex-partner from the police force, Luke McBride. He works with Sam at KnightGuard now."

Marlee gave him the stink-eye. "Why did you call him? I thought you and Sam were going to handle this."

"I called him to bring me two new tires to replace the two you ruined yesterday."

"Humph. You deserved that."

Ben heard Luke chuckling from the chair and realized he was enjoying this exchange way too much.

"I didn't want any strangers coming here to change the tires. I trust Luke completely, and you can too. We can protect you, but not if you keep jumping through windows and thrashing through bushes, making so much noise a child could find you."

"Humph."

Marlee wasn't giving an inch. Ben happened to look over at Luke, who was trying to stop grinning. Unsuccessfully. Yep, he was definitely going to have to turn in his man card.

"So. Marlee." Luke relaxed into the chair and crossed his

legs, that damn shit-eating grin still on his face. "How long have you been seeing our Ben?"

Oh yeah, Ben was so going to kill Luke.

Marlee glanced at Ben and smirked. "We never met before last night."

Luke nodded slowly. "Okaaay then."

Was this nightmare ever going to end? Ben thought yesterday was strange, but here he was again having to explain an embarrassing situation. The worse thing was that Marlee was a tiny thing. How could he ever explain she got the drop on him?

"Luke, Marlee's in a peculiar situation."

Luke snorted. Ben wanted to kill him on the spot, but he let it go.

"She witnessed what she thought was a shooting. Not sure if the guy is dead. Then Marlee was shot at and managed to find her way here. Sam came over last night and promised to do some investigating and get back to us."

Luke sat up straighter now. Ben thought for a moment about the situation. Luke would be a great asset if Sam okayed it.

"Actually, you might be able to help. Check with Sam. I bet she'll have no problem with you getting involved." Ben knew he could trust Luke to have his back.

"Happy to. What's the situation with work? Are you still on the force or coming over to KnightGuard?"

"Yeah, about that. Captain put me on leave because of my injury. I put in a call to her this morning and gave my notice. I'm sure she wasn't surprised. She knows I've been unhappy for a while. Sam is taking me on."

"Great. It'll be good working with you again." Luke got up and thumped Ben on the back. "Let's get those tires changed. I have to get back to work, and it appears you have a lot of explaining to do." He chuckled. Ben wanted to throttle him, but he needed Luke's help.

"HOW THE HELL did you get into my room? I put a chair under the doorknob."

Ben glanced over at Marlee, who hadn't spoken a word since Luke left. She'd been stewing on the couch, and he was already worn out by her energy.

"Oh, Tinkerbell, it would take a lot more than a chair to keep me out." Ben hated to burst her safety bubble, but the woman wasn't good at keeping herself safe. Something he was going to work on the few days they would be at the cabin. "If you paid attention, you would have noticed that the door opened out into the living room, not into the bedroom, so the chair wouldn't stop anybody."

Marlee had the presence of mind to look humble. For a second. "*Humph.* Smart-ass," she finally said.

Ben couldn't help admiring Marlee's attitude. The woman was small and sassy. And fearless and adorable. He shuddered. What was going on with him today? He didn't do adorable, cute, sweet, bubbly or nice. He did busty and lusty. He did big-busted women who were horny. Women who liked sex, knew how to have fun, and then leave. Not adorable. And not women who were running for their lives.

CHAPTER SIX

Ben and Marlee had just finished cleaning up the breakfast dishes when they heard the crunching of stones from a car driving toward the cabin. Ben wasn't expecting anyone. He told Marlee to go to the bedroom and wait.

Pulling out his gun, he walked toward the door. He felt a warm breath on his arm. Turning, he looked down into Marlee's guileless baby blues. *Damn.* Would the woman ever do what she was told? He put his fingers to his lips to be quiet. She nodded but kept close to his elbow.

The car stopped in front. A door slammed. "Ben?" A woman's voice. Sam. Ben opened the door when he realized who it was.

"Why don't you give a person notice you'd be coming?"

Sam smiled at him. "On edge a little?"

"Damn straight." Ben put his gun back in the shoulder holster. Marlee stepped back a little to give him room to open the door fully.

Rubbing his head, he sighed and looked at Marlee. "Sweetlips, when I tell you to do something, you need to listen. What if it wasn't Sam but someone who wanted to hurt you? Do you have a gun?"

She shook her head.

"So, what could you do but get in my way?"

Marlee stared at Ben. He saw tears glistening in her eyes, but he knew she wasn't giving him an inch. "I thought if it were Robert, we would gang up on him. You know, just in case he took you out first."

If Sam didn't have the audacity to snort right then, Ben would have said a lot more to Marlee. But he managed to spit out, "For your information, I'm a trained professional. You're not. If someone took me out, as you so kindly put it, you would run away and hide until Sam or someone came to find you. Understand? *Capische?*"

Sniffing, Marlee squinted at him. "You don't have to get huffy. I was only trying to help. It is my life. Remember?"

Sam closely watched them as if it was an Olympic ping-pong match. *Not a good sign for a new employee.* But he was dealing with a headstrong woman with no regard for her personal safety. How could he protect her if she didn't listen? Ignoring Marlee's last statement, Ben asked Sam if she wanted a cup of coffee and any more information.

"Yes, to the coffee. And yes, I have more information. My friend on the Lakedale police force told me that Robert reported the murder yesterday, told them an employee found the body, but there was no mention of Marlee or any embezzlement. He's trying to pass this off as a random act of robbery gone bad."

"How can he do that? Won't the police look at the books or something?" Marlee's voice got an octave higher.

Sam shook her head and said, "Not unless there's a reason to."

Marlee's shoulders slumped. Ben knew she had been too optimistic thinking this would all sort out, that Robert would be arrested, and she could get back to her job, her life. Not happening.

"Look, Marlee, I know you're disappointed, and staying here isn't the ideal solution, but we have no idea what's going on right now." Sam reached over and rubbed Marlee's arm.

"What about the security cameras? Robert put them everywhere," Marlee asked.

Sam pursed her lips and shook her head. "Turns out most of them were for show. As for the ones that were working, there was nothing to show anyone was there."

"Nothing from the surrounding buildings?" asked Ben.

"It's in a commercial area, not many buildings around," said Marlee. She put her head into her hands and moaned, "I am so screwed."

Crap, that was a bummer. Ben was disappointed with the news. How could they prove Robert shot Jim or that Marlee was even there that night? This scenario was not looking good for Marlee.

"OK then, more bad news." Sam shrugged. "The police found a gun, and it turned out to be unregistered. Jim's wallet and cell phone were taken, as well as some petty cash. So far, they determined some junkie broke in to steal money but ran into Jim instead. They think he put up a fight and that's why whoever killed him."

"That's not what happened," Marlee screeched.

"Calm down, Marlee. We'll get to the bottom of this." Sam turned to Ben. "Luke told me that you've spoken to your captain and resigned. Consider yourself officially hired. And your first assignment, should you accept it," she said with a grin, "is to guard Marlee until we get to the bottom of this."

Ben gave her a little nod. He would guard Marlee, but he suspected that taking on this assignment was going to be the death of him.

"On another note, I took the liberty of speaking with

Seth." She accepted the cup of coffee that he brought her and put it on the table. "He agreed that you could stay here another week if you want. I think it's a good idea. This place is safe, and no one knows Marlee is here."

Ben thought about that for a moment. "I agree. I think staying until the end of the week is a good idea, and then I'll move Marlee to my house if nothing has been resolved by then. No one knows about me or where I live. I have top-notch security. With all the workers renovating around here, I don't want to chance that anyone would see her and talk to the wrong person."

A shrill voice from his side piped up. "Heeello." Marlee waved her finger at them. "Marlee's sitting right here and can hear you." Glaring at Ben, she asked, "What if I don't want to go to your place?"

Could this situation get any worse? His first job, and he had to deal with a pain-in-the-ass sprite who questioned everything he said and did and thought she was invincible. Ben was wondering if he should just quit KnightGuard now before he was accused of murder—hers.

"Marlee," Sam said in a soft voice. "I know this isn't ideal. I know you want to go back to your life. However, if Robert killed once, he'll kill again. You said he tracked you home and tried to shoot you. You're in his sights. Ben is the best person to protect you; I promise you're safe with him." She put her arm on Marlee's shoulder. "Please let us help you."

Ben watched as Marlee mulled it over and then made her decision. Good lord. The woman just didn't understand safety and protection.

"Fine, I'll stay with Ben. But I'm not happy about it." Marlee pouted a bit. Ben wanted to kiss the pout off her face. *What was wrong with him?* This was his chance at a good job. He needed to convince Sam and himself that he could protect Marlee, and all he could think about was kissing her?

"We need to get answers as soon as possible. Not that I don't appreciate all that you're doing. But I need to get on with my life," said Marlee. She crossed her arms and glared at Ben and Sam.

Sam smiled. "Yes, ma'am. We will do our best."

Ben observed the play between Sam and Marlee. Was everyone crazy? They all seemed to be falling under Marlee's spell. Didn't they see what he saw? A contrary, opinionated, stubborn woman? One who was driving him crazy? Although if he were honest with himself, a woman he wanted to protect and get to know better. He was in deep shit.

They talked strategy for a while. Ben walked Sam out to her car. She opened the trunk and pulled out a bag of groceries, indicating that he take the rest. *And be still my heart!* She also brought some fun toys she thought Ben might need.

Damn, he loved a woman who could do one-stop shopping for groceries and gun supplies. Giving him a warning, albeit, with a smile, Sam told him to play nice with Marlee. She waved goodbye, promised to keep in touch, and said she would send someone from the office to help with security.

BEN BROUGHT THE GROCERIES, extra gun, and ammunition into the kitchen. When he came back, he noticed Marlee curled up in a ball in the side chair and sniffling.

He walked over and crouched down next to the chair. "Marlee, everything is going to be all right. You'll see. We'll resolve this, and you'll be back living your normal life in no time."

Inhaling a deep, wet breath, Marlee said, "I know, but I had to leave Jeffrey, and I'm really worried about him."

Jeffrey? Who the hell is Jeffrey? A boyfriend? A kid?

"Who's Jeffrey?" he calmly asked, sure he wasn't going to like the answer.

"Jeffrey is my cat. I couldn't find him when I left and, and ... " Marlee started sobbing.

Ben mentally shook his head. A cat? A goddamned cat named Jeffrey. She's running for her life and worried about a—cat.

Not exactly knowing how to treat a sobbing woman, he patted her back and pulled her close to his chest, murmuring, "We'll figure it out." Letting Marlee cry, Christ, letting any woman cry was not something Ben was comfortable with. Having an older sister, he knew that women cried a lot and usually over stupid things. Still, knowing that, he hated when tears flowed.

Marlee finally stopped sobbing. Hiccupping several times, she managed to pull herself together, grab a tissue and blew hard.

"I need to call my friend Amber. I rent my house from her. I'm sure she'll find Jeffrey and feed him. Jeffrey likes her. Or we could drive by and pick him up." She looked hopefully at Ben. Her small, pink tongue was caressing her lower lip.

Ben followed her tongue back and forth with his eyes. There were places she could use that tongue that would please him. *Stop. What is wrong with me? She's running from a murderer, and I'm thinking about sex?*

He thought about the cat for a minute. "Look, I don't think you should show your face in Lakedale for a while. Why don't you call your friend and have her feed Jeffrey? When things calm down, we can drive up and get him."

BEN GOT up to fix a snack. Marlee settled into a comfy chair and thought about Robert. She wasn't feeling optimistic the issue would be solved any time soon. Robert was arrogant and vindictive. Not a good vibe for a person, let alone a CEO. Robert never liked that she was working there or even liked her. But since her father started the firm, hired her, and was still a partner, there was nothing Robert could do about the situation.

That was the story of her life, though—never fitting in. She was always too smart, too mouthy, too this, too that. Working at the firm finally gave her the peace that she found a job she was good at. It was a respectable job, even if her father hired her.

She had her little home—actually, a renovated garage in the back of her friend Amber's house. She had a couple of good friends who were fun to be around, and she missed them terribly. Not that they frequented bars and danced naked on the counter, but they laughed over coffee, books, and dating. She had her dad and grandma. She had Jeffrey— she missed the big lug. He was her comfort when things got rough, and things got rough several years ago. That was another time when she couldn't keep her mouth shut and created a problem. The secret that she was ashamed of, and she hoped she would never have to share.

And now there was Ben. He was cute, muscular, and appeared very capable of protecting her. She felt safe with him. He awakened sexual urges she didn't think she possessed. They were confusing her because she was running for her life. She shouldn't be thinking of sex right now. Should she?

Ah, well, first things first. Jeffrey. A call to Amber was in order, and maybe she knew what was going on.

Marlee couldn't reach Amber, so she left a voice message asking her to take care of Jeffrey and to call back. She would explain what she could then.

The day was sunny and promising to be warm. White,

puffy clouds lazily moved across the sky. She and Ben had nothing scheduled. Ben asked her if she wanted to go fishing. Fishing!

"Wow, I've never gone fishing. Dad was always working, and my grandma wasn't the fishing type."

"Well, it will be a new experience." Ben was excited. "Seth said I was welcome to use one of the boats down by the docks, and this is a great bass lake. Put on a bathing suit, and let's go."

Marlee gulped and shook her head. "Bathing suit? Really? Do you think I had time to pack for a vacation while dodging bullets?"

Ben closed his eyes and shook his head. "Damn. Marlee, I'm so sorry. I wasn't thinking. Put on something you don't mind getting wet."

Marlee didn't know why she snapped at Ben. It wasn't his fault she didn't have a bathing suit. The whole situation was beginning to irritate her.

She patted his arm. "Sorry I jumped at you. This situation isn't your fault. I'll be right back."

BEN COLLECTED the fishing gear from the back of his truck while Marlee was getting ready. Christ, could he be any more insensitive? Bathing suit? Marlee was running for her life, and he was asking about a bathing suit. He shook his head. *Dumb*.

Marlee walked out to the little porch and asked if he wanted her to make some sandwiches. Nodding yes, he placed his gear on the porch, and went in to collect a small cooler. There wasn't much ice, and Ben put that on his list of things to buy. He packed some beer and water. Marlee placed the sandwiches on top, and they were off.

They walked down the path to the boat docks, their shoes

crunching on the gravel the only noise they heard. There was a gentle breeze, and the docked boats were gently bobbing up and down. There were two flat-bottomed fishing boats with motors tied to the dock. Ben walked over to one, checked for fuel, placed the cooler in it.

"I can't believe I'm finally fishing." She was skipping down the dock, bursting with joy. Ben loved that this was making her day and held out his hand to help Marlee into the boat.

Taking the boat out would be a nice break for them. Ben hadn't been out with a fishing newbie in quite a while. In fact, he hadn't been fishing for ages; work kept him busy. The week at the fishing camp was relaxing even with Marlee's problems.

"My dad never had time to fish, and I don't know if he even liked to. And my grandma? Somehow I can't imagine her fishing." She shrugged her shoulders. "But who knows? She's pretty cool. She might like it."

"Well." Ben smiled. "You're not fishing yet. Sit down in front and put a life jacket on. I don't want to have to fish you out of the water if you fall in."

"Fish me out. Funny. No worries, I can swim," Marlee said. "Maybe you should put one on in case you fall overboard and knock yourself out. I would never be able to haul you in. Besides, I don't know how to steer a boat."

Fall overboard? Knock himself out? Smart mouth. Ben shook his head. The woman kept him on his toes, but he was sure going to teach her about steering and the engine—just in case.

It was a pleasant morning. The boat floated gently with the waves. They hadn't caught any fish yet, just a few nibbles on their lines. But even the nibbles excited Marlee, which in turn excited Ben. Lord, what was wrong with him? He was attracted to Marlee. She was running from a crime. He was supposed to be guarding her, not lusting after her.

The sun was high overhead. Ben heard Marlee's stomach rumble and asked if she was hungry. Marlee nodded, yes. Ben motored over to a small island, jumped out and pulled the boat close to shore. Lifting the cooler on his shoulders, he and Marlee found a cleared area to picnic and lay down a blanket.

Ben wolfed down a couple of sandwiches and was working on a beer while Marlee lay back to soak up some sun. She had taken off her hat. Her long, curly auburn hair was half in/half out of her ponytail. He couldn't help noticing the way her blue top kept sliding up, showing off a toned stomach. His eyes moved south to her slender legs. Legs he wanted wrapped around his waist. Could they do it here? Ben mentally slapped himself. What the hell was he thinking? He was on guard duty. Not sex duty.

"So, Ben, why did you become a cop?" Marlee's question brought him back to reality. "Was your father a cop?"

"Nah. Dad was a mechanic. After I got out of the service, I struggled with what to do with my life. I had all these skills that weren't compatible with most jobs. Luke already started on the police force and asked me to consider it. It was a good move. I loved the job most of the time. But recently, the murders and rapes started to bother me. Then when I got shot this second time, I started thinking I needed less stress in my life."

Marlee grimaced. "I can't imagine being shot. It must hurt a lot."

"Yeah, it does. Plus, you start to get a little jumpy around people, which is not a good attitude for a detective." He shrugged. "Not that I trust many people."

"No, I wouldn't imagine. So now that you're working for Sam, will it all be protection?"

Ben thought for a moment. "I guess I'll find out. I think so."

Marlee reached over and touched his arm. Zap! A shock of electricity surged up his arm. Did she feel that too? Pulling her hand back quickly, he thought, she did. But if she did, she ignored it.

"Well, I couldn't ask for a better bodyguard. Thank you if I haven't said it already."

"Well, sweetcakes, this is far from over, but I'd guard your body any day." Ben winked.

Whoa, what was he of talking to a client like that? Truth was, he wasn't. Ben looked at Marlee all relaxed, stealing glances at him with sleepy eyes—sleepy eyes filled with desire. Did she want him? He didn't understand his attraction to her. He didn't know if it was her feistiness, her can-do attitude, or the vulnerability she exhibited when she thought he wasn't looking. Whatever it was, he felt stirrings of desire. Her touch a few minutes ago zapped him, and Ben knew she felt it too.

"What about you? How did you get into accounting?"

A pain passed over her face, then disappeared. "My dad is an accountant. I floundered around school for a while. Some of my friends went into nursing or became flight attendants. I thought I might like either profession. You know, helping people or traveling."

Ben snorted.

"What? You can't imagine me being in those types of jobs?" She looked hurt.

He laughed. "With your bedside manner? The patients or passengers would jump ship."

"Hardy har har." Marlee grinned. "You're probably right. I have no patience for waiting on people. The sight of blood makes me gag, and I didn't want to be stuck on a plane with difficult passengers. But I like numbers, so I changed my major to accounting. I realized I loved structure. Accounting just made sense, and the fact that my dad was an accountant ... " She shrugged.

"How did your parents feel about that?"

"Dad loved it." Sighing, Marlee blinked rapidly. "My mom died when I was five, but I'm sure she would have been pleased. Dad's mother stepped in and raised me after my mom died."

Ben was so used to Marlee's positive outlook that seeing the sorrow cross her face made him sad.

"That sucks. I'm sorry. How did she die?"

"Cancer." Marlee shrugged. "I never really knew her, but Dad and Grandma made her real for me."

"That's tough, especially when a kid is that young."

"Yeah, but Grandma made life fun. She was strict but kind. Always full of adages that she still doles out regularly. She acted in the community theater and got me involved, which I love too. Dad brought me to his office when he could. Not a perfect life but a pretty darn good one."

Ben thought about his own life with two loving parents, his sister, and brother. Sure, life was tough for a while, but they had each other. He couldn't imagine losing any of them.

Marlee shivered and pulled on a sweater.

"Let's pick up and get back. The fish are laughing at us right now, and I doubt they'll be biting." Ben picked up the trash and placed it in the empty cooler. Marlee folded the blanket and put on her life jacket.

The ride back to the cottage was quiet, and Ben appreciated the sun dancing off the waves as they made their way back. Marlee's admission about her mom dying saddened him, but the brave woman sitting at the helm of the boat with her face upward, catching the sun's rays, was getting to him big time.

CHAPTER SEVEN

R obert Gilligan was furious. It had been days since Marlee Burns disappeared. Marlee hadn't been back to her house, and Amber hadn't heard from her. No one in the office had heard from her. He told the staff Marlee took emergency leave and wouldn't be back, and they believed him.

Everyone was stunned by Jim's murder. He was surprised the police took Jim's death as just that, a robbery gone wrong. Pulling out Jim's cell phone and wallet and tossing them in the trash blocks away was a smart move. Breaking the locks on the front door of the office to make it look like a break-in was another. Leaving the unregistered gun on the floor— genius. The police never asked about the books. They never questioned why Jim was in the office on a Saturday night. They never checked anything.

Was getting away with murder that easy? Well, yes, it was. Just ask John Bennett. Riiight. First, though, they would have to dig him up.

Robert didn't want to make a habit of killing people, but he needed to find Marlee and take care of her for good. He couldn't have her spill the beans and ruin his plans. Plus, there still was the problem of the missing thumb drive.

Driving over to Amber's, he had time to go over the whole scenario with Jim and his accusations. If only that bitch Marlee just minded her own business, he wouldn't be having this problem. Why did she go to Jim at all? Jim didn't need to know the extent of his acquiring cash from the company. He could have deflected Marlee's questions. Why did Jim have to get involved? He had a good job.

And why did Marlee's invalid father hire her anyhow? Just because her father started the business didn't mean he should employ relatives. Well, that was water over the dam now. But now that he thought about it, that problem Marlee had at her last job might come in handy somehow. He wondered if she knew her father confided in the partners. Honest Mike.

Robert pulled into Amber's carport. Marlee was gone, so he didn't need to be as careful not to be seen. Marlee had no idea that he was seeing Amber, and Amber had no idea Marlee was working in his office when she rented the apartment to her. He stopped visiting here when Marlee moved in. He was cursed with her. It was none of her business, and he never wanted her bringing it up. Work was work. Personal was personal. He had enough of people sticking their noses in his personal business.

Besides, with Marlee confiding in Amber, he could keep tabs on her. He'd been cautious not to come to the house when Marlee was around. Amber usually came to his condo, or they got a motel room. How they managed to keep that factoid from Marlee for years, he didn't know. *Dumb bitch.* Didn't matter now, though. He stepped out of the car, noticed Amber moving around the kitchen, and noted when she spotted him. Flinging open the back door, Amber ran out and jumped into his arms.

"Bobby, I've missed you. It has been the hardest week of my life not seeing you."

God, he loved her. Robert gently put her down and went in for a deep kiss. "Same here."

He pulled away from the kiss, took her hand, and looked her over. She cut her long brunette hair into a shoulder length hairstyle, a bob, she called it, and it looked perfect on her. She wore his favorite blue top with the V-neck down to there and God, he loved down there. She was tall, slim, vivacious—he loved all of her. The past few years with Amber were the best years of his life, and there were many more to come—just as soon as he took care of Marlee.

He smiled. Amber was it for him. They kept their affair secret from the office rumor mill. It was serendipity that Marlee rented Amber's refurbished garage. She and Marlee became good friends. Marlee confided in Amber a lot. It was helpful, shit, more than helpful, to have eyes on Marlee. One could never be too cautious in his business. Although he was surprised Marlee never confided her suspicions of the embezzlement to Amber.

When Marlee ran from the office, he assumed she might run home, and sure enough, she did. The woman just wasn't that smart—no sense of personal safety. Amber had no problem shooting Marlee. Unfortunately, she missed.

Because of Jim's murder, they would have to put off their plans to move to Mexico until this little blip was taken care of. His money was safe in the Caymans. If only Marlee kept her nose to the grindstone and not meddled in his business. *Bah, water over the dam.* Just a little while longer. Then he and Amber would build their lives together.

Amber came back and said, "Oh, guess who left a message on my phone earlier?"

Robert thought about it, shook his head. "God, is she stupid or what? What did she say?"

"Something about Jeffrey, and she would explain where she was."

"Jeffrey? Who the hell is Jeffrey?"

"Not who. What. Jeffrey is her cat."

Robert rolled his eyes. The stupid woman cared more about her cat than her life. "Have you called her back?"

"Not yet. I got home a short time ago and wanted to tell you first. Do you want me to call Marlee?"

"Yes." Robert thought for a moment. "What phone number did she use?"

"She called on her cell."

Robert contemplated what Amber said and then laughed. "Stupid, stupid woman." Oh yeah. She would pay for her stupidity.

Amber looked confused. "What difference does that make?"

"Her phone is paid for by the company, and my computer has a 'find my phone' app on it." He chuckled. Robert couldn't believe his good luck. He was finally going to track the bitch down, get the thumb drive, and eliminate her. Problem solved.

CHAPTER EIGHT

Marlee helped Ben unpack the boat and bring everything back to the cabin. It was late afternoon, and they were sitting on the small porch overlooking the lake. The weather was less humid, and the sounds of birds and insects were making Marlee feel mellow. The wooden rocking chairs were quite comfortable, and she was enjoying the views—one of the lake and the other of very masculine Ben, who changed into cargo shorts and another tee and was looking both luscious and serious. His face was the most relaxed she had seen it since their first encounter.

She leaned her head back and sighed. "This day was perfect. It was so much fun fishing that I totally forgot about the trouble I'm in. Thank you." Oh, she had fun all right, ogling Ben's muscular, tanned body, especially as he cast off, or when he bent over as he put bait on her hook, or standing tall while steering the boat. Oh yeah. She was so not telling him that.

Ben reached for her hand and told her he was glad she got a break from worrying. His hand lingered too long. Marlee looked down at their entwined hands and then looked up at Ben. He looked back at her and winked.

There was some definite attraction and heat there. She was in trouble. Not only with the police and Robert but with wanting Ben. The big "but" was, did he want her too? Would he understand her situation, or would it turn him off?

His hands were so warm and comforting. His lids were hooded, and his baby-blue eyes deepened almost to midnight blue. Marlee never noticed before how dark and long his lashes were. Ben took her hand and guided her onto his lap. He moved his hands to her back and pulled her in closer. Something hard rubbed against her rear. *Oh yeah, he wanted her.*

Soft kisses. Warm lips. Marlee thought she was in heaven. She moved even closer and put her arms around Ben's neck. His kiss deepened. *Oh my!* This man could kiss. She moaned, and he took the opportunity to assault her mouth, entwined his tongue with hers, and made love to her mouth. Making Marlee feel warm and fuzzy things much lower and much more exciting. *Was this how making love with Ben would be?*

She was almost lying on top of him in the chair when Ben groaned and pushed her away.

Marlee was stunned. She stared at him. "Did I do something wrong?"

He took a deep breath and gave her a small smile. "No, honey. You didn't. I did. I'm supposed to be guarding you, not hanging on you like a horndog."

"Oh. I'm sorry if I was tempting you." Disappointment flooded her body. Her confession would be hard. "I don't have a lot of experience, but it seemed like you wanted me too."

"God, yes," he grumbled. "I want you. But we aren't doing anything about that until this situation you're in is over." He pulled her even closer and whispered, "Then, all bets are off."

Ben grinned, gave Marlee a chaste kiss, and let her up.

There were no fish to fry, so dinner was spaghetti. Ben was cooking. He told her it was one of the few dishes outside of grilling meat he knew how to make. Marlee was grateful for the chance to watch him cook. Ben's body filled the tiny kitchen, and watching his muscles move under the black tee was an eye exercise she appreciated. Lord, he had muscles. And he was cute. And kind. Although she wondered if kind would undermine his bad-boy persona. Nah, she decided it made him more desirable. Marlee still couldn't believe she was in the cabin with the sexiest, most masculine male ever.

They ate dinner on the picnic table outside by the kitchen. When mosquitoes got too bad and were making a meal of them, Marlee helped Ben clean up. Ben watched a game on TV while she read. She thought they looked like an old married couple.

Marlee caught herself nodding off, her eyes drooping. Sleep. She needed sleep, although she didn't want to leave Ben. But she didn't want to fall asleep in the chair either. Gathering her energy, she said goodnight, walked into the bedroom, changed and got into bed.

But sleep wasn't easy in coming. Nightmares about Jim lying on the floor, not knowing if she could have done something still troubled her. Dreams about being in Ben's arms and making love with him excited her. Every thought that could disrupt her sleeping decided to play havoc with her mind tonight. It was hours before she finally fell into a dreamless sleep.

JUST BEFORE SUNRISE, Robert drove to the address he found on the "find my phone" app on his computer. The bitch just wasn't smart. Dumb enough to involve Jim. Dumb enough to call Amber on a company phone. Dumb enough to die.

He followed the GPS instructions to a fish camp. Fish camp? That made no sense. What the hell was Marlee doing at a fish camp?

He turned onto a long dirt driveway. Palm trees and live oaks lined the drive, which led down to a lake that he could barely see in the distance. Not sure what he was going to find farther down the road or exactly where Marlee was, he parked the car off the road in some bushes. It wasn't completely hidden but close enough to the road that he would be able to get out quickly.

The camp looked deserted or closed. There were several cabins on either side of the road. Robert pulled up a black mask to cover his face and snuck up on each, peering in. He tried each door, but they were locked. It looked like the cabins were under construction or renovation. Materials were lying on the ground. Stupid. People would steal anything they could get their hands on for a few pennies.

There were a couple of cabins off the road nestled in the woods, and he checked them out. No Marlee.

There was one last cabin to check out, tucked farther away in the woods overlooking the lake. Thankfully, the sun was barely up. He didn't think the construction workers would start working until at least 8 a.m. He came up from the backside of the cabin, and as quietly as he could, walked over and peeked into a window—the kitchen. Empty. He walked to the other side of the cabin and peered in.

Holy shit! There she was. Sleeping like a baby. Like she didn't have a care in the world. Like she hadn't turned his world upside down, got Jim killed and was running for her life.

His gun, he needed his gun. He accidentally knocked the gun on the window in his hurry to pull it out. Shhhhhh. Did he wake Marlee up? Peering in again, he watched in horror as Marlee opened her eyes and stared right into his.

Confusion etched her face. Then disbelief. Then she screamed. Damn. That scared the shit out of him. Robert thought he had time to aim. He took a pot shot. Glass broke. She screamed again. Robert aimed again but didn't have time to take a second shot when he saw a man run into the bedroom.

Did he shoot Marlee? He hoped so, but when he saw the man run into the bedroom, he knew he needed to get out of there. Now. He turned and ran around the front of the cabin. Too late, Robert noticed a truck parked on the other side of the cabin. *Sure, now, I see it.* The thought that he should have checked the whole cabin out before he took aim at Marlee flew through his mind. Next time, he would be more careful.

He was panting and sweating. He didn't have time to wipe the sweat racing down his face. He could hear heavy footsteps thumping on the gravel road behind him. But he had the advantage of time—a few seconds, but it was enough. He hoped. He jumped into his car, started the engine and backed out, almost hitting the angry man, who was yelling and brandishing a gun. He hightailed it out of the camp just as he heard a ping on the side of his car.

Would his heart ever settle down? It was pounding so loudly, he thought he would pass out. What the hell? When did Marlee have time pick up a guy? And who the hell was he? How did she find this fishing camp? Didn't matter. He was still one step ahead of her—*stupid woman.*

The more he thought about it, the more excited he became. Finding Marlee was becoming a game. A hunt. He loved being a hunter. Marlee was the game, and she was going to die. When? He didn't know. He hoped Marlee didn't realize how easy it was to track her phone.

He needed to make plans to end this situation. How? He had another idea, but first, he needed to talk to Amber.

BEN WAS in the middle of a sexy dream where Marlee was naked, bent over the sofa. He was pumping the hell out of her. Marlee was screaming his name as he brought her to orgasm. It took a second in his dream state to realize it wasn't a sexy scream he heard but one of terror.

He jumped up from the sofa, grabbed his gun from beneath the pillow, and ran toward the bedroom when he heard a gunshot. His heart stopped as he raced into the room. Marlee was sitting up in bed, her eyes terrified. Hyperventilating. Glass was all over the bed and on the floor. Ben ran over to the bed and wrapped his arms around her. She was trembling hard. He rubbed her arms trying to calm her.

"Marlee, sweetheart, tell me what's wrong. Are you hurt?"

Marlee gulped in air and finally pointed out the window. "Masked. Man.

What? Masked man? Who was here? Ben jumped up, careful of the glass, and peered out. He didn't see anyone.

Shouting at her to hide in the bathroom, he ran out the front door. A rather large man was hoofing it down the road. Ben raced after him. However, the man was far enough ahead of him that he was able to get into his car and back up before Ben could catch up to him. Ben aimed his gun, but the car was fishtailing as he shot. His shot went wide. Damn. Then the car was gone, leaving just a dust trail. Ben bent over, clutching his stomach, breathing heavily. That was too close for comfort.

How the hell did Robert find them? Was it even Robert? He couldn't see his face; a black mask covered it. He only got a partial on the license plate. Did Marlee call anyone besides Amber? Some bodyguard he was. How could he not have talked to Marlee about safety precautions? Civilians were too innocent to understand criminal minds.

Shit. Shit. Shit. Punching the air, Ben couldn't believe he missed the car and couldn't catch Robert or whoever shot at Marlee. Ben was furious with himself. Some protector he was.

Could this get any worse?

He turned to walk back to the cabin and watched as Marlee came running barefoot down the road in her pink shorty pajamas, her Taser in her hand.

Sighing, he answered yes. But damn if Marlee didn't look sexy with her hair all tousled and those naked slender legs he wanted wrapped around his waist. *What the hell am I thinking? She could have been killed, and I'm thinking about her legs. And sex.* Shit, he was in trouble.

Marlee jumped into his arms and clung to his neck the minute she caught up to him. "Oh, my God."

He put her down. She rubbed her hands all over his body, tears running down her cheeks. "Are you OK? Did he shoot you? Did you shoot him?"

Marlee was trembling. Ben pulled her into his chest, wiped her tears with his thumb. He hugged her for a minute before he let her go.

"Sweetcakes." He held on to her arms and stared into her eyes. "I told you to hide in the bathroom. What part of hiding didn't you understand?"

She looked at him all innocent, her guileless blue eyes wide. "But I did hide. After I heard the shooting, I thought you might need some help if you were down, so I came running." She held up her Taser. "See, I brought my Taser."

Oh, sweet Jesus. What am I going to do with this ninja? She looked so frightened and yet fierce. *And adorable?* What the good fuck was he thinking? She shouldn't look adorable after a shooting or any other time. He was in deep, deep shit.

He shook his head as he started walking back to the cabin. What the hell was he going to do with her? She had no regard for his role as a bodyguard or her own safety, something he needed to remedy soon before one of them got hurt.

Marlee reached for his hand, and he grabbed hers. Then he remembered she was barefoot. He turned and picked her up in his arms, much to her chagrin.

"Hey, put me down. I can walk."

"No way, Mighty Mouse. You're barefoot, and there are too many rocks on the road that could cut your feet."

"Humph," she said, giggling into his shoulder. "You're barefoot too."

Ben laughed. *Got me there.* "OK, then you can carry me." Marlee slapped his arm.

They were high on adrenaline, but when that wore off, he was going to have a "come to Jesus" moment with Marlee.

But first, he needed to call Sam and tell her what happened.

"MARLEE, get dressed. I've called Sam, and she's going to be here soon."

She nodded. Well, not nodded but sniffed a couple of times and went into the bedroom. The adrenaline had worn off, and while Ben was used to the feeling of coming down from a high, Marlee wasn't. When she came out, she still looked distressed. He made Marlee a cup of tea, and he drank a beer while they waited for Sam, who was bringing Luke and Joe Harkin with her. He hadn't met Joe yet but heard good things about him.

Marlee was still trembling but didn't say anything, just stared at her cup of tea. Ben didn't want to approach her about the safety subject yet. He also wanted to wait for Sam and the guys to arrive to tell them what happened, and hopefully, they would have some suggestions. The waiting was killing him.

Finally, hearing voices, he looked out the window. It was only the construction crew. Marlee ducked down when she heard the voices, and Ben hated that she was suffering like this.

He sat down next to her and rubbed her back. She leaned into him and started sniffling harder. Jesus, why? He didn't do tears. He stroked her back and murmured, "everything is going to be OK."

She mumbled something. Then started crying again. Minutes later, Marlee hiccupped and looked up at him with the tear-stained face.

"I was so scared."

"I know, sprite, I know." He wanted to break something, anything to get rid of the anger and frustration building up. How did Robert or whoever find them? He was still pissed he missed that shot and upset that Marlee felt the need to rescue him. Him? No woman ever thought to rescue him.

Marlee leaned closer to him, murmuring, "I know I've said it already, but thank you for protecting me."

Ben felt movement in his lower body. Shit. Now was not the time for little Ben to come out and seek attention. Marlee was upset, not asking for sex. Or was she? Her body kept moving closer. Her eyes were half-closed; her lips slightly pursed. Did she want to kiss him? Lordy. A kiss that he desperately wanted.

Closer still, their lips were almost touching. Ben could smell the light floral scent of the tea she had been sipping on. She was aroused, her blue eyes liquid ink.

He leaned over, their lips barely brushing. Just as he was going to complete the kiss, he heard car tires crunching on the road. Damn.

Putting off the thought of consoling Marlee with kisses or more, Ben slid away from her.

He pulled out his gun and looked out the window. Finally. Reinforcements arrived. Sam, Luke, and Joe got out of the car and walked up to the door. Ben put his gun away and opened the door, ushering them in.

Sam immediately went over to Marlee and put her arms around her. "Marlee, are you all right?"

Marlee nodded. "Yeah, I'm fine. I'm sorry you have to keep running out here."

"It's part of the job. Don't worry about it."

Sam introduced Joe to Marlee and Ben and pointed her hand toward Luke. "I think you've met Luke."

Marlee's face turned red. Luke smiled and winked at her.

"Luke and I have met." She gave a little finger wave.

They sat down, and Sam asked Marlee to tell them what happened. Marlee described how she was sleeping but sensed someone was watching her. When she opened her eyes and looked out the window, a man in a mask was staring at her, holding a gun. He grinned, took a shot, but missed her. She was sure it was Robert. Who else could it be?

Then Ben took over. He told Sam he heard Marlee screaming. He was definitely not telling Sam and the guys that he thought she was screaming his name while she orgasmed. He raced into the bedroom and saw Marlee sitting up, pointing at the window. It took him a few seconds to focus and understand what she was saying. By the time he ran out the door and chased the shooter up the road, the man reached his car and was driving off. Ben didn't think he shot him but did think he hit the car even though it was fishtailing.

Ben did not add that Marlee came racing out in her shorty pajamas, which were incredibly sexy, and holding her Taser. His man card was already severely dented.

Taking in all the information, Sam thought for a moment. "Thoughts, anyone?"

Joe had been sitting there quietly and spoke up. "My first question is, how did the shooter find Marlee?"

They all turned and looked at Marlee.

"Whaaat?" she said indignantly, raising her shoulders. "Do you think I invited him here?"

"Calm down, Marlee," Sam said. "Hon, we're not blaming you, only gathering information. Have you made any calls since you've been here? Used the internet?"

Four pairs of serious eyes returned to stare at her.

"Hmmm, well, I haven't been on the computer. I finally charged my cellphone and called a friend at my office to tell her that I wouldn't be in and to see if there was any gossip about Jim."

Groans. *Do they think I'm a complete idiot?* Well, maybe. Look how many mistakes she already made—water over the dam.

"I didn't tell her anything," she hurriedly added. "My friend said Robert already mentioned that I was on vacation." She thought for a moment. "Oh. I also called my friend Amber to watch Jeffrey." Marlee saw Ben grimace when Jeffrey's name was mentioned. Tough. Jeffrey was a calming force in her life.

Darn, even Sam rolled her eyes. "I hate to ask, but who is Jeffrey?"

The sarcasm didn't deter Marlee. "Jeffrey is my cat. I couldn't find him when I left, so I called Amber, my friend, and landlord, to find him. Besides, Amber doesn't even know Robert," she added.

Sam held out her hand to Marlee and said, "Phone, please."

———

BEN COULD HAVE KICKED HIMSELF. Her phone should have been the first thing he thought about.

Marlee got up, went into the bedroom, and returned with her phone. "How could someone have tracked me here?" she asked as she handed Sam the phone.

Thinking about it for a moment, Sam asked, "Is this your personal phone or a company phone?"

"It's a company phone, one of my few perks."

Groans and head shakes, again.

"Okaaay then. Marlee, you probably wouldn't know this, but if your company is paying for your cell phone, they can track it from the office. I bet that's how whoever and I'm betting it was Robert, got your location." Sam opened the phone and pulled out the battery.

Ben didn't think this could get any worse. But how would a layperson know how criminals work? And what was wrong with him that he didn't think about someone tracking her phone? Marlee had his mind swimming in the land of sex and orgasms. Some protector he was.

Marlee looked horrified. She hid her face in her hands.

"Look," Sam continued, "we can sit here and point fingers, or we can come up with another game plan."

She glanced around at the small group in front of her. "I'm frustrated that we haven't found out more about Robert. KnightGuard will keep searching."

Nodding at Ben and Marlee, she focused on Luke and Joe. "I've already told Ben and Marlee that Robert reported Jim's murder. The police determined it was a robbery gone bad.

His wallet was taken, and petty cash stolen from the office. They also took some computer equipment."

"What about security cameras?" asked Luke.

Sam pursed her lips, shook her head. "The security cameras were worthless, hadn't recorded anything helpful."

"So, you think we probably shouldn't expose Marlee until we have more information," asked Joe.

"Right. She should still talk to the Lakedale police."

Marlee shook her head vehemently.

Sam ignored her and continued, "Until we can establish the partial on the plate, having Ben guard Marlee is probably the safest bet. We need definite proof it was Robert."

"I'm positive it was Robert," Marlee said, looking around, defying anyone to contradict her.

Sam leaned over and patted Marlee's arm. "Marlee, we believe you, but we just can't accuse somebody of a crime, and nothing we have so far points to him except what you told us."

Luke cleared his throat. "Ben, you have excellent security at your house. I think you and Marlee should pack up and go there. The fishing camp was a good idea, but it's compromised now. Someone knows where Marlee is now, and you know he'll be back."

Ben thought about it and nodded. "That's a great idea. I can keep Marlee safe there until we catch him."

Crying out, Marlee said, "Guys, all I want is to go home. I want to snuggle with Jeffrey. I'm tired of being a prisoner and having a guard. I just want to go home." She sat back and hugged herself.

Sam shook her head. "Marlee, I know you want to go home and lead a normal life. But that ship has sailed. Robert, or whoever shot at you, appears intent on killing you. You'll never have a normal life until we catch him. Ben is more than capable of keeping you safe. Luke and Joe will help."

Marlee took a deep breath and nodded. Ben's heart sank as Marlee swiped at a tear running down her face. It had to be difficult, depending upon other people for safety. To not be able to live your normal life.

"I do appreciate your help." She scrunched her face. "I'm sorry my mistake brought trouble here."

Ben bent over, kissed her cheek, and held her face. "You have nothing to be sorry for. It was my mistake for not paying more attention."

Ben heard a snort. He turned and noticed the glances and smiles between Sam, Luke, and Joe. *Humph, nothing going on here, folks. Just comforting a client.*

SAM HELPED Marlee pack her meager belongings. They walked outside to watch Luke and Joe pack up Ben's truck. Ben took Marlee's suitcase from Sam and placed it in the back seat of his super cab and helped Marlee up and in.

Luke drove Marlee's car, Sam and Joe followed in her car to Ben's house.

His house was only forty-five minutes from the camp on the outskirts of Black Pointe. Ben was unsure how this was all going to work out having Marlee at his home. They assumed it was Robert who found them so quickly at the camp—company phone. App on the computer. Didn't take a genius to figure that one out.

Marlee was mortified thinking she led Robert to them. but that was all on him. He got caught up in rescuing Marlee without thinking things through. Checking her phone should have been his first—or second—thought. Reality was setting in. He questioned himself again about whether or not he could protect Marlee. The mistakes he was making were ones a first-year rookie would make. His attraction to Marlee and having his mind on sex was embarrassing.

Marlee didn't say a word on the ride over. She stared out at the passing landscape, hands clasped, sniffling. Usually, Marlee would be chatting nonstop, and Ben was worried. Ben kept glancing over at her, unable to help her. But he knew she needed time to adjust to her new normal. Shit, he needed time to adjust too.

Breaking the silence, Ben said to Marlee, "Sweetheart, you'll be safe at my home. It's fully secure. In fact, I went overboard with security."

Silence.

Ben grasped her hand, brought it to his mouth, and kissed it. "I promise you'll be OK."

Silence.

Finally, Marlee glanced over at him, her voice trembling. "I'm sure it's safe. I can't believe this is my life. I'm an accountant. A junior accountant at that. Nothing special. But I like..." she hesitated. "Liked my life, my cat, my little home."

She sniffled a little and then gave him a weak smile. "I'm sorry. I'll feel better soon, I promise. At this moment, I'm having a mini-pity party that only I'm invited to."

"Sweetheart, you have a right to feel sorry for yourself. You shouldn't be going through this. I'm so used to criminals, liars, cheaters." He sighed. "I've become immune to the stupid things they do." Ben let go of her hand and stared at the road. Sure, he was immune to the senseless criminal acts he encountered, but he was a detective, not an accountant.

"I've never experienced this kind of violence and deceit before. I don't understand why Robert felt entitled to steal from the company and kill Jim." She shook her head. "Or for that matter, want to kill me."

Ben grunted. "Welcome to my world. I've never understood criminals either."

They were almost at his house. Ben hoped Marlee would feel at home. He didn't have a lot of furniture and extras, but the house had everything he needed and was comfortable. It was small, but he was fortunate to own the house outright. In fact, he owned the homes on either side of him. They made nice rentals, and he could control who lived next door to him.

Ben pulled up to the neat, nondescript, beige ranch on a quiet street. The sidewalks were empty, but there were cars in the driveways. It was a family neighborhood, and Ben knew the kids were in school.

The front of the house showcased a couple of colorful short bushes in front and a planter filled with bright red and yellow blooms that his mom gave him when he moved in. A few pygmy date palms dotted the front yard. Marlee said her grandma was into gardening, and Ben hoped the little landscaping he had would make Marlee feel at home.

He parked his truck in the driveway and opened the two-car garage door so that Luke could pull Marlee's car into it. Marlee got out and reached back for her suitcase.

"Let me get that."

"It's fine. I have it. You can get the other things."

Keying in the house code, Ben carried his bag through the front entrance.

MARLEE FOLLOWED Ben down a short hallway that ended in a pale, yellow kitchen. She put her bag down and looked around at the spare but spotless space.

It wasn't a gourmet kitchen, but the stainless-steel appliances were new, and the counters were granite and clean. They were bare except for a microwave and coffee pot. Ben wasn't into curtains, but there were plenty of oaks and palm trees surrounding the fenced-in yard, and Marlee didn't think Robert or the neighbors could look in. Other than the scratched wooden four-person table and chairs, he didn't have much.

Marlee's stomach rumbled. Ben looked around the bare kitchen and then in the fridge.

"Looks like I don't have much, but I'll get some food this afternoon." He looked at Marlee sheepishly. "I have some cheese and crackers if you're hungry."

"No," Marlee said, rubbing her head. "I have a headache. I want to wash up and take something for it. Will you show me where I'll be staying?"

Ben picked up her suitcase and led her through the living room, past the master bedroom, and opened the door to another bedroom.

"I'm across the hall, and the bathroom for your room is the next door over. The sheets are clean, as are the towels in the bathroom. I'm going to talk to Sam and the guys for a few minutes while you freshen up. Come out when you're ready."

Marlee thanked him and closed the door. Home. Marlee glanced around the smallish bedroom. Beige walls, queen-size bed with a white coverlet, a single chair, and light on the nightstand. Basic but home for now. She collapsed in the chair and closed her eyes. How did her life get so complicated?

LUKE WAS HELPING himself to a soda when Ben walked back into the kitchen. "Sparse pickings here, dude. You might want to go shopping."

"Yeah." Ben sighed heavily. "Man, this has been a really

shitty day. I can't believe that asshole shot at Marlee and that I missed him."

He turned back to the living room and saw that Sam and Joe arrived and were walking up the sidewalk.

"Okay, loosen up, boys. We need to sit down and come up with a plan to keep Marlee safe," Sam said as she and Joe came into the kitchen.

Sam swiped Luke's soda as she was passing and walked into the living room.

"Please, have a soda," Luke sarcastically said as he grabbed a couple more cans from the fridge and followed Sam into the living room.

"Marlee?" Sam cocked her head.

"She's washing up and will be here in a minute."

"OK, then. I have to leave soon. You can catch her up. Ben, I think Luke should stay with you guys for today. Joe can pick up the slack tomorrow. I can have someone drive by every hour or so during the day on the off-chance Robert finds Marlee."

Ben rubbed his hands over his face. "Having Joe or Luke as backup is probably a good idea for now. Although I'm not sure we need someone to drive by. Especially if someone is always in the house with her."

"That's fine, but our first priority is to keep her safe," Sam said.

"Marlee is feeling low about the circumstances right now. She needs closure." Ben realized he wasn't telling Sam anything she didn't know.

"Heeello." Marlee apparently overheard some of the conversation. She raised her hand, her eyes like saucers, and waved. "Right here."

Oh yeah. There was his girl. *His girl?* Sassy as ever.

"Sam, regardless of how Ben feels, if you want the National Guard, the Army, the Navy, or alien puppies surrounding the house, I'm for it," Marlee said, turning to frown at Ben.

Sam laughed. "I don't think we need to go to that extreme, but we'll keep you safe. I'll get Phil on that partial plate when I get back to the office. Maybe he can use his magic fingers to get some information with all the special equipment that he insisted I buy."

Agreeing on the arrangements, Sam and Joe left. Luke stretched himself out on the sofa and turned on the TV. Marlee decided to take a shower and rest for a while.

Walking into the kitchen to take stock of supplies, Ben opened the fridge. Great. Beer, beer, soda, and cheese. Opening the cabinets, he saw some cereal, crackers, pasta, and cans of vegetables. Sparse wasn't the word. Vowing to go to the grocery store after he showered, Ben went into his bedroom and closed the door. His vacation was a bust, but he had a new job and a woman to protect.

BEN LOADED up at the store with everything he thought Marlee would like—make that Marlee might eat—yogurt, lettuce, fresh vegetables, fish, and chicken—and drove home. He walked into the kitchen with the bags and spied Luke munching on cheese and crackers.

Then he heard voices coming from the living room that sounded like women talking.

"Good times going on here while you were grocery shopping," Luke said. He had the same shit-eating Cheshire Cat grin he sported at the cabin.

"What the hell is going on?" Ben asked as he put the groceries on the counter.

"Well, your new girl is having a coffee klatch with your old girlfriend."

"Old girlfriend?"

"Yeah. Someone named Patty showed up. She was concerned that you might be 'sick' and stopped by." Luke looked away, his shoulders shaking.

Could this get any more embarrassing? Ben was going to kill him outright.

He'd forgotten Patty flew in last night. They had a standing date and fuck session every month or so whenever she was in town. How could he have forgotten that?

Luke continued. "I gotta tell you, I like your woman. She's sassy as hell, funny and fearless. But the woman has no sense of personal safety. She let Patty in before I could get to the door. Now they're BFFs."

Ben shook his head. "She's not my woman."

Luke smirked. "Riiight. You are such a bullshit artist, and you are in so deep, man."

Ben peered around the corner into the living room and saw Marlee and Patty drinking coffee and laughing. *Probably at him.* Just then, Marlee spied Ben, put her cup down and waved to him.

Damn. There was no choice but to go in. He couldn't run away, and he couldn't melt into the carpet. Ben shuffled into the room, feeling like a doomed convict.

"Hey, you're home." Marlee sounded decidedly more upbeat than before her nap. "Patty stopped by because you stood her up last night."

Could this get any worse?

Marlee's eyes twinkled. "I told her you were working. Guess what? Patty's a flight attendant, and you know how much I wanted to be one. She and I have a lot in common."

Ben snorted. Patty and Marlee grinned like two fools at each other. Lord save him.

Patty gave him an enormous smile and stood up. "I'm sorry to interrupt your 'work,' but I have to leave. I stopped by because I thought you might be sick and need something. But apparently, you're all set, or so Marlee tells me."

Ben wished she would stop with the shit-eating grin and get on with it.

"I also stopped by to tell you that my schedule changed, and I won't be coming through Jacksonville anymore."

Wow, Patty was fun, always keeping it light, loving sex a lot. They had some good times, and Ben felt a little sad. But his future was looking up, and it looked a lot like the small, slender, sassy woman grinning at him.

Patty and Marlee hugged goodbye. God, this lovefest with her and Marlee was getting a bit strange. Thankfully they didn't make plans to get together—he hoped.

"Thanks for stopping by and telling me." *Gotta get Patty moving before this gets any more embarrassing.* He inched toward the door. "I'll walk you out."

Ben opened the door for Patty and stepped outside with her. On her way out, Patty leaned over, kissed him on the cheek, and whispered, "I like her. Don't mess this one up."

CHAPTER NINE

The next few days Ben and Marlee spent settling into a routine. Luke or Joe would come over during the day to watch Marlee if Ben needed to go out. Ben took her wherever she wanted to go. He knew it was boring for her. But he was enjoying the bodyguard business. Marlee was so darn cute and entertaining. And sexy. Things were going well, at least on his end. She was upbeat most of the time and good about not complaining about her situation.

KnightGuard hadn't turned up anything new on Robert. He was still going to the office like nothing was wrong.

Sam had Phil Donovan, her IT guy and reformed hacker looking into Robert's background. Ben couldn't prove Robert shot at Marlee. He'd only seen the man's back, and the man had a mask over his face. Phil ran the partial on the plate, but a partial number on a beige car made it impossible to know for sure whose car it was. Phil could only tell them that it wasn't Robert's car. He owned a black Jeep. The plates were stolen. It was odd that Robert was so well-versed in the criminal life. Ben wondered how he knew how to stay under the radar.

The only thing Marlee asked for was a new cell phone to replace the one Sam had thrown away. Ben bought her several burner phones paid for in cash. They didn't want to use her identification or credit cards to get one. She promised to pay him back. He ignored that.

Ben was watching a game while Marlee called her family.

"Grandma." Silence.

"No, everything's fine. Just wanted to hear your voice and check-in to make sure everything is okay."

Silence. "Uh, uh."

Silence. "Uh, uh."

"I'll try to get up there soon. I love you." Ben saw Marlee place the phone on the table, wipe a tear and turn her head. Not being able to visit family when you wanted to had to hurt, and Ben was feeling her pain. A few sniffles later, she sat down opposite him and stared at him.

"What?"

"I'd like to see my family."

"OK."

Marlee's eyes opened wide in surprise, then she clapped her hands and gave him one of her gorgeous smiles. "Just like that?"

"There's no reason not to see them." Ben shrugged. "Besides, I'd like to meet your grandma. She sounds like a pistol."

Marlee laughed. "She is. But don't tell her that. She'll get a swelled head."

Hearing Marlee's stomach growl, Ben turned the TV off. "Hungry?"

She nodded.

"I'll make tacos. How does that sound?"

"Yummy. I'm impressed you know how to make anything other than spaghetti."

Ben laughed. "Hey, I may be single, but if I ate out every night, I would have to get a second job."

"I have to say, you cook a lot better than I do. Opening cans is a skill I perfected," Marlee said as they set the table.

"If that's the case why don't you show me those skills tomorrow night?"

"A challenge?" She cocked her head.

"You're on big guy. I can show you more useless skills than you ever imagined. You'll be amazed and awed and never the same again," quipped Marlee.

He looked at Marlee's flushed face. He was already amazed and awed. Marlee was one of a kind. He couldn't wait to explore wherever this fascination with her and see where it might lead. But only after she was safe. It was an odd feeling for a confirmed bachelor who loved women—a lot. Ben decided not to spend too much time thinking about that and concentrate on the spunky woman in front of him.

Rubbing her stomach, Marlee smiled and informed Ben she thought tacos were her new favorite meal. He told her he would make them as often as she liked.

As they were cleaning up the table, Ben asked, "Do you want to go see your family tomorrow?"

"That would be great."

Plans made. Dishes put away. They watched TV for a little while, but Marlee couldn't keep her eyes open anymore.

She yawned and told Ben she would see him in the morning. He double-checked the locks on the doors and got ready for bed. But dreams—nightmares—invaded his sleep. Marlee was screaming. He couldn't get to her in time. He was terrified that he couldn't keep Marlee safe. After all, he couldn't save Kimmie. Then his dreams turned to her father and grandma, who were calling out for help. He was too late to help them. Marlee would be devasted if they got hurt. He was afraid KnightGuard would come up empty. And Marlee wouldn't be able to enjoy a full life. He thrashed and turned. Tomorrow couldn't come fast enough.

———

BEN DROVE and followed Marlee's directions to her father's house. Her family lived about forty-five minutes from his house. Marlee talked nonstop about her grandma. Ben felt like he knew grandma's entire history by the time they arrived. Pulling into the driveway of a small Mediterranean-style home on a quiet street, he stopped and looked at Marlee.

"Are you ready for this?"

Marlee sighed.

"I'm not looking forward to telling them what happened," she said. "And I'm afraid for them. Do you think Robert will go after them?"

Ben shrugged his shoulders. "Sweetheart, I don't know. I think it might be a good idea to have someone watch the house. I'll ask Sam if someone can watch it or drive by occasionally."

"That would be great. Maybe an occasional drive-by." She stopped talking. Ben glanced over at her. Her eyes darkened, and sadness came over them. "Although," she said, "I'm currently not working or getting paid, so I can't afford full-time security."

She took a deep breath and exhaled lightly. "Or any security for that matter."

He had forgotten that. He leaned over and held her head between his hands. "Marlee, don't worry about that right now. Let's keep you and them safe as safe we can."

Damn, he felt like a heel. He totally forgot Robert stopped paying her since she hadn't quit or shown up for work. He promised himself tomorrow he would talk to Sam or pay for security himself.

"Come on," he said and took her hand. "Let's go meet the parents."

They walked up the manicured path. Someone, probably the grandma, had planted all sorts of colorful flowers. Ben thought his mom, who also liked to garden, would love the country look.

The front door opened just as they approached it, and Ben heard a woman's voice yell, "Marlee!" A pair of arms reached out to her.

Marlee fell into her grandma's arms, and they both started crying. *Sheesh, women.* Ben would never get used to the crying. He was amazed that grandma was even shorter than Marlee.

A tall, thin man stood behind them and pulled them both in. "You two," he said with a small smile.

He put out his hand to Ben, and they shook hands. Ben followed him into a small living room. Her father told him to sit down. Marlee and her grandmother sat on the sofa. Her father sat opposite Ben. The house was smaller than his, and Ben glanced around the comfy, sun-filled room. Pictures of Marlee in various activities covered a bench pushed against a wall. The furniture was older but clean and didn't have the grandma look. Marlee mentioned grandma was an energy force and into all sorts of activities from acting to yoga.

Marlee looked so much like her dad, Michael. Both were thin, but Marlee was delicate-looking—although Ben knew she had some muscle underneath that exterior. He almost grinned thinking about how she got the best of him. Almost.

He didn't notice before they sat down that her dad was on oxygen. Mike, as he asked Ben to call him, saw him looking. "Emphysema," he said and pointed to the oxygen machine. "The result of a bad habit. It's the reason I retired."

"Tough disease." Ben didn't quite know what to say. A disease like that would be hard on the family.

"Yeah. Fortunately, I made a good living with my company before I couldn't handle the work anymore," Mike said.

Marlee's grandma got up and told them she was going to put a pot of coffee on. A few minutes later, she came back with mugs and a coffee cake. Setting up plates for everyone, Barb, as she liked to be called, looked at Ben and asked if he was Marlee's boyfriend.

"Grandma," Marlee squeaked. "You can't just come out and ask that."

Her grandma ignored Marlee's outburst and stared at Ben, apparently waiting for an answer. Ben laughed. "No, ma'am, I'm Marlee's protection."

Her dad and grandma stopped what they were doing and looked at Marlee, questions in their eyes.

"Something you need to tell us, child?" her dad asked softly.

The ordinarily talkative Marlee sat there like a deer in the highlights, picking at the pillow she held in her lap. Ben watched her eyes fill with tears, and her lips moved, but no sound came out. He decided to speak up.

"Yes, sir. Marlee, she, er, we have a problem. Hopefully, it won't affect you or Barb, but it certainly is affecting Marlee. That's why she has protection."

They spent the next half hour explaining the embezzlement, the murder, the attempt on Marlee's life, and their inability to pin it all on Robert. He told them that she was living at Ben's house and gave them the address just in case they had a problem.

Mike and Barb were shocked and frightened for Marlee.

"Bah, I never trusted that man. He's a sleaze bag." spat grandma.

"Ma, please don't get upset. What's done is done." Mike tried to placate his mom.

They talked about it for a while. Then Barb picked up the cups and walked toward the kitchen. Ben asked if he could help her, and she nodded. Picking up the coffeepot, he followed her in.

She placed the cups in the dishwasher and turned to Ben, whispering so Marlee and her son couldn't hear her. "I didn't want to say anything in front of those two. They have enough on their plates. I wondered why the company checks we've been receiving each month had been cut in half. Now I know why. That man, Robert Gilligan, told me the company wasn't doing well and he couldn't send as much. I'm concerned because the medical bills are quite high, and I'm stretching our budget as best I can and trying not to stress my son out. I haven't said anything to him."

Shit. That was heartbreaking, being ill, and having to choose between your health or food. Ben took the tiny, gray-haired woman's hand in his. "Barb, we are going to do everything possible to resolve this and keep Marlee safe."

She gave him a big smile so like Marlee's, hugged Ben, then pulled away. "As I always say, 'Better a thousand times careful than once dead.' So be smart. Be careful. And keep my granddaughter safe."

Looking at him slyly, she added, "And don't take advantage of her. She's innocent and has much love to give to the right person."

Oh, man. Even Grandma Burns? What the hell was he doing that everyone thought that he had a thing for Marlee? She was a pain in his ass, plain and simple. She was spirited, headstrong, and brave but charming. *Charming?* He might as well admit she was adorable too. Damn, Marlee was getting to him big time.

Marlee walked into the kitchen. "Dad is getting tired and needs to rest. I'm ready if you are."

Saying their goodbyes, they got into Ben's truck to head home. Marlee was quiet for a few minutes. "Grandma and dad liked you. Thank you for bringing me. I've missed them both and wanted to make sure they're safe. I don't trust Robert to leave them alone. He's so vindictive."

"When we get home, we'll sit down and come up with some ways to make sure they're safe." Ben looked over at Marlee, who was sniffling and wiping her nose. "OK?"

Marlee wiped a tear, nodded, and then gave him a megawatt smile. Then proceeded to regale him all the way home with hilarious stories of growing up with Grandma Burns's disastrous choices in after-school activities for her.

CHAPTER TEN

Robert couldn't calm down after locating Marlee's cellphone and following the app to that fishing camp, shooting at her, missing, and then being chased by the Hulk. Close call.

But now he had to come up with another idea to get to Marlee. The police put Jim's death down to a robbery gone wrong. Fine by him. He didn't want to call attention and have someone look at the books. Jim must have been lying when he told him he'd given Marlee a thumb drive with the second sets of books on it. Or was he? Didn't matter. He needed to come up with a Plan B if things went south. He sure couldn't count on Marlee keeping her mouth shut. Although he wasn't too worried, his cousin would give him a head's up if, or when she came into the station. A couple of extra bucks and a whisper in his cousin's ear, Robert was confident that it wouldn't go anywhere.

What to do now?

Well, he wasn't an accountant for nothing. He enjoyed a good reputation in town. John Bennett, the Bennett in Burns, Gilligan, and Bennett, died several years ago with a little help

—from him. Thank you very much. Too bad Bennett had gotten so nosy. Michael Burns was wasting away in Black Pointe and would probably kick the bucket soon. So, the firm was basically his.

He couldn't coax Marlee from her protection detail, but the police could. *Let's think. Yes.* He'd already created an account in her name, added some significant numbers to her bank account, and the night he shot Jim, he siphoned some money from the accounts she oversaw. She was a wealthy woman. She just didn't know it yet.

He wasn't worried anymore about anyone finding the second set of books. Maybe a really sharp forensics guy could find them, but he and Amber would be long gone before that happened. He knew the money was well hidden.

When Jim found some discrepancies in the books, he had been surprised. But then, Jim was always too smart for his own good, and look where being too smart got him. *Are you happy now, Jim?* As for Marlee, she found some discrepancies because of a phone call meant for him. And they were only on a small account that he hadn't had a chance to clean up. Not smart on his end, but they were scrubbed clean now.

Robert sat down at his home computer. It was a good decision having the accounting program here. Under the guise of working at home, everything the office had, he put on his home computer. Plus, all the extras.

He pulled up Marlee's bank account. She hadn't used her credit or debit cards to withdraw any money while she was hiding, but that didn't matter. When he presented the police with his evidence, the dumb bitch wouldn't be able to hide anymore. Now, time for a call.

THE SKY WAS DARKENING, and it smelled like rain. Sam had received a disturbing call and was driving over to Ben's house with the news. Ben told her they just got back from Marlee's dad's house and were making dinner. The news was going to ruin their dinner for sure.

She pulled into the driveway, got out of the car, and rang the doorbell. Ben opened the door, took one look at her face, and asked what was wrong.

"Why don't you get Marlee, and I'll explain everything to both of you."

Ben called Marlee from the kitchen, and they all sat down in the living room.

There was no easy way to tell them the news, but still, Sam hesitated. "Marlee."

That was as far as she got. Marlee immediately interrupted her, panic in her voice. "Is ... it, dad?" She started rubbing her arms, turning pale. "Oh my God, are he and Grandma OK?"

Ben rubbed Marlee's back. Sam shook her head. "Nothing to do with them; it's about you."

Marlee squeaked, "Me?"

"Unfortunately. I just got a call from a friend on the Lakedale force. Seems like Robert has reported to them that he suspects you embezzled funds from the company."

Marlee jumped up. "Are you kidding me? When I see that bastard, I'm going to squeeze his balls until they shoot out his mouth. I'm gonna ... "

Ben stood up and covered her mouth. "Shhh, sweetheart, let's hear what Sam has to say."

"Girl, you're a, woman after my own heart," said Sam. She looked at the small but fierce warrior in front of her, ready to do battle. That was one of the reasons she liked Marlee so much.

"However, squeezing his balls isn't going to get you out of

this. The police want to ask you some questions about the embezzlement based on Robert's statement and proof."

"Proof? What proof?" Marlee sat down and put her head in her hands. "Oh my God, what am I going to do? I swear I'm innocent." She looked imploringly at Sam.

"Marlee, we know you're innocent, but this has to play out. I hope to get more information from the police about what they want to talk to you about, and if they have specific charges against you. It might be best to go there without them coming after you."

"Ohmygodohmygodohmygod."

"Marlee, calm down. This isn't the end of the world," said Sam. Watching Marlee break down was stressful. She hoped Marlee could keep it together when she spoke with the police. The woman would probably confess to anything in the state she was in.

"Maybe not for you," Marlee retorted. "This is horrible. My dad and grandma are going to be so upset or worse. I can't afford a lawyer right now. I'm going to jail." She started to wail and wring her hands. "I'm going to die alone. A lonely old woman in a tiny cell."

Ben shook his head and put his arms around her. "Marlee, you're not going to jail if you didn't do anything wrong, and you are certainly not going to die a lonely old woman in jail." He continued, "Besides, we'll come to visit you. Maybe bake a cake and put a knife in it for your birthday."

Sam could only shake her head. Ben was trying for levity, but she knew that was going to fall short.

Marlee stopped crying and looked astonished. "You're a giant asshole, you know?" She smacked him alongside his head. "I think I hate you."

"Ow."

Sam grinned. "Marlee, everything's going to be all right.

You don't need to involve your family right now. I'll get the firm's lawyer to go with you."

Marlee sniffed, patted her pants for a tissue, blew, and then nodded.

"Well, I've done my duty as the bearer of bad news. I have a date I'm late for." She stood and hugged Marlee. "We'll talk tomorrow and decide the best time for you to talk to our lawyer, and the police."

Sam walked to her car, reflecting on the conversation she had with Ben and Marlee. She wanted to be optimistic about the outcome, and certainly, KnightGuard was pulling out all the stops, but every day something else was coming up against Marlee. It wasn't looking good for her friend, but she wasn't giving up. They would find evidence against Robert.

———

BEN CLOSED the door after Sam left and walked over to Marlee. He sat on the sofa and pulled her into his arms. "Sweetheart, this will turn out all right. Have a little faith; Sam is good at these sorts of problems."

"You're right." She left his hold and stood up. "Listen, I'm not hungry right now. I'm going to take a bath and climb into bed if that's all right." She pressed her palm to her mouth and let it fall. "This is not going to end well. I just know it."

Shaking her head, she said, "not well at all."

"You don't know that. You're innocent. Nothing bad is going to happen. Trust us." He hugged her and told her to take a bath.

He had no idea what the police knew or were going to ask. He could only guess based on personal experience. He didn't know anyone on the Lakedale police force, nor did he think anyone at his old precinct knew about the case. The police didn't know he was sheltering Marlee at his house. A feeling of helplessness settled in like an old friend. But for Marlee, he would ask or beg to watch her interrogation as a professional courtesy.

SOMETHING WOKE HIM UP. Ben cocked his ear, struggling to hear what it was. Then he heard noises coming from the hall. Was someone in the house? The alarm didn't go off. Grabbing his gun from beneath his pillow, he quietly opened the door and peered out. No one there. He listened again. Sniffling noises were coming from Marlee's bedroom.

What the hell? Was someone in her room? His bare feet made no noise as he stepped closer to her room. Standing beside the door, he slowly opened it with his gun and looked in.

The noises were coming from Marlee. She was whimpering in her sleep and thrashing around. Nightmares.

Ben went to the side of the bed and gently shook her. "Marlee, honey, wake up."

Her eyes snapped open, and she suddenly sat up. "Ben, is there something wrong? Are you hurt? Is someone in the house? Do you need anything? Should I get my Taser?"

Ben groaned. *Please, no Taser.* Wow. Marlee talked nonstop, even in the middle of the night. "No, sweet cheeks. I heard noises, and it appears you are having bad dreams. I came to check on you."

She snuggled back down in the bed, pulling the covers up to her chin and sighed. "Yeah, I can't keep thoughts of being arrested and going to jail out of my mind."

"Marlee, you're not going to jail. Come on. Turn over. Let me rub your back." It was the least he could do. He couldn't do anything about the police interview. Robert was still out there. A shit storm was on the way, but he could rub her back.

Marlee turned on her stomach. Ben rubbed her back until he felt her muscles relax. Marlee groaned. His cock was getting hard. Not going there, he stopped and started to stand.

In a small voice, she asked, "Will you stay with me until I fall asleep?"

Oh, yes, he would. Unfortunately, his cock was getting too excited just from rubbing her back. He needed to get his body under control. Could he do this? For Marlee, he would, even though he would be uncomfortable.

"Sure, honey, turn on your side, and I'll hold you until you fall asleep."

They cuddled for a couple of hours. Ben lay there with her butt tucked into his stomach, his cock hard as a rock. Occasionally, she would wiggle her sweet rear around, and his cock would get harder. It was agony, pure agony. He stayed awake listening to her breathing and smiled to himself when she started snoring. Thank God, she finally fell asleep.

He'd just closed his eyes when Marlee started whimpering again. Ben rubbed her back, hoping she wouldn't wake up.

Marlee turned over, wide awake, and gazed into his eyes. "You know, I think I would feel better if you were to make love to me."

Ben choked. "Excuse me."

"You heard me, big boy. Make love to me."

Holy shit. Did Marlee understand what she just asked him? Did he want to make love to her? Oh yeah. But was this the right time? No.

YES, please! That was little Ben answering. Down, boy. Ben knew he was in trouble. He couldn't think clearly, he wanted her. He needed her, and, by God, he was going to have her.

"Marlee, are you sure? I mean, I would love to, but we've barely kissed."

Marlee murmured, "I know that. But I know you're

attracted to me. I'm attracted to you and making love will make me forget about tomorrow for a while."

"Oh, sweet cheeks, you're going to be the death of me yet." Telling her to hold that thought, Ben hurried into his room for condoms. He pulled out the contents of his side table. Junk but no condoms. Shit, where did he put that new box? Marlee was waiting. Then he remembered he put the box under the sink in the bathroom, thinking he didn't have an immediate need for condoms. He grabbed the box, and hurried back to Marlee, hopeful she was still awake and willing.

Oh yeah, she was awake all right and lying on top of the sheets. Naked. Ben took in her slim body glowing in the moonlight. She wasn't heavy-breasted the way he usually liked his women, but he thought her breasts were perfect. She also wasn't as curvy and full-figured as he usually liked. Easier to pound into a woman with a little meat on her. But he savored her slim, delicate figure, and he wanted to explore every inch of it. Oh God, he had it bad.

Marlee reached out her arms and brought him close. "Ben, I'm not very experienced doing this."

Ben smirked. "Oh honey, I'm very experienced, not to worry."

Ben slowly ran his hands up and down her body. He stopped at her breasts and stared at the small nipples peaking under his touch. He leaned over and started licking and sucking each one.

Marlee groaned. "Oh my, that feels really good."

Ben chuckled and sucked harder. "Well, hold on, honey, because something else is going to feel even better."

He moved his hands down to her mound. She squeaked. He rubbed in circles, and she pushed harder into his hand. Marlee was more responsive than he thought. Especially since she already told him she wasn't very experienced.

He inserted one long finger into her folds, she clenched it tightly. She was hot, wet, but not wet enough. He kissed her breasts and moved his body downward, all the while kissing her knees, her inner thighs, her clit, her pussy. Marlee was getting wetter and moaning.

"Oh, my God. Ben, are you going to make love to me or not? I can't wait anymore." She was bucking into his mouth.

What an invitation. Ben nodded as he licked her pussy. He stopped to put a condom on, and his cock headed home.

God, she was tight. Really tight. Ben thought he made her wet enough for his cock and making love.

He pushed in a little harder, and Marlee grunted a little. He pushed a little more. Her pussy clamped around his cock like a vise. "Relax, honey. Am I hurting you?"

"No," she groaned. "Just move."

He tried to move again, but she was so tight. Damn, he never had this problem before. He wanted to make it good for her, and he was failing. A little thought popped into his head. *No. She couldn't be.*

"Sweetheart, you're not a virgin, are you?"

Marlee nodded into Ben's chest. Shit. Fuck. No way. He was not deflowering her. He had no experience with virgins. Virgins wanted marriage and kids. He wasn't ready for that.

He started to pull out. Marlee wrapped her legs around him, and with all her strength, pushed herself on his cock. He was thrust into her and entered heaven. Tight. Warm. Wet.

"Marlee?" He was afraid to move. Afraid he was hurting her.

Marlee was breathing heavily. Her brows furrowed. Taking a deep breath, she said, "Give me a minute, then move, damn you."

Ben gave her a minute to get used to his girth. He knew he was large. He knew it hurt. He knew a lot of things, but that didn't stop the intense need that was taking over.

He started thrusting slowly, she moaned. He stopped and then started again.

Marlee was getting wetter and looser. He started a rhythm that she matched.

Faster and faster. His balls were aching, but he wanted to make it last, make it good for her.

He was trying hard not to come too soon. Couldn't. Stop. Himself. He pumped harder.

Ben thought if he didn't come soon, his balls would explode. Marlee begged him to come. With a gush, he exploded into the condom and gushed and gushed. Where the hell did all the cum come from?

He collapsed on top of her. Realizing he was heavy, he turned so Marlee was resting on his chest.

Marlee was breathing as heavily as he was. She let out a deep sigh and opened her eyes. "Wow."

Wow was right, but Ben was embarrassed. He felt like he deflowered Bambi.

He kissed her cheek and gently moved her body to the side. He got up to dispose of the condom and noticed the red spots on the sheet—a vivid reminder. Going into the bathroom, he returned with a warm washcloth.

Lying next to Marlee, Ben told her to open her legs. He washed her gently, hoping he hadn't hurt her too much.

"Marlee. Honey, you should have told me you were a virgin ahead of time. I would have done things differently."

"How differently?" She cocked her head, looked at him, puzzled.

"Just differently. Spend more time getting you aroused. I'm sorry I hurt you."

"Aroused more? How? What could I have done to help?"

Only his sprite would want to get into a discussion about sex and orgasms. Ben thought about the question. On the one hand, he shouldn't make love with her again. Ever. He was supposed to be protecting her, not screwing her. On the other, Ben didn't think he could ever get enough of Marlee. Devil or angel. Both battling on his shoulder. Shit. The devil won every time. He wanted to make love to her again.

She snorted. "Besides, if I waited for you to make a move, I would be that old woman in jail. I wanted you to be my first. Is that so wrong?"

"It was my pleasure to be your first. I feel privileged, although I wish I'd known. A woman should orgasm first before she makes love."

"Did I have an orgasm?"

Such an innocent question. But then she had been a virgin until a short time ago.

"I don't think so. You would know if you did." Ben closed his eyes. His heart was clenching. Great. He was the experienced one, and he only took care of himself. He wanted to hit his head on the sideboard. He was a horndog all right, but he would make this good for her.

"Sweetheart, the next time we make love, which will be as soon as I catch my breath, I'm giving you an orgasm, and trust me, you'll know it. C'mere, let me hold you." He held out his arms.

MARLEE SNUGGLED INTO BEN. Every idea she had about sex flew out the window. It was more wonderful than anything she could have imagined. Well, except for that little obstruction. Ben was an enthusiastic lover. She was a bit concerned when she saw the size of his cock, but *oh my*, he knew how to use it and make her feel good.

But she wondered what an orgasm felt like. Would she even recognize it if she had one? She smiled to herself. Ben said *next time*.

They fell asleep for a while. It was early dawn when Ben woke her up to make love again. He made sweet, gentle love this time and she got to explore that snake tattoo.

Afterward, there was no doubt in Marlee's mind she had an orgasm, probably two. Smiling, she fell asleep.

CHAPTER ELEVEN

Sam called Ben early the next morning to tell him to expect her in an hour. She hated the way they left the conversation the previous day with Marlee so upset. After speaking with Earle Conway, the firm's lawyer, she had a better sense of how to talk to the police.

Ben handed her a cup of coffee, and they all sat in the same seats they'd occupied the previous night, but something was different. She was perplexed by the sizzling looks Ben and Marlee exchanged and thought she didn't see. If she was a betting woman ...

She'd heard rumors about Ben being a love'em and leave'em guy. Marlee was an innocent. Ben was so out of her league. She shook her head, not going there right now. She had more important things to discuss.

"I understand why you didn't go to the police right away after you heard Jim being shot," said Sam. "The police are still interested in hearing your version. But why did you keep quiet about the embezzling?"

Sam was bewildered by the way Marlee hemmed, hawed, and wouldn't answer the question. She waited patiently.

Taking a deep breath, Marlee finally confessed. "I didn't go to the police for a couple of reasons."

She held up one finger. "One, I was afraid. I didn't actually see Robert shoot Jim. I heard them arguing and then heard a shot. I did see Jim on the floor but didn't stick around to know if he was alive. All I could think of was that Robert would kill me before I told the police. And, if you remember, I told you Robert's cousin is the police chief and supposedly on the take. As for the embezzlement, Jim wanted to make sure we had all the facts before we accused Robert or went to the police, and two ... "

Marlee gulped and held up two trembling fingers. "Two is, I have a history."

Sam and Ben looked at each other. A history? What the hell did that mean? Marlee was a mystery that just kept unfolding.

"Explain," Sam said. Could this story get any more complicated or confusing?

"THIS IS EMBARRASSING," Marlee said, clearing her throat. "When I first started working as an accountant with another firm, I noticed one of the employees writing himself checks and signing them, which was against company policy. I reported him to my boss, who told me to mind my own business."

"But could I? Noooo." Marlee paused. The whole event had been embarrassing and avoidable. She still felt terrible about it after all this time.

"I reported Jerod's actions to the CEO and let everyone in the office know what he was doing. It turns out Jerod got permission to write a check for reimbursement for a loan he made. However, he was supposed to have the CEO sign them, and he didn't. Because of the stink I made, they fired Jerod, and reprimanded my boss."

Marlee couldn't look at either Sam or Ben. Sam looked surprised, but Ben's brows scrunched together, and he was scowling. Did her story bother him? Was he embarrassed by her admission?

She took a deep breath. It was painful to recount a moment in her life when she hadn't used her best judgment. *Would Sam and Ben think less of her?* Didn't matter now. So why was her stomach churning and her chest hurt?

"Why did they fire Jerod? It sounds like a lapse in judgment, not a capital crime," asked Sam.

"Well." Marlee cleared her throat. "They were making an example of him. It wasn't up to him to make his own rules. If he did that, then it would be all right for everyone to do so."

"Hmmm. I guess that's right," said Sam.

"Eventually, I was fired. My boss claimed for poor performance. It turned out that nobody trusted me at the company anymore. I was called a troublemaker. Jerod made sure to tell everyone that I got him fired for no reason. And then rumors started. I couldn't get a job for months. No one would talk to me. Thankfully, my father believed in me and hired me."

She sat back on the sofa. "Grandma was right when she said, 'Believe nothing that you hear and only half of what you see.' If I only gathered more information, none of this would've happened. And, I definitely would have handled the situation differently."

It sounded so simplistic when she spoke about the problem. But it took her a couple of years to feel better about herself. And now this mess. A setback for sure.

SAM LISTENED to Marlee retell how she bungled a crappy situation. There was no good solution for something like that. No winners, for sure. But as Marlee learned, sometimes you have to hold your tongue and let others handle it.

Besides, it wasn't as if Sam hadn't made some bad judgment calls in her career. She could tell Marlee felt terrible about what happened. Now, this thing with Robert. Not good. If Robert knew about Marlee's history, and he told the police, they would have a hard time believing anything she said. What a mess.

Marlee continued, "I was embarrassed. You can see why I didn't report Robert was embezzling or Jim's murder, besides the fact that Robert's cousin is police chief. The partners had to know about my previous accusation. For sure, my father wouldn't have hired me without telling them. So, you see, accusing yet a second person of mishandling accounts wouldn't have made me a good witness."

Sam sighed. "I understand what you're saying. But a man was killed."

"Tell me something I don't know." Marlee wiped a tear. "Given my history, if Robert's spoken to them, they'll accuse me of telling tales. My word is probably no good, and they won't believe me about Robert killing Jim."

Sam agreed with Marlee's perception. It wasn't looking good for her. She glanced over at Ben, who hadn't said a word. He sat rigid in the chair with a dazed expression on his face. What was going on with him? Weird.

"Ben, you look lost in thought. What do you think?"

BEN HESITATED FOR A MOMENT. What did he think? He wasn't thinking good thoughts, that's for sure.

"Well, I think this whole situation is messy. I don't know

what information the Lakedale police have, but they're not going to arrest her without doing an investigation."

Sam nodded. "That's what Earle said."

"I'm sure Robert doesn't want the police looking into the accounts, so that part of it doesn't make sense."

"I agree."

"And I keep wondering, what's his end game?"

Ben couldn't look at Marlee. He'd been devastated listening to her story. Hearing her speak about ruining a man's life even if she was partly right but didn't get all the facts straight brought back memories of a rough time in his own life. Memories he didn't want to revisit. *Too late.* How could she do that? Was she only thinking of herself? Maybe she was one of those people who had to follow the rules and never give anyone a break.

Ben shook his head, trying to clear the negative thoughts away. Marlee was due to talk to the police soon. He didn't want her any more stressed. They needed to make a plan.

MARLEE WAS uncomfortable talking about her mistake in judgment. It was not the avenue she wanted to go down or have anyone know. She took responsibility for that a long time ago. What did Ben and Sam think of her now that she gave her secret up? Would they believe her about Robert? About Robert shooting Jim? About anything, she told them.

She had been in the wrong at the time. It wasn't her place to say anything to her CEO. And saying "I'm sorry" to Jerod didn't cut it. How do you ruin a man's life and just say, "Oh, by the way, I'm sorry I made a mistake that cost you your job and reputation?" How do you apologize to his wife and kids?

When she got the call about the discrepancies in the account, she did a little investigating herself before realizing something odd was going on. After bringing it to Robert's attention, and not being satisfied with his response, she told Jim. It was his responsibility as her boss to handle it. Thankfully, he believed her, but Jim wanted all his ducks in a row before he approached Robert or the police. Jim told her he suspected that something squirrelly was going on, and Robert might be fudging the books. He had a backup plan just in case Robert found out. But Jim died before he told her what the backup plan was. Too late now.

If Robert told the police about her lying at her previous company, they would have a hard time believing her now. How could she tell them that she and Jim suspected Robert of stealing without any proof? And what about Jim? Would he ever get justice?

What was that adage grandma liked?

Oh, right. If you "cry wolf" too many times, no one will believe you when something was true. Well, Grandma Burns was right. Again.

CHAPTER TWELVE

"Benny, eat your sandwich, or you'll be late for your game. Daddy won't be home in time to watch it, but I'll be there." He picked up a half of a peanut butter sandwich with the crusts cut off and thought his mom made the best sandwiches in the world.

It was the last T-ball game of the season, and he couldn't wait to get to the field. He played catcher most games, and he hoped today he would too. The back door opened as Benny was finishing his glass of milk. Dad walked in. He didn't look so good.

"Aaron, what's wrong? Are you sick?" His mom rushed over to Dad.

"Not sick," he whispered. His mom hugged Dad. They were talking low, but Benny could hear them. He had good hearing. His dad was telling her he'd been fired for stealing. Stealing? His dad? His dad would never steal. He always told Benny and his sister and brother that stealers were the lowest of the low.

Mom started crying. Benny wanted to rush over to her. But his dad put his arm around mom, and they walked toward their bedroom. Benny heard his mom ask Dad, "What are we going to do?"

Benny wasn't sure what was happening with his parents, but he *was going to be late for the game. He left his plate and glass, walked over to his parents' bedroom door, and knocked.*

"Mom, Dad? Coach won't let me play if I'm late. Mom?"

His mom opened the door, wiping her eyes. What did Dad say to make her cry? He would ask later. Right now, they needed to get going.

"Benny, good news. Dad is going to come to your game too." Benny was excited. It wasn't often Dad could take time off during the week to go to a game.

He didn't think any more about Dad's problem. School was letting out soon, and he would be free. Summer. Yeah. This would be the first year he would go to summer camp with his sister, Ashley, and his brother, Charlie. Last year he was too young, but his parents promised he could go to camp this year. He couldn't wait.

Dad was grouchy for weeks. Ashley and Charlie would talk about it, but Benny didn't understand why Dad couldn't get a job. Something about his "putation." Whatever a "putation" was, Dad didn't have it anymore.

It was a hot night in June, and they were having hot dogs from the grill for dinner when Dad told Benny and his siblings that they wouldn't be going to summer camp that summer.

Ashley and Charlie didn't say anything, but Benny couldn't stop himself. "Why not? I've been waiting all year to go. You promised."

"Benny," his dad said, rubbing his chin. "I haven't been able to get a job, and we don't have the money to pay for camp. I'm sorry to disappoint you, but that's the way it is. I'm starting my own business, and mom is going to help me. All our money will be tied up for a while. Maybe you can go to camp next year."

He stood up and started crying. His mom reached out to him, but he ran to his bedroom. Life was so unfair. Why did dad have to get fired?

Ben woke up in a sweat. It was still dark outside, but there was a glow from the TV. What time was it? He fumbled for his phone. Found it. Shit, it was 3 a.m. Fell asleep again in the living room. Damn, his back hurt. He needed to get a new couch for sure. He lay there missing Marlee, but he wasn't ready to go into the bedroom. Her confession the other day knocked him for a loop, and he didn't know how to respond to it. But he missed her and her sweet body. And he desperately wanted her arms around him, moaning while he plunged into her tight pussy.

He got up and peeked into the bedroom and watched Marlee as she peacefully slept—aching to go to her. They made love a couple of days ago after Sam's visit, although Ben's mind wasn't in it. His body, oh yeah, nothing stopped the body, but he felt like a horndog now and a hypocrite. He couldn't get over what she did, how she ruined a man's life. Maybe she was young and inexperienced, but you didn't throw a man under the bus just to be right. Did you?

If he were honest about it, Marlee's confession was coloring the way he looked at her. Maybe he was wrong, but the effect on his family of his dad's firing for borrowing some tools was still as strong in his mind today as it was when he was younger. And it hurt. He'd forgotten how much.

Ben hadn't thought about his dad getting fired in a while. His father's garage had done well. His mom worked there helping in the office, and he and his siblings went in to help occasionally. Not to work on the cars but to clean the garage and pick up. It was hard on his family for a while until business picked up.

He learned a few years later that his dad had been blackballed, and that was the reason he couldn't get a mechanic's job anywhere. Just like Jerod after Marlee went after him. All for borrowing a few tools to work on his car at home or, in Jerod's case, signing his name to the check instead of the CEO. Sure, they weren't smart moves, but they were small in the scheme of things.

He never believed everything was black or white. Even

being a cop didn't change that. He had lots of experience with the dregs of society. He believed in shades of gray. So why did this bother him so much? It didn't make sense to him. When he had time, he would ask his dad what happened.

He knew he was short with Marlee several times over the past couple of days. Not just short but sarcastic. He saw the hurt on her face. He was sleeping on the couch, telling her that he fell asleep watching television or working. Ben was sure she didn't understand what was going on. She asked him if everything was OK several times, but he couldn't talk about it yet.

If he thought they had a future, he would, but first, he needed to come to grips with the fact Marlee ruined one man's life, and maybe another's. How many times had she lied?

He wanted to trust his woman, but right now, that trust was in short supply.

CHAPTER THIRTEEN

Marlee was betwixt and between. Fed up with being guarded, although having a couple of hunks guarding her, was certainly not a hardship. She enjoyed talking to Luke and Joe. They entertained her with stories of stupid things some of their clients did when they were only trying to keep them safe.

She was fed up with not having a job or her things.

And she was fed up with not seeing her friends or having the ability to drive herself to the store without a bodyguard.

Sam called to tell her that Earle made an appointment for them to talk to the police in a day. The interview was weighing heavy on her mind, and she was terrified that she would end up in jail. Although Earle called earlier and told her not to worry—as if.

Marlee liked the smart-mouthed Sam. A woman after her own heart. Small but strong. No pushover. Loyal to her friends. But at the same time, the woman was intense. Sam didn't do anything overtly to make Marlee feel that way, but there was edginess about her, a wariness that Marlee couldn't identify. She was just glad Sam was her friend.

The fact remained; she wanted her old boring life back. Well, parts of it anyhow. She wanted to talk to her friends and go out for coffee. She wanted to laugh and go to work. She wanted Robert behind bars. She wanted Jeffrey, and she wanted Ben—a lot. But what did Grandma Burns always say? "If wishes were horses, beggars would ride."

Something was off with Ben lately. Sure, he was still around and guarding her. But at night, instead of making love, he was making excuses. If he worked late, he fell asleep on the couch. Or if he stayed up late watching TV, he fell asleep on the couch. In short, he was spending a lot of time on the couch and not in bed with her. She noticed he was distant during the day too. Not overtly, but there were no kisses or hugs, no teasing, no Ben participating in their relationship like he had been.

Marlee couldn't imagine what was going on with him. Was he bored? Did he still want a relationship with her? Although she didn't have a lot of experience in the relationship department, she thought their relationship was going great. But not now. She shook her head. *What to do?*

She was tired of wishing her life away. She made up her mind to confront Ben when he came home. She was no coward, and if he had a problem with her, she wanted to know what it was. Either they could get past whatever the issue was or not.

IT HAD BEEN a few months since Ben was able to get away to visit his parents. Sure, they talked every couple of weeks, but it wasn't the same as seeing them in person. He was grateful his sister Ashley lived close to his parents and took the grand-kids over to visit with them once a week.

Marlee's confession bothered him on so many levels. He

thought they had something going but ruining a man's life—Ben couldn't go there with her right now. Sure, they made love a couple of days ago; he couldn't keep away from her. But now that the drama was in the past and he had more time to hash over what Marlee said, it still disturbed him. He never got to hear the whole story from his dad, and now he needed to.

Pulling up to the light-green ranch house he grew up in, Ben took in the manicured garden in front and the recently mowed lawn. The house always looked well-maintained. Even though his parents still worked at the garage, his mom found time to garden.

His mom's car was in the driveway. He walked up the front path and debated ringing the doorbell, but history was, no matter how many times he cautioned his parents, they very seldom locked the door. Ben made a mental note to remind his mother of the dangers of an unlocked door. He met too many nut jobs who would love to help themselves to whatever his parents had or worse.

"Ma? Dad?"

No answer. Where the heck was his mother? The open door, no parents greeting him—this was a disaster waiting to happen. Why didn't they just put a sign out front, "Burglars welcome."

He walked through the small living room into the kitchen. No one. Looking outside, he saw his mother bent over, weeding the vegetable garden.

"Ma," he called out as he walked out the back door.

Looking up, his mother gave him a broad smile. "Ben! What brings you here?"

"Can't a son visit his mother without an ulterior motive?" he teased as he kissed her on the cheek.

"Of course. I'm glad to see you; it's been a while."

Standing up and removing her gardening gloves, she said, "Let's go in and have a cup of coffee."

Following her, Ben couldn't help noticing there were a few more gray hairs in her auburn hair than the last time he was here. She was still an attractive woman though.

The kitchen soon smelled of his favorite coffee. Call him a sissy, but he loved the caramel-flavored coffee his mother favored.

She handed him a mug and sat down at the kitchen table across from him. "Saw Ashley and the kids yesterday. Those boys are getting so big."

"Yeah, she sent me some pictures. They're gonna be bruisers like Tim." Tim, Ashley's husband, use to play college football and still kept in top physical condition.

"You seem anxious. You never visit during the day, so tell me what's going on. Is everything OK?"

Ben wasn't shocked that his mom picked up on his discomfort. She could always sense when something was wrong with one of her children.

"Everything's cool. My job is going well. You know I left the force to start at KnightGuard Security. You've met Sam Knight, haven't you?"

She nodded. "Smart gal. Do you like working there?"

"I do." Ben paused, rubbing his brow. "Hmmm."

"Ben, whatever it is, just spit it out." She gave him a small smile and touched his hand.

Ben swallowed hard. "I came today to ask you some questions about when dad lost his job at the garage."

"Oh," she sighed. "That was such a long time ago. I can tell you what I know, but your dad never told me the whole story. You'll need to talk to him. He's at the garage today. One of the mechanics called in sick."

For the next half hour, his mother told him what she

could. Ben knew most of the story, so there wasn't much new he learned.

Kissing his mother goodbye, he promised to visit more often and mentally noted that the next time he came, they were going to talk about safety issues.

He headed toward his father's garage. Ben wasn't looking forward to this part of his trip. He hoped his dad would fill in the blanks. He needed to get over thinking about this or break up with Marlee. If he couldn't trust her, there was no other way. All in or all out was his motto.

The lot was located in a now rundown part of town and filled with cars in various states of repair. The garage had taken off after his father bought it. Fair prices and good work made a huge difference.

"Ben!" His father spotted him, walked over and clapped him on the back. "Son, how are you? Have you seen your mother yet?"

"I'm fine. Yes, I just came from home."

His father put down his wrench and yelled over to one of the mechanics that he was taking a short break. Wiping his hands on a rag, he looked at Ben. "Come on to the break room. Let's catch up."

Ben followed him down a narrow hall with the familiar smell of grease and oil wafting around him. The garage was clean, but certain smells never went away. The garage was his childhood. He always loved the smell of used oil, the sound of hydraulic tools, and the men joking with each other.

"Here you go." Ben's father pulled a chair over for him. "What's up? You hardly ever come to the garage anymore. Is everything OK?"

"Everything's fine. I'm at KnightGuard Security now and on a case. But something came up on a case I'm working on that I wanted to ask you about."

His dad lifted his brow, his blue eyes questioning. "Okaaay."

Hemming and hawing, Ben finally said, "I'm just curious about why you left your job at Richardson's." Ben hated to ask and bring back bad memories for his dad, but he needed to understand why Marlee's confession bothered him so much, and they could, hopefully, move on.

"Ah, Richardson's. That was so long ago. A gray day in my life for sure."

Ben looked at his dad. His light brown hair turned gray years ago. Life had been hard, and it showed in the many wrinkles on his face, however, he always had a positive attitude.

"There's no way to rephrase this, but I need to know. What happened that day? I know you were let go, but did you steal those tools as they claimed?"

His dad's eyes blinked rapidly, and his ears turned red. Ben knew he was embarrassed, and he felt terrible that he was bringing up hurtful memories, but he needed to know the truth of what happened and not rely on his boyhood memory.

"Steal." His dad paused, shook his head, and sighed. "Such a strong word. You know I worked at Richardson's for about ten years and was a supervisor."

Ben nodded.

"About five other mechanics were working under me, and it was up to me to keep track of tools, money, etc. We were having some problems with your mother's car, and she couldn't drive it. So, I borrowed some tools to fix it at home. Figured it would be easier and cheaper than having it towed to the garage."

He stared at his hands and then at the wall, finally letting out a deep breath. "Unfortunately, one of the more expensive tools was stolen from the house. Never found out who did that. I had to tell my boss the next day. One of the ironclad rules at the shop was that no tools were to be taken out. Ever. So not only did I borrow the tools without permission but lost a very expensive tool. And to compound the problem, several weeks before my incident, I had to fire a man for the same thing."

Oh, Dad. Ben's stomach clenched.

His dad sat there and twiddled his thumbs.

Grimacing, his father continued. "My boss was livid. Mostly because I was the supervisor and supposed to set the example for the other mechanics, he had no choice but to fire me. Unfortunately, the mechanic I fired weeks before was popular, so the men were already upset about his firing. Rumors started. I couldn't get a job in any established garages. I was desperate to make money. That's why I started my own."

Ben was astounded. Everything he believed was not true. His dad broke the rules and suffered for it.

"Were you angry?"

"You bet. Blamed my co-worker. Blamed God. In retrospect, I realized it was my own damn fault. I thought I was above the rules of the garage. I was mad for a while, most of all blamed my boss. But it wasn't his fault. He was following company rules."

He gave Ben a small smile. "It was hit and miss for a while. You might remember money was short for a long time, but your mother stepped up, and we made a go of this garage." Reaching for Ben's arm, his father asked, "You're not in any trouble like that, are you?"

"No," Ben said emphatically. "But the woman I'm guarding had a similar incident. She reported someone she thought was stealing. Turns out, he didn't steal, but he didn't follow proper procedure. He lost his job and couldn't get another one. It just reminded me of your situation."

"So, you thought she was wrong to do what she did and potentially ruin someone's life."

"Something like that."

"Ben, in life, we all have choices to make. Rules are there for the good of all. They may not be fair or just, but as you know, it only takes one person to break a rule and make it hard for everyone else. Don't put too much blame on this woman; she probably did what was right even if she suffered the consequences."

Could Dad be right? He had been a detective long enough to know what happened when people bent the rules to help themselves. In retrospect, Marlee could have handled the situation better, and his dad should not have taken the tools home.

He was an ass. Exhaling a pent-up breath, Ben looked at his dad. "So, when did you get so wise?"

His dad laughed. "Wise? I don't think so, but if you're impressed, we'll let it go."

Ben stood. "I've got to go." He clasped his father's shoulders. "I love you. You've been an inspiration to me all my life. Thanks for sharing this with me."

"Love you too, son. Now don't stay away so long." His dad smiled. "And bring that woman of yours around."

"I don't have a woman."

"Ah. I think you do. If this woman's story affected you, you must have feelings for her. Otherwise, you wouldn't have cared what happened to me in the past or be bothered by what she did."

Ben shook his head and snorted. "Well, I think that ship has sailed. She hates me right now, and I don't know what to do."

"You go back and throw yourself on her mercy. Apologize profusely. If she has feelings for you, she'll take you back. Women are like that when they care about someone. Trust me. A sincere apology goes a long way." He smiled and added, "So do flowers and candy."

"I'll try but not holding my breath. I've been really shitty to her."

"Well, don't stop trying. Good luck then." His dad pulled him in for a hug and gave him one last look. "Love you."

Ben got back into his car and thought about how he was treating Marlee, how he pushed her away. What could he do to get her back? Was it too late? She knew something was up. She was no good at holding in her emotions. The hurt showed all over her face. He was wrong to assume she was in the wrong or that his dad was unjustly accused. Baggage had a way of doing that to a person, but his dad's insight might get him back in her good graces. He just had to come up with a plan and flowers—lots of flowers and begging.

CHAPTER FOURTEEN

Driving back to Black Pointe after his visit to his parents, Ben thought a lot about what his father said to him. Had he been too harsh with Marlee without knowing all the facts? Probably. For that matter, why did he have to forgive her? He didn't. She hadn't hurt him. Besides, she hadn't forgiven herself after all these years. It was a judgment call. What was wrong with him that he was pointing fingers?

He knew he was in love with Marlee, but the baggage they both carried had gotten in the way. His childhood baggage was just that—childhood baggage. Ben knew that when he was a kid, he wouldn't have understood what his father told him today. Sure, they were broke for a while, but his parents loved each other and their kids. In all honesty, his childhood didn't suffer too much. His siblings suffered more because they enjoyed, then lost, more activities then he had.

Come to think about it, neither Ashley nor Charlie ever mentioned missing sleepaway camp that year. When the garage was up and running, they were able to attend the camp. Plus, his parents made that first summer as much fun as they could. They went on lots of camping and hiking trips.

Maybe he should call Ashley and get her perspective.

A car honk startled him out of his thoughts. *What the fuck?* He was daydreaming and almost hit another car. Marlee had him in knots. Ben knew what he needed to do.

HE STILL HAD a little time before he got home, so Ben called his sister. They spoke once a month, and he tried to get over to see his nephews as often as he could. At six, nine and ten, three active boys kept Ashley busy. Tim, her husband, was a fireman and wasn't home as much as she liked; however, he knew his mom helped them out a lot.

Ashley answered on the second ring. She sounded winded.

"Hey, sis. How's it going? You sound out of breath."

"Oh, Ben. Hi. Yeah, well, the spawn of Satan are driving me crazy."

Ben laughed. "Well, you wanted kids."

"I wanted sweet little girls who liked tea parties and dresses, not three hellions who are bent on terrorizing the neighborhood."

"I'm sure you're exaggerating, but I'll try to get over soon and spend some time with said hellions."

"Great."

Silence. "So, you hardly ever call. What's up?"

Ah, Ashley. So direct. "Well, I wanted to ask you what you remember about dad losing his job when we were little."

She was silent for a minute. "Well, not much. I remember when he opened the garage and mom helped him. We worked there in the summer and after school. They were stressed for a while, but it worked out. Why?"

"Oh, nothing." He hesitated. "Do you remember not going to camp that first year?"

"Ben." Ashley laughed. "You're never letting that go, are you? You were such a brat about that. I remember every day that summer you made mom and dad feel guilty that they couldn't send us to camp. I knew it was going to be your first year, but you did go the next year."

Hmmm. Ben didn't remember that. He recalled being disappointed, but making his parents feel guilty, not so much.

"What did I do?"

"Ah, let me think."

Ben was pretty sure that was sarcasm.

"Oh yeah, you pouted all summer. You were sarcastic and cried when you weren't pouting. You kept slamming your bedroom door when they tried to talk to you. You didn't want to go camping or hiking and resisted going to the garage. You ... "

"OK. OK. Stop. I get the point. Wow, I'd forgotten how I acted. Mom and Dad must have been really upset with me." Ben was embarrassed. He had been awful to his parents that summer. They were only trying to make the best of a bad situation, and he acted like a spoiled brat.

"Well, you asked. But why bring that up now?"

"Something at work reminded me of Dad losing his job. Look, I've got to hang up now. I'll visit the hooligans in a week or so. Love you."

"Back at you."

Ben hung up. He was confused and embarrassed. Nothing was how he remembered it, and he was blaming Marlee? Ugh. That bouquet of flowers was getting larger and larger.

MARLEE WAS grateful Ben was still guarding her. However, the past couple of days he had been acting squirrelly. His smile didn't reach his eyes. He didn't laugh as much. In all honesty, he wasn't much of a laugher, but she did see encouraging signs that he was changing. She wasn't positive about his inner anger but thought it had something to do with her confession about Jerod.

They needed to talk; the awkwardness between them had gone on long enough. When Ben got home, she was going to get him to open up or else. Or else what? Well, she'd figure that out later.

It was Joe Harkin's turn to babysit her or guard her—whichever. Marlee liked the quiet, brooding man. He didn't speak much, but when he did, it was always insightful. He was an observer, and he missed nothing.

In fact, the man himself was walking toward her holding sandwiches. They sat at the kitchen table to eat, and Joe cleared his throat.

"You know, I've only known Ben a short time, but from what I've seen, he's a man who takes action. You usually know what is going on with him."

Marlee sighed. "I know. I don't know what his problem is. Maybe he doesn't want me anymore. He won't talk to me about it."

Joe gave her a small smile. "I don't think that's it. I'm positive Ben cares about you. He doesn't talk much about your relationship, but I see it in his eyes." He took a bite of the sandwich and put it down. "We all carry baggage, and I've found it best to deal with it before it ruins a relationship."

Wow, that was the most conversation she ever had with the taciturn Joe. Marlee wondered if Joe was speaking about himself and what kind of baggage he carried. Interesting. Thoughts for another day. Right now, she wondered what baggage Ben was carrying and how and if it affected their relationship.

She thought about what Joe said for a while, tapping her fingers on the table. "You're right. When Ben gets home, I'm going to sit him down or sit on him, whichever works, and not let him get up until he tells me."

Joe laughed. "Oh Lordy, I would love to stick around to see that, but thankfully, I have a date."

Just then the object of their discussion walked in the door with a huge bouquet of colorful flowers in his hands.

BEN LOOKED at the cozy scene in front of him. Marlee and Joe both gawked at him and stopped talking. Joe got up, put his plate in the sink, told him to have a great afternoon and winked at him.

What the hell was that about? Ben shrugged—didn't matter. He handed Marlee the huge bouquet of flowers and sat down. He was having this talk.

Marlee took the flowers and cocked her head. "Hello to you too."

He gave her a little smile.

"The flowers are beautiful. Thank you." She brought them up to her nose. "Hmmm. Let me put them in some water. Then you can tell me the special occasion." She got up to go to the sink and stood there staring out the window.

Ben was at a loss for words. Everything he planned to say disappeared from his mind the moment he saw Marlee looking like a sexy fairy sitting at the table. His cock throbbed. He wanted her to be in his arms but first ...

"Ben."

"Marlee."

She came back, sat down and in one huffy breath said,

"We need to talk and clear the air. I don't know what is going on, but I know you are unhappy with me, and if you're going to break up with me, do it now so I can get on with my life."

Break up with her? What the fuck was the woman talking about? Was their relationship so meaningless to Marlee that he would break up with her over this before even talking about it?

Marlee looked at him expectantly, her bottom lip trembling. "Well?"

God, he loved this woman. Why did he ever doubt her? She was afraid of his answer yet still direct, fearless, no fooling around or playing games. He knew he'd hurt her big time. Even if she made a mistake that reminded him of his father's problem, it wasn't enough to break up over.

Ben leaned forward and took Marlee's hand. "Your story about Jerod brought back some bad memories from my childhood. I didn't understand how you could ruin a man's life."

Marlee gulped.

Ben went on to tell her the story of his dad losing his job and the impact on his family. He left out the part of him acting like a spoiled brat. He had a feeling Ashley would gleefully bring that up when she met Marlee.

As he was talking, Marlee covered her mouth and moaned.

When he finished, he said, "I get why you felt you had to do that, and you were probably right to do so. But how did you live with the knowledge that you damaged a person so profoundly?"

"First, I'm so sorry you went through that as a child." Marlee took a deep breath and grimaced. "Second, it bothered me for a long time, still does."

Ben watched the gamut of emotions on her face. Finally, she made up her mind.

"I'll tell you what happened about a year later. I saw Jerod walking down the street, and I was ready to hide. I wasn't sure how I would handle the situation if he was going to yell at me. But I was too late, and unfortunately, he saw me. We talked for a minute. I apologized. He told me he had been angry for a while. It took time, but he finally got a new job—a better job. He was thrilled. He said in retrospect what he did was wrong. He knew it at the time, and the CEO was right to fire him."

She sniffed. "I felt like a giant stone was lifted from my shoulders." Then she smiled sweetly. "Of course, his last words to me were that he was glad I had been fired too."

Ben guffawed.

Marlee looked at him sharply. "You think that's funny?"

"Nooo?"

A small smile formed on her face, which turned into a big grin.

They both started laughing and then laughing so hard, Marlee bent over, clutching her stomach.

When she was down to giggles, she said, "Yeah, that sucked to hear, but if it made Jerod feel better, who cares? I might have, probably would have, said the same thing to him if our positions were reversed. Of course, at the time I told the CEO about Jerod, I thought I was so smart and righteous. As Grandma Burns always says, 'pride goeth before a fall,' and I sure did fall."

"Oh Marlee, you're a pistol. C'mere. Let me hold you." Ben opened his arms, and she went over and sat on his lap. "I've been in such a funk. I told you that I saw my dad today, and we had a good discussion about what happened to him. Like Jerod, he had been made an example that the rules apply to everyone. It made me see things differently."

He covered her hand with his. "I'm sorry I've been such an ass." She didn't pull away, so that was a good sign.

He leaned over and started nibbling on her earlobe, whispering, "Will you forgive me?"

Marlee groaned.

He placed soft kisses on her forehead and chin. "Will you forgive me?"

Marlee nodded. He started rubbing her breasts through her top. "Will you forgive me?"

She leaned over and kissed him.

He slid his hands under her top, pushed it up and at the same time pulled her bra down.

Staring at her breasts, Ben licked his lips. "Perfect." Tweaking one nipple, then the other, he leaned in and started sucking each rigid peak.

Marlee pulled away.

"If you don't take me to bed this second, I will never forgive you," she murmured.

Smirking, Ben let her up. He got up, tossed a giggling Marlee over his shoulder and carried her into the bedroom.

It's going to be some makeup session was Ben's last thought as he gently lay her on the bed.

CHAPTER FIFTEEN

Marlee shivered. It was not a tiny shiver but one that started at her toes and took over her entire body. The impersonal conference room at the police station might have had something to do with it, but it was fear. Fear she was doomed. Fear she would go to jail and be forgotten.

She and Earle were a few minutes early. She came to the meeting determined to tell the police about Robert being the one who shot Jim. Her courage built up overnight by some—lots of—wine and good sex. She dressed conservatively but comfortably.

They gave the information officer their names and were buzzed in. All was going well until she heard a voice.

"Ah, Ms. Burns, I'm glad you finally decided to pay us a visit."

She turned toward the voice and recognized a familiar face—Robert's cousin. He smiled at her, but his smile didn't reach his cold, brown eyes.

Marlee took a deep breath, she was going to do this. She was going to do...

"And, how is your father? I heard he is sick."

Not do this. No, no, no. That was a warning if she ever heard one. She was not going to put her family in danger.

She pasted on her best smile. "Dad's doing great, thank you."

"I hope he continues to get better and nothing else happens to him. I know Robert misses him at work"

Liar.

"Detective Monelli will be taking your statement. I understand I will be overseeing the interview with a friend of yours, Ben Green. Special request. We try to honor requests from our brothers in blue," he said smirking.

He turned to walk down the hall. "Good luck."

Marlee gulped. She looked at Earle. His lips were pursed, and his eyebrows looked like angry caterpillars. He didn't say anything but gave her a slight shake of his head. She wouldn't be saying any more today. They were led into a small interview room.

The smell of unwashed bodies permeated the room, and she tried to remember if she used deodorant this morning. What did she care? She was sitting in a police station, for God's sake, not out on the town having fun. Sitting in a police station because they thought she was a criminal. And here she was worried about a little body odor.

She sat at a small, gray metal rectangular table that held four straight-back chairs, one of which was occupied by the detective looking into her case. Earle occupied the other. On the opposite wall, she saw a window and a height chart behind it. *What did they call it?* Certainly not a height chart— gah, didn't matter. As long as she was on this side of the window and not on the other, she was OK. *How did my life become so messed up?*

Marlee wasn't sure what she had been expecting when they arrived at the police station, but it was quieter and not as beat-up as she'd imagined. No yelling, no hustle, and bustle of cops and prisoners, no one puking. Nothing like the cop shows on TV portrayed. She only saw one man sitting at a desk talking quietly to a cop as they walked in. Maybe it was a slow day for arrests.

The detective—what was his name? *Monelli, that's it*, just started asking her questions about a $250,000 deposit into her personal account that never contained more than a few thousand dollars before. It showed the deposit was made the night Jim was killed. From her computer. In the office.

Bile was snaking up her chest; her hands were shaking as she held the report in her hand. Why? Why would anyone do this to her? She suspected it was Robert. Hell, no. She knew it was Robert. He'd already told the detective about her getting fired for poor performance at her last job and that she was a troublemaker. Her credibility was now in question. She suspected her father would have told both partners—he was honest like that. Robert was also kind enough to throw in that no one would hire her after she was fired, and she couldn't get a job without her father stepping in.

Robert even had the nerve to suggest that she had a reason to kill Jim. He indicated to the police that she and Jim were having an affair, and Jim wanted to call it off. *An affair? How could he lie like that?* She and Jim went out once, and they both realized there were no sparks there. They were just friends.

As if that wasn't damaging enough, he told the police he'd been planning to fire her for sticking her nose into business that didn't concern her. He also said that she was a distraction in the office with her accusations, pretty much fingering her as a liar and a bitch. He even told the police that her siphoning off money from the company meant that her father wasn't getting his full monthly amount. Marlee thought if she got a minute alone with Robert, she would be satisfied siphoning off his body parts.

The detective seemed to believe Robert's side of the story hook, line, and sinker. At least, that was the impression Marlee got by the questions he was asking. Robert was good. The facts all looked terrible—for her. Marlee couldn't imagine how any of this could turn out in her favor.

Earle Conway was quiet, patient, and reminded her of her dad. She felt a little more confident with him sitting there. He was doing all the talking and not letting the detective dictate the conversation. Marlee didn't think she would be able to answer any questions without crying.

Her lawyer, well, Sam's lawyer, already informed her she wouldn't be arrested. He told her just because someone was suspected of a crime, the detectives would have to thoroughly investigate before they gave it to the prosecutor.

Good lord. She closed her eyes. She was a criminal—a potential criminal, anyhow. How did her life go down the toilet so fast? This is what happened when you tried to do the right thing. If the case was turned over to the district attorney for prosecution, Earle said he would represent her. As if that was good news. As if she had any money to pay him or even to hire another attorney.

She groaned. Well, yes, she did have money—lots of it. It just wasn't hers.

The other good news was that nothing was said about Jim's murder. Marlee snorted. If that was the good news, she didn't want to think of the bad.

Sam told her the other day that KnightGuard's IT person was working on finding Robert's accounts and was a genius at digging up information. Marlee thought he seemed to be taking a long time. What if they couldn't prove anything? She would go to jail. *Jail?* She realized she groaned out loud when the detective and Earle looked over at her.

Marlee couldn't imagine how this could get any more embarrassing.

How could she face Ben? Her father and grandma? Herself? She wasn't a thief. She wasn't a murderer. She didn't lie about what she saw or found.

She had the misfortune of being in the office when Jim was shot, which turned into a murder.

Marlee suspected there was a second or third set of books Robert was keeping because the accounts she was working on didn't show what Jim discovered. Robert probably hid the withdrawals even deeper since he had the time. She still didn't know what evidence Jim claimed to have. Just a cryptic message that he had proof. Robert also had time to put that money in her account. It must have been after he killed Jim. But how to prove it? The deposit was made from her computer. She couldn't even prove what time she ran out of the office. The cameras inside weren't working, and the few around the complex weren't aimed at their office. She was in deep doo.

After what seemed like hours of questioning, she was free to go. The detective told her he would be in touch if he had more questions.

Marlee's legs barely supported her body. She clung to Earle's arm as they walked out of the station and through the front door. She wiped away the tears that formed and were racing down her cheeks.

She looked around for her car and then remembered Earle drove her. Ben said he would pick her up.

Where was he? Did he leave her to fend for herself? Did he believe her? Was she too much trouble? Was he embarrassed the police were looking at her for a crime? He had been a detective. Probably saw all kinds of people like her, claiming they were innocent but lying through their teeth. God, she didn't want to think about Ben abandoning her right now. She needed him. She needed to feel his arms around her, surrounding her with his warmth and security.

Earle patted her arm, told her not to worry and he would be in touch if he heard anything, and walked down the stairs toward the parking garage. Not to worry? Riiight, like that wouldn't happen.

She stood at the top of the stairs for what seemed like a long time. Alone again. People were coming and going. Laughing and talking with each other or crying.

Oh well, time to pull up her big girl panties, find a ride and go—where? Home? To her dad's? Ben's place? Her legs were trembling, but she managed to get to the bottom stair without falling and looked around for a cab. Before she took another step, a warm pair of arms surrounded her, kissed her head, and turned her into his chest. Ben! Ben was here. He didn't desert her. Marlee almost wept in relief.

"Hey, sweet cheeks, why so glum?" Ben whispered in her ear and turned her around.

Marlee couldn't answer. Her heart was racing; she felt weak and relieved at the same time.

"I spoke with the detective on your case a few minutes ago. He talked to me as a professional courtesy seeing as I was a hotshot detective in Black Pointe." Ben winked at her.

BEN HOPED to put some humor into the situation. Marlee looked like an abandoned kitten walking down the stairs. He wanted to pummel Robert, Jim Matthews, the police, anyone who was responsible for making her sad. And the police chief. What was going on with him? He never said a word to Ben, but he got the look. The look that implied they were going to get Marlee for something.

Marlee looked into Ben's eyes and burst into tears. She sobbed uncontrollably, and Ben pulled her in closer.

"Shhhh, it's gonna be okay, Marlee," whispered Ben. "Sam is working her end; Earle will represent you. I will keep you safe. You need to believe this is going to be all right."

He needed to be her strength. People were clogging the stairs. Calling for taxis. Jumping into cars. It was a free-for-all. He hugged her tighter to his body, hoping to impart a sense of security for her, but part of him, the non-thinking part that was now standing up and begging for attention, wasn't listening. Damn, she didn't need a horny bodyguard-slash-boyfriend distracting her right now.

Sobbing into his chest, Marlee just held him tight. It was a good five minutes before she got control of herself. She pulled a tissue out of her purse, hiccupped a couple of times, then blew her nose.

"Feel better?" asked Ben.

She rubbed her eyes, smearing mascara, and looking somewhat like she did when he first met her at the cabin. Marlee told him she was embarrassed and worried about telling her dad that she'd been called to the police station and accused of embezzling. And, that somehow, they might accuse her of killing Jim.

"Maybe you should put off telling your dad for a little while," he suggested and shrugged. "Or at the very least wait until Sam has more information. There isn't anything he can do but worry."

Marlee said she wasn't sure Sam was going to be of help, but she did agree to wait a little while. She told him about the police chief's implied threat against her family, and Ben was ready to go back in and have words with him.

"Let it go," she said. "Nothing you can say or do is going to change the course of this fiasco. After all, how much worse can it get?"

CHAPTER SIXTEEN

Ben was driving too slowly. Although the speedometer showed he was going faster than the speed limit, the drive to her home was taking too long. At least it felt like that to Marlee. But when she received the call from her friend Amber that her little house had been trashed, she needed to be there now. As in yesterday.

I'm not going to cry. I'm not going to cry. Marlee kept reciting the mantra as she watched neighborhoods fly by. Ben didn't talk much on the drive over. Marlee was thankful because she didn't think she could carry on a conversation. How could things go from really bad to worse? The list was growing, Jim being shot, her being shot at, being accused of embezzling, grilled by the police, and now her house was trashed.

Ben asked Joe to follow them. They pulled up to the neat ranch on a busy street. Marlee pointed to a space next to an attached carport for Ben to park in. Her friend Amber was pacing the front walk.

He'd barely stopped the car when Marlee opened the car door and ran over to her friend.

BEN FOLLOWED, and when he reached Marlee, the women were hugging and crying.

Amber kept saying she was sorry, and Marlee kept asking, "Sorry for what?"

The women finally got control and broke apart. Joe parked and walked over to them, and Marlee made introductions.

Ben glanced around and was confused. He didn't see another structure. So where was her house?

"Marlee, I'm not seeing your house."

"Oh, Ben, remember I told you Amber converted her original garage into a studio apartment?" She pointed down the walkway toward some bushes. "There it is."

Ben didn't realize the little cottage, aka garage behind the bushes was hers until she pointed it out. He thought it belonged to a neighbor.

They walked through a narrow path that led to her house. It was a private little oasis. Someone did an excellent job renovating it to look like a home. A driveway stopped just before the door. Marlee had a small porch that contained two wicker chairs and a small round table. Ben didn't notice at first glance that a front door was cut into the solid garage door. Colorful potted plants surrounded the blue door, and a small window box with bright flowers decorated the one front window. Ben liked the homey feel and knew it was something his mom would also like.

"Marlee, I'm so sorry this happened." Her friend Amber followed behind and began to apologize again. "I can't believe I didn't see or hear anything."

Marlee gulped. "Jeffrey?"

Amber gave a little smile. "If the saying is that a cat has nine lives, then Jeffrey is living proof. Thankfully he wasn't in the house when this happened. I brought him inside my house already."

"Thank God. I can't wait to see him. Has he been any trouble?"

"You know I love him, so no."

Ben hated to break up the lovefest. "Did you call the police?" he asked Amber.

Amber replied she did. "The cops came, took fingerprints, made a report but didn't think they could do anything. They thought it was probably kids, since nothing of value appeared to be missing."

Ben made a note to contact the police later. He didn't think it was kids.

Joe told him he would check out the back of the house for any clues that might have been missed.

They reached Marlee's front door, and she pulled out her key to open the door. Amber placed a hand on her arm. "Hon, they broke this lock, too, and I haven't gotten a locksmith over here yet."

"Oh, dear." Marlee's shoulders slumped.

Ben motioned for the women to step back until he checked inside. Pushing the door wide open, he peered in but didn't see anyone. Telling Marlee and Amber to stay put for a moment, Ben walked into the small house and sighed when he saw the destruction. A tornado had gone through. Everything in the little house was tossed or broken, not something Marlee needed to see. He and Joe would take care of it. He turned to tell Marlee not to come in, but in stepping back, he almost fell over a person—Marlee. *Would that woman ever do what she was told?*

Marlee looked wide-eyed at the cut-up cushions, the food tossed around, the smashed TV, the broken furniture, and wailed, "Everything is ruined."

She headed into her bedroom before Ben could stop her.

Marlee stopped, gasped and covered her mouth. Ben wanted to kill someone as Marlee stood and stared at the black paint splashed on every article of clothing in her closet and dresser.

"Shit, shit, shit." Tears were running down her face. "I know I didn't have anything of value, but this is too mean."

Ben came over and wiped the tears from her face with his thumbs. He kissed her forehead and told her he was sorry. He couldn't believe the destruction either. Marlee had been through enough. He was fuming she had to go through this too.

"Grab whatever you can that isn't ruined. I'll talk to my friend about getting people to come over, clean, and paint."

Joe walked in and just stared at the destruction. "Shit, what a mess."

"Thank you, Mr. Obvious," Marlee said. Amber came in with some plastic bags.

"Find anything outside?" Ben asked Joe.

"No, it's been dry, so no footprints. It looks like the lock was forced on the back door. They must have come in through the back. It's private. But why break this lock?" He sighed. "Kids, maybe?"

Ben shook his head. He didn't want to say anything in front of Joe. Joe nodded.

"Is anything missing?" Joe asked.

Marlee said she didn't think anything was missing since she didn't have much to begin with, and now, she had even less. The TV was about the only thing of value, and that was smashed. Thankfully, she'd brought her laptop with her to Ben's house.

Ben could only watch and empathize as Amber and Marlee poked through her belongings and filled the plastic bag with what was salvageable. When Marlee got to a family picture with a broken frame, she sniffled but put it in the bag. She looked at Ben with sad eyes and said she was grateful that most of her family pictures and mementos were still at her dad's house. Ben knew at that moment she was a survivor and was so proud of her. Here her life was going to shit, her home was destroyed, but she was still grateful to have her family pictures.

Ben clenched his fists. The destruction was so personal. He just knew it was Robert. But how to prove it? Why destroy Marlee's home? What did Robert get out of it? Didn't make any sense unless Robert wanted to scare her—just because he could. They needed proof. However, Amber didn't have a security camera and didn't hear anything.

The list of what they didn't know or had proof of was growing longer. They still didn't have any evidence that Robert was embezzling from the company. Phil was still digging and finding bits of information but nothing that could help them. They couldn't prove that Robert killed Jim Matthews, which was a moot point since the police considered it a robbery gone bad, and the gun was unregistered.

They had nothing to tie Robert to shooting Marlee at the camp. They had no evidence Robert was involved in Marlee's house destruction. Basically, they had nothing. Robert was clever. Was he getting help? If so, from who? Ben promised himself to talk to Sam about another course of action.

The two women walked arm in arm over to Amber's house so Marlee could get her Jeffrey fix. Joe left, promising to meet them back at Ben's house. Ben told the women he would meet them in the house. He picked up and placed the small bag of Marlee's belongings in his truck. Amber's front door was open, and he followed the two women's voices coming from the living room. He stopped short when he saw a small black and white dog sitting on Marlee's lap. A dog? He was confused for a moment until he realized it was the largest cat he ever saw.

"Feed him much?"

"Hey, Jeffrey is big-boned; he needs lots of nourishment." Marlee looked affronted. But Jesus, the cat was enormous.

The gigantic mutant cat purred as Marlee rubbed his head, then looked over at Ben, smirked—that is if a cat could smirk—squinted his eyes, then actually growled at him.

Ben shook his head. He was thankful that Amber was keeping the cat for Marlee while she got her life together. He didn't think the big-boned beast would ever let him get close to Marlee or, for that matter, let him into his house.

Watching her love the cat, Ben hated to disturb the happy twosome, but they needed to leave. Marlee kissed Jeffrey one more time, stood, and tried to brush his hair off her shirt. *Oh yeah, glad the shedding mutant ill-natured cat isn't coming home with us.* Ben promised Amber that he would get someone to clean Marlee's house, and they left.

The drive home was quieter than the trip over. Marlee was sniffling quietly, trying not to let Ben hear. Ben wanted to punch someone, anyone. It hurt him to see her so upset.

Marlee broke the silence. "You know, I didn't have much. I just don't know who would be so mean as to destroy it all." Marlee wiped her eyes and in a small voice, asked, "Do you think it was Robert?"

Ben thought for a moment. It would be easy to accuse Robert, but without positive proof, he was reluctant to do so.

"I don't know, sweet cheeks. If I were a betting man, I would say hell, yes. But there is no way to prove it. I can't imagine why he would even bother. If he killed Jim and shot at you, tossing your house is a few steps down from that."

"I was curious about that too. It's probably kids. Mean, vicious kids." She took a deep breath. "I'm so glad Amber doesn't know Robert; she could be in danger too."

Marlee stared out the window the rest of the drive. Ben took advantage of the quiet time to mentally make a list of everything that he needed to do—get the cleaners to Marlee's house, buy her new clothes, and talk to Sam. Well, it was a short list, but there was plenty to do to keep Marlee safe and happy.

He was anxious to get Marlee home and hold her. Oh yeah, hold her tight while they were both naked. Naked and making sweaty love—definitely making hot, sweaty love.

CHAPTER SEVENTEEN

R obert was lamenting the fact that they couldn't find out where Marlee was living. She hadn't confided in Amber, only told her she didn't want her involved. It was frustrating because Amber was anxious to move on with their lives and harassing him every day about what he was going to do to take care of Marlee. He needed to come up with a plan to find out where she was staying.

What he knew them was: Marlee had hooked up with a cop, detective—whatever. She was living somewhere in Black Pointe. She threw away or broke her company phone. He didn't think she was smart enough to take out the battery, but the cop should have known. He knew she had an unlisted number that she had given to Amber. It was probably a burner phone. He knew she missed Jeffrey. God. He hated that cat, but Amber was a cat lover and wouldn't let him touch the damn thing. Although know how much Marlee loved Jeffrey might come in handy later if he couldn't come up with something else.

They were still looking for the thumb drive that Jim confessed he gave to Marlee just before he died. They trashed

Marlee's house hoping to find it. No luck. When Amber called Marlee to tell her about the house, they hoped she would come alone. But did that bitch do anything the way they wanted? Nooo. When she came up to look at the damage, she brought two rather large, muscular men with her. Robert couldn't take them all out. Well, he didn't think he could, so he hid in Amber's house while she dealt with Marlee and her friends. He purposely parked on the next block so Marlee wouldn't see his car.

Amber squealed, "I have an idea." She looked at him, her eyes sparkling. She skipped around the kitchen. "This is a good one."

"Spill."

"Marlee's grandmother and dad live in Black Pointe, right?

"Yeah?"

"Isn't her dad still a partner in the firm?" she asked.

Robert nodded. Mike Burns was a partner in name only. Pain-in-the-neck, straight-as-an-arrow Mike Burns. Robert was glad when Burns got sick, had to retire, and sell most of his shares in the company to him. When Burns was working there every day, he was always looking over his shoulder. Robert had to be extra vigilant that Burns didn't catch on to what he was doing.

John Bennett, the third partner, was even nosier. Too bad he kicked the bucket so soon—with a little—well, a lot of help from him. It didn't hurt that Bennett's heart was weak and that it just happened to give out before his time.

Amber could hardly contain herself when she was excited, and she couldn't control her hand gestures. "Why don't we take pictures of her dad and grandma moving about and send them to Marlee's email account? We can disguise ourselves and use one of those internet cafés. They won't be able to tell who sent the pictures."

Robert processed that thought for a minute. "You know, that's a great idea."

Clapping her hands, she said, "She'll come up to make sure they're OK, and then we can follow her to wherever she's staying and take care of her."

"Amber, you're a genius. It's a win-win for us."

Excited they finally made a plan to find Marlee, Robert looked over at a flushed Amber. His cock decided at that moment to make his wishes known. Robert knew just how to appease his insatiable appetite for Amber. Putting his arms around Amber and kissing her neck, he said, "Sweetheart, lose the clothes. We're celebrating."

MARLEE LOVED mornings that started with sex. Sometimes she contemplated why she ever waited so long to have it. But now she knew why. She'd been waiting for Ben.

Just this morning, after drinking their coffee, Ben stared at her, licked his lips, then told her to bend over the sofa— another new position for her. Leaning over her, Ben slowly pulled down her pajama bottoms, all the while kissing her back, her rear end, her thighs, calves, *oh my*. Then he knelt on the floor, pushed her legs apart and proceeded to suck, lick, blow and kiss until she had an orgasm, then he slipped a condom on and thrust into her. And thrust and thrust. *Oh my, this new position is going to be a new favorite* was the last thought Marlee had before they orgasmed together.

Ben withdrew while Marlee was still bent over the sofa, gently pulled her pajama bottoms up, and lightly slapped her rear. "You're going to be the death of me, sweet cheeks."

Marlee thought that dying after having sex, especially with Ben, wouldn't be a bad way to go.

Ben went into the kitchen and started fixing breakfast.

Good smells of bacon and eggs wafted toward her. Yum, she was starving after all that good sex.

"Have a cup of coffee. Breakfast is going to take a few more minutes."

Marlee grabbed a mug and sat at the table to turn on her laptop. The pictures took her by surprise, and a squeak came out. Then a full-blown scream.

"Oh, my God." *This can't be happening. Oh, sweet Jesus.* Someone had taken pictures of her family.

"What's wrong, sweetheart?" Ben raced over.

Marlee turned her laptop toward him and showed him the pictures that arrived.

Ben pulled up a chair and gaped at the computer

They looked at pictures of grandma tending her front flower gardens; her dad was resting on a chaise lounge, his oxygen tank beside him. Every day innocent actions. Marlee felt sick to her stomach. These threats were Robert's doing for sure. Why was he targeting her family? Would he really hurt them? But what was Robert's end game? None of this made sense.

"That son of a bitch. I'm going to rip his balls off his body and go bowling with them," Marlee snarled. She felt her face reddening, and anger clenched her heart. She beat her fists on the table. No one messed with her family. No. One.

WHOA. Did that just come out of his sweet Marlee's mouth? Well, she wasn't sweet, and Ben was glad she could be her usual sassy self. He knew she was as devastated by the pictures as he was.

Ben kissed her on the head, and they leaned over the laptop, looking at the individual pictures, each one with a caption. "Maybe we'll bury granny in her garden and see what pops up," said one. Another said, "How long can daddy live without his oxygen?"

Raw anger shot through him. What kind of sicko goes after the old and infirmed?

Marlee was already on the phone with her dad, and Ben saw relief on her face after she asked how they were. She didn't want to tell them about the pictures until she saw them in person. He was proud that she kept hysteria out of her voice, although her face was pale, and she was panting for air. She told them she and Ben would visit later that day.

He had to call Sam and find out where KnightGuard was in terms of watching Marlee's family. Sam did say they were shorthanded but would have someone drive by occasionally until she had a full-time person available. That wasn't good enough now. Damn, he would hire someone full-time himself if that was the case. Those two innocent people were going to get protection.

They also needed Phil to find out who sent the pictures. Ben was sure Robert was ratcheting up the stakes with the pictures, but why target Marlee's family? They had nothing to do with the embezzlement or Jim's death, unless Robert was sending a message. But what was it?

Marlee hung up the phone and looked at Ben with tears in her eyes. "I should never have run. I can't have my dad and grandma go through this. I wish I kept my mouth shut." Rubbing the tears from her eyes, she asked in a small voice, "Can we drive up there right now?"

Ben was furious that his woman was going through this. He hated her tears and felt her pain. "Yes, but first, I'm calling Sam. She must have someone full-time to watch them by now."

He finally reached Sam on her cell phone, and Ben explained the problem. Sam was pissed and promised to send Caleb Brown up since he was free and new to the company like Ben. It would be a good experience for him. Ben thanked her and hung up.

Looking hopefully at Ben, Marlee asked if Sam was going to protect her family. After assuring her that someone was going to guard them full-time, he told her to get ready, and they would drive over.

THE FORTY-FIVE-MINUTE DRIVE to her family couldn't go fast enough for Marlee. She needed to see and touch them. Seeing the pictures on her laptop reminded her that she or her family weren't safe anywhere.

However, no one, and she meant no one, was going to hurt her family. She wasn't sure what she would do but would do everything within her power to protect them. Thank God, Ben had the presence of mind to call Sam. Knowing someone from KnightGuard would be watching her dad and grandma full-time made her feel a little better. She hadn't met Caleb Brown yet but was confident he was as muscular and well-armed as everyone else she'd met at KnightGuard. Well, except for Sam. She was petite, well-armed and a kick-ass attitude. Not because of her size but because she excelled in determination and tenacity and wasn't afraid of anyone or anything. If Ben weren't around, Sam would be her number one choice to guard her.

Ben pulled into her dad's driveway and hadn't even turned off the car when she opened the car door and ran into the house.

She burst into tears seeing the familiar scene before her. Grandma and dad were having tea and watching TV.

They were startled when she came running in.

"Baby. What's wrong?" Her dad got up and drew her into his arms while rubbing her back. "Did something happen?

Are you hurt?" Marlee couldn't stop crying. Ben came up behind her, led her over to the sofa, and sat down beside her.

"MIKE." Ben took over because Marlee was still sobbing and couldn't get a coherent word out. "We told you about some of the problems Marlee was having at the company. Well, today, we received disturbing images of you and Barb with threatening captions."

"What the hell?" growled her dad.

"I'll kill whoever tries to hurt us," Barb shouted as she pulled a baseball bat from the side of her chair and stood up, brandishing it.

Oh, good lord. Ben saw where Marlee got her sass and spunk from. *Down, Grandma.*

Ben gently said, "Now Barb, I would prefer it if you didn't try to take on anyone by yourself."

He proceeded to tell them what happened. "Someone from KnightGuard had been driving by occasionally, but the situation has changed. Caleb Brown will be here soon to introduce himself. Caleb and others will take shifts watching the house full-time until the problem is resolved."

Barb lowered her arm with a humph. Mike gave her a little smile and shook his head. "Mom, you're a pistol. But if we have a young, strong, armed man outside, you're going to let him take care of things, right?"

Silence.

"Right?"

Barb pursed her lips and finally nodded.

"Ben, I appreciate that you've arranged for someone to watch us." Mike let out a slow breath. "I hate to say this, but we can't afford guard services."

Mike looked at his mother. "Mom, we can take out a bank loan, mortgage the house, whatever ... "

"Stop right there." Ben was not going to let these two sweet people worry about money. "You don't have to worry about paying anyone. It's all part of our service when we guard a client. We're guarding Marlee, and that includes you too."

Mike looked over at his mother, who was still agitated but sat down holding the bat. He turned toward Ben, shook his head and he thankfully accepted Ben's explanation. Ben wasn't sure what he would have done if Mike didn't accept the service or if he felt like they were a charity case.

Ben and Marlee stayed until Caleb arrived and introduced himself.

"I'll be parked outside by the curb and patrol the back of the house occasionally if that's all right," said Caleb.

Ben had to stop Barb from following him with her bat. "Barb, Caleb is trained, please let him do his job."

Caleb gave Barb a big smile and told her he would get fired if she helped. She reluctantly put the bat down and told him to call her if he needed help.

Good God, so this is where Marlee got her guts from. Grandma.

They said their goodbyes, and Ben helped Marlee into his truck then he went over to talk to Caleb.

"Keep me in the loop, OK? This whole situation is so squirrelly."

Caleb nodded.

Marlee was strangely silent on the way back, and Ben let her be while she processed all that happened.

He didn't think Robert would physically attack her dad and grandma. But he had been wrong about so many things with this case. Something else was going on. Robert was targeting her family for a reason. He just wished he knew what it was.

CHAPTER EIGHTEEN

obert and Amber were careful following Ben so he wouldn't suspect they were behind him. Marlee knew their cars, so they borrowed two and then would trade off as they followed Ben to his house.

He doubted Marlee would look for a tail. Ben might or might not. Although the bodyguard didn't seem to be too sharp, considering he hadn't been caught yet. Or maybe he was just smarter than the bodyguard. Robert doubted anyone knew that he was dating Amber. He kept a low profile since the fiasco at the fishing camp except for going to the police about Jim's death and Marlee's embezzlement. He sure didn't move any more money around. Anything outside of those two events, he was at the office. With alibis—ten alibis.

Besides, Ben and Marlee couldn't prove he had anything to do with the pictures of her family or trashing Marlee's place. They might suspect him, but with no proof, he wasn't worried.

Amber turned around a mile ago to go home. Robert was several blocks behind Ben on a semi-busy street when he watched Ben pull into the garage of a neat, beige one-story home. Gotcha!

Robert knew he had to be careful that he wasn't spotted. Slinking down, he drove past Ben's driveway, not slowing down, noting the address, then drove home.

Marlee told Amber that someone was guarding her when Ben wasn't there. A Joe somebody. But he wasn't there now. There were no other cars in the driveway. Well, it didn't matter. God bless Amber. If she weren't friends with Marlee, all of this would have been a lot more difficult. He needed that thumb drive. He'd hoped to get a few more years out of the firm, but curious Marlee squashed that dream.

Right now, different scenarios were going through his mind. He discarded the kidnapping idea for the time being. He had in mind something bigger,

He drove back to Amber's house and parked down the street. He wasn't worried about someone recognizing him or the car. The rental car he was using was under a fictitious name. It would throw off anyone trying to follow him.

Amber told him the cleaning service would be there in two days to take care of Marlee's house. After today, Robert decided it would be too dangerous to meet at Amber's house until they and he thought meeting at his condo was dangerous too. He wasn't sure if he was being followed or not. As a precaution, he had rented a room downtown by the week, again under an alias, and took different routes to get there in case he was followed.

Today had been a thrill, and Robert couldn't wait to see Amber. He saw her shadow by the door, and she flung it open. She pulled him in and gave him a warm welcome.

When she stepped back, she laughed and asked him if he found out where Marlee was staying and what he was going to do.

He told her they were successful in finding the guard's house and explained what he discussed with his cousin.

"Make it soon, baby. Please. I want to leave this dump, sit on a beach, inhaling piña coladas, and having wild monkey sex with you." Amber fluttered around the kitchen, excitement emanating from her body.

Oh yeah, he wanted that too, and it couldn't happen soon enough. But first, he had an appointment with "Double T." Someone he hoped never to see again.

CHAPTER NINETEEN

I t was a perfect Florida day with blue skies, a few puffy white clouds floating gently about, and temperatures hovering around eighty-five degrees, ideal for the beach. Everything was quiet with Marlee's family. Ben and she had settled into a routine. Whoever from KnightGuard was checking up on Robert reported he was keeping to himself and just going to work. They needed a break. Ben picked up a beach towel and put on his swim trunks with beach balls all over.

He walked not the kitchen to find her cleaning up. "Marlee, you and I need to get out of this house. The weather is great and going to the beach would be perfect. We could swim, take in some rays, catch a drink at one of the bars overlooking the ocean. Relax. It will be perfect."

"Sounds good."

"Hurry up, sweet cheeks." Ben swatted Marlee's behind. "I can't wait to see you in a bikini."

"Hold your horses, big guy. Give me an hour, I want to finish picking up. And, I hate to disappoint, but I don't do bikini's, tankini's, or anything with kini in it."

Damn, there went that vision. They were heading to the store first since everything of hers was destroyed. Maybe she would model a few. A man could only hope.

Marlee was puttering around, dusting, putting dishes away, keeping herself busy. He helped a little, but she shooed him away, telling him she liked the way she cleaned. Fine by him. He had other things to do, like check in with Sam.

The hour went by quickly, and Ben hollered to Marlee to grab her purse, they were going shopping and then to the beach. He put the chairs and umbrella in the truck and waited for Marlee. She came racing out. Before he could question whether she set the alarm or not, Marlee guessed what he was going to ask. She pursed her lips, rolled her eyes, and said yes, she set the alarm. *Good girl.*

They were finally on their way.

"This is so much fun. I haven't been to the beach in a long time."

"For purely selfish reasons, I'm hoping that you'll try on and model some bikinis for me."

Ben gave her a smile and a wink. She snorted.

MARLEE TOOK one more look around Ben's house; it was spick-and-span, just the way she liked it. Oh, sure, Ben volunteered to help, but she liked the way she cleaned, plus it was faster. Every time she bent over, Ben was there rubbing her ass or trying to unzip her pants. Men!

She picked up her purse when she heard Ben opening the door to the garage.

The doorbell rang, and she wondered who was there. Joe wouldn't be over unless Ben was going out without her. She didn't have any friends stopping by. She looked through the peephole and saw a deliveryman. Opening the door, she saw a national delivery truck parked in front.

The man was holding a package marked "fragile," and she saw the return address was her dad's. Reaching for the small box, she thanked the man, closed and locked the door. She debated opening the package. She couldn't imagine what her dad would be sending her, but he often found little things in the garage or attic of hers that he thought she would like and mailed them to her. But Ben was waiting and ...

"Marlee, let's get going. Now."

OK, Mr. Impatient. She laid the package on the coffee table, grabbed her purse, set the alarm, and walked into the garage. Ben held the truck door open and raised his brows. She knew exactly what he was going to ask. "Yes, I set the alarm."

Since she lost everything when her apartment was trashed, they were going to stop to buy a bathing suit and cover-up for her. Ben wanted her to model bikinis, the one thing she had never bought in her life. Give her a plain ole one-piece, but maybe, just for Ben, she would model some bikinis. Didn't make sense to her since he saw her naked all the time. Naked. Sex. Naked Ben. Dang, why did those thoughts pop in her head? She laughed.

Ben looked at her, his brows raised.

"Don't ask."

They were a few blocks from the house when they heard a tremendous boom.

"What the hell?" yelled Ben. "That was too loud to be an accident. Wonder what it was?"

———

BEN'S PHONE RANG. Reaching for it, he looked and saw it was his security company. *Shit, this isn't good.* Putting them on speaker, they told him that his fire alarm went off. Marlee gasped.

Fire? Coincidence?

Goddamn. What the hell happened?

With his heart racing and bile burning its way up his throat, he quickly turned around and floored the truck.

Marlee reached over and rubbed his arm. "Ben?"

Shaking his head, he swallowed hard and tried to answer, but no sound came out. Marlee turned and faced forward, fear written over her face.

When Ben got to his street, he noticed a black cloud of soot positioned over his house. Angry red flames and black, billowing clouds of smoke were reaching for the sky through the roof of the house.

His heart stopped. *Goddamn.* It was his house! His hands were sweating. This was unreal. What happened?

Inching his truck down the street until he got as close as possible, he threw the truck in park, and he and Marlee sprinted over. The neighbors were already filing out, staring. He could hear shrieking sirens getting closer. Someone called the fire department. Good.

Marlee took his hand. Concern etched on her face. Tears ran down her cheeks. "Oh, my God. Ben, your house.

He shook his head. He wiped her tears with his thumb and kissed her head.

Ben was grateful they were alive and that they weren't in the house. But what could have caused the noise and fire? Did he leave something on the stove? Did Marlee?

He would find out more when the fire marshal got here. The fire was so random—why his house? Why now? He had a sneaking suspicion it might be Robert. But how would he have found his house? His phone number wasn't listed anywhere, and he didn't think Robert knew Marlee was with him or where he lived. Or did he?

CHAPTER TWENTY

S am found a safe house for Ben and Marlee to stay at that night. It was a small, well-kept bungalow just outside town. Away from any close neighbors, in case they had another unwanted visitor with a bomb. Sam pulled in a couple more employees to provide extra security, in addition to the state-of-the-art alarm system at the house.

Ben wanted to believe they were safe, but after his house was bombed so easily, he needed to redefine safe.

The fire marshal told Ben that a package bomb destroyed his house. They were still combing through the embers and would let him know when they got more information.

A package bomb.

When Marlee heard that, she felt faint and had to sit down. When she confessed that she received a package addressed to her from her father just before they left, Ben's stomach dropped, and he swiped at the sweat forming on his brow. Thank God he called Marlee to come out to the garage when he did. Otherwise, she would have been killed instantly. Actually, they both would have been. He didn't care about the house. There wasn't anything of value in it, and it was insured.

Nevertheless, he was furious. Furious that someone found out where he lived, furious someone firebombed his house, furious that someone wanted to kill Marlee and now him, furious they couldn't pin anything on Robert. Furious with himself that he couldn't keep Marlee safe.

He was sure everything that had happened was Robert's handiwork, but how to prove it? Robert had ten alibis; he was in his office when the bomb went off. Someone was helping. But who?

Sam was going to have Phil check security cameras on his street. It was a long shot, but just maybe they could spot something unusual.

MARLEE WOKE UP FROM A NAP. She walked into the living room and asked if he wanted a cup of coffee. She looked so sad and forlorn, it hurt him. There were deep shadows under her blue eyes. Her face was pale, and he knew she wasn't sleeping much. How much more could his woman take? Or lose? She didn't have the security of a home or a job, and what little she'd salvaged from her home just blew up in his.

She brought in two mugs and settled in a chair across from him. "I'm so sorry your home was blown up," she said in a small voice. Her shoulders slumped, and she stared at her hands. "I shouldn't have accepted that package, but dad sends me things all the time. I didn't think it was dangerous." There was a catch in her voice. "I don't know what's wrong with me." Her hands trembled as she lifted the cup to her mouth. She put the cup down. "This is all my fault. I shouldn't have stayed with you, putting you in danger."

"But babe. Danger is my middle name." Ben winked at

her. Marlee gave him a weak smile. His trying to put a little humor into a shitty situation didn't help.

"Marlee, none of this is your fault. Blame Robert. Blame me. I'm supposed to be the expert." Damn. He should have suspected Robert wouldn't give up. Although blowing up his house was a little extreme.

Walking over to her, he pulled Marlee into his arms and whispered, "It's gonna be all right. Promise."

Nodding into his chest, Marlee muttered, "I know, but when?"

Ben felt his shirt getting wet. "Oh shit. Honey, please don't cry. We're alive. Sam has people looking for information; we have people guarding your dad and grandma. We'll be OK."

She looked up at him, rubbed her eyes, and told him she knew, but it was hard waiting. Ben leaned over and kissed the tears falling down her cheeks. Shit, he shouldn't have done that. He had no control over his cock. It was rock-hard. However, now was not the time to be thinking about sex. Marlee was in distress.

"Hmmm, Ben?"

"What sweet cheeks?"

"Something hard has come between us."

Oh, shit yeah. Ben couldn't control himself around Marlee. She was it for him, and just thinking about her got him hard.

"Always, sweet cheeks. But I don't want you to worry about me. You need to relax." *Oh lord, was that difficult to say or what?* Especially when his cock just kept getting harder.

"Well ... " She winked. "I know how I would like to relax." With that, she took his hand and led him to the bedroom, where she proceeded to show him how to unwind.

JOE WALKED into the safe house later that day and sniffed. Something familiar—what? He looked around the basic three-bedroom no-frills bungalow that Sam moved Ben and Marlee into. It reminded him of a house from long ago.

This safe house was a step down from Ben's comfortable ranch, but that house was blowing in the wind, so to speak.

But then, this one was ten steps up from the last foster home he stayed in years ago. And that one had been many steps above the group foster home he came from before that.

He found Marlee sitting in the kitchen. She looked up and smiled at him when he walked in.

She made lunch and offered him a tuna fish sandwich. That's what that smell was — tuna fish.

It didn't take much for him to remember the fishy smell of tuna fish sandwiches permeating the foster home. They served tuna fish at least three times a week. Couple that aroma with the taste of stale chocolate chip cookies and potato chips for dinner, and he swore off tuna fish for the rest of his life.

"Joe ... "

"Joe?"

Fingers snapped. "Hey, what's going on? You're a million miles away."

Joe looked at Marlee. He shook his head and smiled at her.

"What?"

"I asked if you wanted a tuna fish sandwich?"

He shook his head. "Nah, I'm good." *Damn straight.* He needed his head in the present case. Not rummaging through old memories.

He was here to spell Ben and guard Marlee. Although being with her was more like hanging out with a friend. Shaking his head, he thought that this little bit of a woman was going to be the death of Ben for sure. She was energetic, sassy, fearless, and innocent all rolled up in one small woman. But she wasn't Joe's type. His type was tall, blond, and curvy. Shit. Who was he kidding? His type was any woman who was going out with him at the moment.

But he was older, ready to settle down. Was he? Well, maybe. If it was with the right woman. *A woman with brunette hair that glistened like whiskey.* Nope. Not going there.

That was a lifetime ago. Being a SEAL provided the edgy, adrenaline high he needed when he was younger. When he left the Navy to work for the government agency, it provided the intrigue of working clandestinely. Now working for KnightGuard, he found the stable working relationship he was looking for with a dose of edginess thrown in.

"OK, then. I'm bored," she sighed. "Why don't you sit down and tell me your life story?"

"Whaaat?" Joe sputtered. "No way. Get your kicks some other way."

Marlee giggled. "Sorry. Just yanking your chain. How about a cup of coffee? Maybe you know something about my case that Ben doesn't?"

She looked so hopeful.

"Well," he said as he sat across from Marlee. "I just heard that Phil found a security camera that shows the delivery truck arriving at Ben's house. After checking with the firm, the truck was legitimate. The company had a record of the package being mailed from Black Pointe. We're still investigating who sent it."

Her shoulders slumped. "Damn."

THE SUN WAS high in the sky the next day. Ben and Marlee were relaxing in the kitchen with a cup of coffee when his cell phone rang. Marlee watched him answer it and grunt a few times, then hang up.

"Pull out your party clothes, sweet cheeks. We're going out tonight." Ben pulled her up and twirled her.

"What?"

"That was Luke. He and Grace decided to have a barbecue tonight and invited a few friends over, plus a few guys from work. It'll be fun. I think you'll like their friends. You already know Sam. Grace's friends Hailey, Anne, and probably Laura will be there."

Marlee hesitated. She missed her girlfriends and hadn't spoken to them for fear something would happen to them. It would be nice to meet other women, but she usually came off quirky and weird. Mouthy and always too smart for her own good. Marlee was sure they wouldn't like her. But it would be nice to get out of the house. Plus, Ben looked excited to meet up with his friends.

Kissing him on the lips as she rubbed his cock, she said, "Sounds great." Sweet Jesus. He was hard again. "We have a little time before we have to leave. Why don't we have our own mini-party here first?"

"Woman, you're going to kill me. I think I've turned a virgin into a sex kitten." His blue eyes twinkled, and he gave her that little half smile that he used when he wanted his way with her.

IT TOOK them a half hour to get to Luke's place. Marlee liked the cute ranch, and she could see a river in the background. There were houses close by, but they were still farther apart than in town. It was a nice, quiet neighborhood. She noticed several trucks and cars parked on the lawn and could hear raucous voices as they walked around to the back of the house. There was a slight breeze coming from the river that cooled the air.

Luke's patio was lit up with strands and strands of tiny, twinkling white lights. They illuminated the patio, giving it a party mood. She felt the vibrations from the music playing in the background, but not so loud as to fill the neighborhood. Marlee counted about a dozen men and women standing around the grill, talking over the music and laughing. She recognized Luke, Joe, and Sam but not anyone else.

The scent of cooked meat wafted toward her, and she realized she was starving. Had they eaten today? Marlee couldn't remember. They must have, or they wouldn't have the energy for all that sex. *Sex.* Marlee looked over at Ben and winked.

His eyes widened. Smirking, Ben shook his head and went back to talking to Luke.

A slender, very pregnant, dark-haired woman came over to her and smiled. "You must be Marlee. Luke's told me so much about you. I'm Grace." Marlee noticed a twinkle in her hazel eyes and wondered what that was about.

Sam spotted Marlee and walked over with two tall, dark-haired men in tow and introduced Marlee to her brother, Danny, and her friend Mark. Mark's eyebrows shot up when she said that. He gave Sam a smirk before he swooped in, bent her over, and gave her a deep kiss with lots of tongue. Sam laughed as he let her up and then slapped her rear. Marlee never saw Sam looking so relaxed and was curious about Sam's friend. If she was a betting woman, they were a lot more than friends.

They chatted for a few minutes, and Ben came over and took her hand.

"Come on. I'll introduce you to everyone else."

Marlee couldn't get over how many hunks were hanging out around the grill. The men looked relaxed, but she noticed they were still very alert. Their eyes were always moving and searching. For what? Didn't matter. She felt safe here.

Since she already knew Joe and Luke, Ben introduced her to Pete, Steve, and Harrison. The testosterone emanating from all the men was palpable and a bit intense. But the guys were nice. She didn't think she would remember who was who, though.

A couple of the men had dates with them, and God almighty, even the women were gorgeous. Harrison was with a redhead who hung all over him. He introduced her as Juliette. Steve and Joe were there by themselves, and Pete had his arm around a serious-looking, blond-haired woman.

Grace walked over with hamburger buns and handed them to Luke. As he took them from her, he looked at her and said, "Grace, sit down right now."

She gave him an angry pout. "I'm fine. Please don't baby me."

He laughed. "I'll baby my baby's mother whenever I want." He pointed to a bench. "Sit."

Grace rolled her eyes and took Marlee's arm, dragging her over to an empty bench. Sam and the two other women she was talking to also came over. Grace introduced Marlee to Hailey and Anne, two of her and Sam's best friends. Grace told Marlee she knew a little of what was going on in her life, and she wondered if Marlee could fill them in more. Marlee looked to Sam for guidance. Sam nodded. She was sure Ben and Sam didn't want her to give them an in-depth overview, so gave them the basics. Sam then filled them in on what KnightGuard was doing.

The women were appalled and asked Marlee how she was handling everything. Then they told her stories of how they all met and what they did for a living. Anne, who taught kindergarten, kept them entertained with stories of her curious and rambunctious youngsters.

Marlee enjoyed talking to Hailey. She owned a bookstore downtown and was up on the latest authors. Marlee missed talking about books with her girlfriends. She noticed the way Danny Knight was hovering over Hailey. Marlee suspected he really liked Hailey too. She wondered if Hailey knew that. She seemed to ignore him most of the time, but occasionally, Marlee caught Hailey watching Danny out of the corner of her eye.

"I'm sorry you can't meet our other good friend, Laura Clark. She was disappointed she couldn't be here, but her nighttime manager called in sick," said Grace. She explained that Laura owned Salt & Sea, a popular bistro downtown, and suggested that she and Ben grab dinner there sometime.

"Speaking of Ben." Grace looked at Marlee slyly. "How is he handling all this?" Then she slipped in, "Are you two a couple now?"

Four pairs of curious eyes turned to look at her. *Oh shit. Did they know she and Ben were doing the nasty? Did he tell?*

Gulping and sputtering, she said he was fine. She knew she'd turned all sorts of shades of red. Grace patted her arm and told her it was OK; they all knew Ben was head over heels for her. Marlee laughed and said that if this was an initiation into the club, she hoped she passed.

"I've got to give it to you, Marlee. Anyone who can tame a man-whore like Ben is OK in my book," said a husky voice from behind her.

What?

Marlee turned to see who it was. It was Harrison, with the redhead still hanging on to him. *Oh no. He didn't say that, did he?*

"Excuse me?" *Should she stay quiet or plant her fist in his mouth?*

"I said anyone who can tame a man-whore like Ben is OK in my book."

Marlee couldn't believe Harrison just said that—twice. It

was insulting to Ben and her. Silence. All eyes were on her, wondering what she was going to do. Well, she wasn't letting the insult go. If her speaking up offended anyone, too bad. It wouldn't be the first time. She took a deep breath, stood up, got right in front of Harrison, and the clingy redhead. She pulled herself up to her full five-foot-two height and looked Harrison straight in the eye—well, sort of. Harrison was at least a foot taller, so she was staring at his chest.

"Harrison, as my grandma says, 'Speak ill of no one,' and she is the smartest woman I know," she said, swallowing hard and shaking her finger at him. "I know we just met, and you don't know me, but that's my man you're disrespecting. So, you should know that I don't appreciate your talking about him like that, now or ever." She glared up at a now embarrassed Harrison.

She prayed Ben wouldn't get in trouble with Sam. Or that she embarrassed him. But she wasn't going to be apologetic about getting in the face of someone belittling another person. Especially her other person. No way.

Everyone was staring at her now, their mouths open. Was she out of line? Had she been too loud? Too forward? Would Ben be mad at her? Would the group be mad at her?

Not that she cared if they were. She didn't do anything wrong. She wasn't going to let anyone talk about Ben or anyone like that.

Harrison stood there looking very uncomfortable. Everyone was staring at him now.

Sheepishly looking around and finally realizing he made a very bad faux pas, he put his hands up. "Whoa, little lady."

What the hell? Was he living in the nineteenth century? Little lady?

Marlee stopped him right there and jabbed her finger hard into his chest. "Excuuuse me?"

She heard lots of "oohs" and "you're in trouble now."

Harrison looked confused for a minute. "Huh?"

She stared him down.

Finally, he got it.

He let out a deep breath and looked her straight in the eye, "Marlee, I was out of line, and I apologize. You're right. I shouldn't have said that."

"Got that right." Marlee turned to sit down.

Ben walked over and caught the last of the conversation.

"What's going on here, bro?" He punched Harrison in the arm. "Are you harassing my woman? I have to warn you, she can take care of herself."

Harrison opened his mouth, but Marlee was faster. "Ben, nothing is going on. Harrison and I just had a little disagreement, but everything is okay now. Right?" She looked at Harrison, who was standing there, mouth hanging open. "Harrison?"

Harrison laughed and shook his head. "Marlee, you're a pistol. I like you. Yes, everything is fine, and I apologize again."

Crisis over. Ben bent over Marlee, held her head between his hands and gave her a long hard kiss with lots of tongue. People shouted, "Get a room." He pulled away from the kiss and grinned. Marlee wanted to crawl under the table. She had never been with a man who didn't mind showing affection in private or public as Ben. She thought she would be more embarrassed, but everyone took it for what it was, laughed, and continued with their conversations.

Grace stood up at that point and asked for help in the kitchen. Several people got up to help and carry out the salads and corn on the cob. Marlee followed Grace into the kitchen.

They were now the only two in the house, and Grace put her hand on Marlee's shoulder and grinned. "Marlee, Luke told me you were spunky and a good fit for Ben. I'm glad you stood up for him. These guys can be a little rough with each other. Ben's a great guy, and Harrison was so out of line. "

Swallowing hard, Marlee thanked Grace. Giving her a little hug, Grace walked out to the patio.

Ben was waiting for Marlee when she left the kitchen. Pulling her close, he gave her a long hard kiss and released her. "I heard what went down. I've never had a woman stand up for me before, but you didn't have to. Harrison wasn't far from wrong. I was a ... " He gave a little cough. "Ladies' man. But that was before I met you. You're one of a kind, sweet cheeks."

Marlee slapped his arm. "I don't care whether he was right or wrong. No one is going to disrespect you or any other person in front of me."

Ben kissed her again.

It was long after dark when they said goodbye. After promising the girls to get together soon, Marlee felt like she made some new girlfriends. She enjoyed being with them, talking about clothes, books, and girly things. She was exhausted but in a good way. It had been too long since she was able to relax and have fun.

Ben was quiet on the drive home, concentrating on the road. Marlee felt herself nodding off. It had been a wonderful evening, even with Harrison's remark.

"Why don't you take a little nap? I'll wake you when we get home," Ben said.

"Okay."

Marlee no sooner closed her eyes than she felt herself being lifted up and out of the car by a pair of warm arms. Sleepily, she asked Ben what he was doing.

"You were sleeping so soundly, I didn't want to wake you. Come on, sleeping beauty, let's get you into bed."

Marlee looked up Ben. It was written all over his face,

from his lusting eyes to his hard-on, that he wanted her but was gallant enough to let her sleep. *Not happening*.

"Oh, mister, I'm not going to bed alone and especially not to sleep."

Laughing, Ben carried her into the house and dumped her on the bed. He crawled on top of her and started kissing her forehead, her cheeks, her lips. She felt his hands creeping under her blouse. His nimble fingers pulled down her bra and began playing with her nipples, which were rigid and begging for his touch.

"Oh yeah, sweet cheeks, you're going to come for daddy before we make love, aren't you?"

Nodding, Marlee could only lie there and experience the orgasm Ben planned for her. She knew that when he was finished, she was going to pull his clothes off and get him under her. Then she was going to kiss his magnificent body all over, and finally, when she got to his rock-hard cock, she was going to tease, lick and nip, then envelop it with her mouth and send him to paradise. *Oh yeah, he's in for a good time*.

CHAPTER TWENTY-ONE

Marlee woke slowly to the Florida sun peeping through the blinds creating shadows on the bed. Her body was relaxed, no doubt due to good loving. She stretched her arms and legs and then reached over for Ben. No Ben. She patted his side of the bed—cold. He probably got up at dawn and left her to sleep. Marlee was disappointed he wasn't there cuddling with her, although he probably needed a break after last night's sexathon. They made love several times until Ben pleaded with her to stop looking so sexy; his body couldn't handle all the loving.

Getting up, Marlee stripped off her pajamas and turned on the bath. When it was ready, she stepped in and relished soaking and scrubbing her sore body. Getting out, she lathered her body in lotion, put on a pair of shorts and top, and walked into the kitchen. No Ben, but he'd laid out a covered breakfast for her. Pulling a mug out of the cabinet, she poured herself a cup of coffee. Noticing his plate was in the sink, Marlee wondered where he was. She knew he wouldn't leave her and not tell her. She dug into the warm eggs and toast. As she lifted her fork for another bite, she felt arms around her shoulders and sniffed. She would recognize that clean, masculine scent anywhere. Ben kissed her head, pulled out the opposite chair, and sat down.

How did one man look so sexy in the morning? She wanted to eat him up. He hadn't shaved yet. His shoulders filled out the black tee and then some. Sexy. Ben. Sex. Gah. He turned her into a sex fiend. As if he knew what she was thinking, he grinned and shook his head.

"Sweetcakes hold that thought. Last night I remembered that Luke insisted Grace take self-defense and shooting lessons when she was being stalked. I just talked to Sam, and she suggested we come down to KnightGuard. Pete can teach you some self-defense moves. Later, I'll take you to the range and teach you how to shoot a gun."

"Why can't you help me with the self-defense?" Marlee asked. She would be more comfortable with Ben tossing her around than Pete.

Ben grunted. "We wouldn't get very far if I taught you. The only moves I want to make on you are in the bedroom." He winked and then took a sip of coffee.

Oh yeah, two could play that game. Marlee stood up and took his hand. "Well then, let's try some of those moves on now."

BEN GLANCED at Marlee on the bed, naked and lying on her stomach, looking very satisfied. "This is why I won't teach you self-defense. My defenses are always down around you." He lightly slapped her rear. "Now get up, sweet cheeks, shower, and we'll head over to Sam's place."

Yelping, Marlee turned over and tried to tug Ben back to bed.

"Oh no, you minx. Up you go, or I'll throw you into a cold shower."

Marlee looked at him in horror. "You ... " she started to say and stopped. Ben could only guess the next part was "you wouldn't," but he would.

She got up slowly, shook her ass, leaving him cursing his decision not to stay in bed, and walked into the shower.

Thirty minutes later, they were on their way downtown to the warehouse Sam converted into the business and her living quarters. Formerly a manufacturing plant, the imposing two-story brick building was set back from the street. The electric gate was open. They drove in, and Ben waved to the guard. The lot wasn't crowded today, and Ben found an empty parking space close to the door.

Marcia Briggs greeted them at the door from the reception desk. The gray-haired grandma was Sam and Danny's aunt and worked there part-time. He introduced Marlee to Marcia, and the older woman shook hands and welcomed her. She informed them that Pete was in the fitness room waiting for Marlee.

Ben led her down an expansive open room filled with cubbies and large floor-to-ceiling windows. There were few people around, but a couple poked their heads up to say hello, and Ben introduced Marlee. Arriving at the fitness room, Marlee walked in, stopped, and stared.

"Ben, this place is enormous," she said, her mouth falling open.

He looked around at all the mats, punching bags, dumb-bells, treadmills, and all types of exercise equipment that Sam purchased for the convenience of the staff. Yeah, it was enormous and well-used.

"This room is twice the size of my little house," she said as she stood there gawking.

"Yeah, lots of people work out here when they're around. We all need to stay in shape, and it's convenient."

"Oh, there's Pete," she said as the tall, muscular, dark-haired man walked toward them. Ben kissed her on the cheek, told her she was in good hands with Pete and that he needed to check in with Sam.

"MARLEE, COME ON IN," Pete said as he walked her over to a mat. They spent about ten minutes going over what she knew —not a lot. What she didn't know—apparently a lot. Marlee knew she was fit because she spent a good amount of her time in the gym weightlifting, doing yoga, and boxing. Well, that was before she had to hide from Robert.

Pete introduced her to some basic Krav Maga moves.

"Marlee, you're a natural," he said as he avoided her latest kick. "I'm going to warn Ben to watch himself."

"Damn straight," she said.

That got a laugh from Pete. They went through an open hand strike, a grab, and how to use the heel of her hand to push in an assailant's face. All skills Marlee hoped she would never have to use.

BEN WALKED BACK through the office to meet with Sam, then he had some paperwork to do, and this was as good a time as any. Leaving Marlee in Pete's capable hands to learn self-defense was a smart move. While Marlee was scrappy and didn't take shit from anyone, she was still a babe in the woods when it came to personal safety. Plus, she was a tiny thing. She needed all the advantages KnightGuard Security could offer, especially if nobody were around to help her.

Sam motioned him to her office. Sitting down, Ben glanced around the tall glass walls, big conference table, and comfy beige chairs. While it had a calmness about it, Ben knew a lot of serious strategies had been discussed around the large table.

"I heard you were bringing Marlee in today. Everything okay with her and Pete?" Sam asked.

Ben shrugged his shoulders. "Yeah, they get along fine. I wish I thought about doing this earlier."

"I'm glad you did. Marlee is going to need all the support we can give her."

"Damn straight. I wish she were more cautious with her personal safety, so these lessons should help."

"So did Marlee have a good time at Luke and Grace's party?" she asked as she pushed around a stack of papers on her desk until she found one and set it aside.

Ben nodded. "It was nice to get out of the house for sure. She really liked the girls."

"I have to say Marlee is a pistol. The girls liked her, too, and we plan on taking her out on the town soon."

"That would be great. She needs some female time." Ben had been confident that as soon as Sam's friends met Marlee, they would like her. Plus, Marlee needed girlfriends. She hadn't complained, but he could tell she was missing her friends. Ben didn't like keeping her from them, but it was safer for everyone right now, especially with Robert targeting anyone who had a connection to Marlee.

And while Joe and Luke kept Marlee entertained, Ben knew it wasn't the same. The guys weren't into romance novels ... well, maybe Luke was, but the point was that they didn't talk about fashion, giggle over a glass of wine, and basically do girl stuff.

"I swear if guts alone could take down a man, she would never have a problem," Sam said.

He laughed. "You have that right." Ben decided Sam didn't call him in to pass the time bullshitting, so he asked, "So what do we have so far on Robert?"

Sam pulled over the sheet of paper and handed it to Ben. "As you can see, Phil has been digging into Robert's finances. Robert's been keeping a low profile at the office. He's there every day, goes home to his condo alone and doesn't go out much. We found out he has two brothers up north. Both clean, married with kids. The three men have different fathers. Robert keeps to himself, doesn't spend a lot of money. Stays under the radar.

She grimaced and shook her head. "We're still looking deeper into his background. It's been slow going." Sam put her palms up. "I'm sorry we don't have more. It's just a matter of time."

THREE HOURS LATER, Ben walked into the fitness room, and Marlee saw him observing her from the corner. She was exhausted and hoped that she and Pete were at the end of their lesson.

She was watching Pete show her another move when she felt someone grab her from behind and cover her mouth. Marlee instantly stomped down on his foot, turned and kicked out, connecting with soft tissue.

"Shit," a male voice bellowed.

What? A blond-haired guy was bent over, holding his crotch and looking quite pale, his eyes watering.

"Oh, my God. I'm so sorry," she cried. "Are you all right? Oh God that has to hurt. Can I help you up?"

She reached over to help him up, but the man shook his head vigorously and held up a finger to give him a minute. This situation was awful and awkward. Was she supposed to strike like that? Getting kicked in the balls had to hurt—a lot. But it had been a reflex on her part.

She glared at Pete. "I can't believe I hurt him. Is there anything we can do?"

But Pete was laughing so hard, he couldn't answer her. She turned to Ben, who looked away from the scene, his shoulders shaking.

"What the hell? Why are you two laughing? The man is in pain," she yelled.

When Ben finally got control of himself, he walked over to them. "Oh, sweet cheeks, you can guard my body anytime." He bent and gave the blond guy a hand up.

"That'll teach you to try to take on a ninja sprite," Ben said to the guy. "Are you okay?"

The blond guy groaned and said, "I will be when my balls settle down."

Ben introduced Marlee to Hank Peterman.

"I'm mortified that I kicked you ... " She gulped and stared at his crotch, which he was still covering. "There."

Hank winced, his voice a little weak. "My bad. I thought I would surprise you and test your reflexes." He grimaced. "I'm happy to say they're in great working order. You reacted exactly the way you're supposed to do."

Leaving Hank to catch his breath and find his balls, Ben and Marlee left.

As they were leaving, Pete shouted out, "Great job, Marlee. Come tomorrow, and we'll keep practicing."

BEN ASKED Marlee to try out a couple of guns before they left KnightGuard. He knew he was in gun heaven the first time Sam brought him into the weapons room. It would be easy to spend hours here, but he had a woman who needed to learn to shoot.

Sam made a couple of suggestions for Marlee. They were

both small women. A lot of guns were too heavy for them or the handles too big to hold. They decided on a Ruger LC9 for Marlee's first time out.

Marlee rubbed her fingers over the gray steel gun. "Ben, I gotta tell you I'm really nervous about shooting a gun. What if I shoot you accidentally?"

"Ah, sweet cheeks, if you shoot me, I haven't done my job right and deserve to be shot." Ben gave Marlee a big hug. "Trust me, okay?"

Nodding, she and Ben left. They would hit up the shooting range later. Returning to the safe house, they unloaded the gun and shells on the kitchen table. Marlee just stared at them.

"I can't believe this is my life."

Ben hugged her. "There's nothing wrong with learning how to protect yourself. It's a big, bad world out there. So does grandma have an adage about protecting yourself?" He was curious. Grandma had a saying for every situation.

Marlee thought for a moment. "You know the only one I can think of is, 'A woman must not depend upon the protection of man but must be taught to protect herself.'"

"Smart. Who said that? Do you know?"

"I do. It was Susan B. Anthony. She was a great believer in women's rights," said Marlee. "I'm thankful that my grandma is a great believer in women being able to take care of themselves and instilling those values in me." Sighing, she said, "Although I still think carrying a gun is a little over the edge."

"I have to say, thinking about you carrying is turning me on," Ben smirked. "How about practicing your hand-eye coordination a little in the bedroom?"

Marlee wiggled her eyebrows and bit her lips to hide a smile. "You're incorrigible."

She turned and raced to the bedroom, but not before Ben caught up to her and threw her over his shoulder.

CHAPTER TWENTY-TWO

A mber and Robert spent the afternoon at Pelican Beach about a half hour from Lakedale. The Atlantic water was warm, and the tide was coming in. The sun was low in the western sky. A faint shadow of the full moon could be seen on the horizon. They were enjoying the quiet time that came when the lifeguards and families with kids went home, leaving a few diehard beachgoers and the gulls to clean up after them.

Robert studied Amber, who was sleeping and snuggled into his arm, her hand across his waist. He loved watching her sleep. Her brunette hair was fanned out on the blanket. He was always amazed at how long her eyelashes were. She had a little half smile on her face, and Robert felt his cock getting hard. It didn't help that occasionally her hand would move farther south. Not X-rated but close. God, he loved her. Corny as it sounded, she completed him. He had always been concerned with money, status, and having someone love him unconditionally. He had the money for now, unless that Marlee Burns ruined that somehow. He had the status—

owning an accounting firm. And he had someone to love him —that was Amber, in spades.

Feeling sleepy himself, he closed his eyes for a moment. The waves were crashing into the shore, and the call of the seagulls and other birds lulled him asleep.

"Bobby, get your ass over here now and help me. You know I can't take care of your brothers alone."

Bobby walked back to the beach, where his mother lay in the sand, lathering suntan oil on her arms and surrounded by two little boys. His brothers. His brothers each by a different father.

His mother had on her favorite bikini, and while he was just fourteen, even he could appreciate her body. Although just once, he wished she would go for a one-piece like all the other moms. But his mother liked to show off her "assets" as she called her boobs and ass. Apparently, the jerks she dated appreciated them as well.

"Help me build a sandcastle," demanded his four-year-old brother Davey. Bobby looked at the golden-haired blue-eyed child so unlike his brown-haired, brown-eyed self. Davey was a good little boy, even if their mother couldn't cope with him.

"Sure thing, sport. Let's get some water in the bucket." They walked to the water with the bucket.

"Wait for me," yelled his other brother, Richie. The red-haired, blue-eyed five-year-old was as different from him as Davey was. Compliments of Jerome Taylor and Bernie Peters. Thank you, mom. His dad, Roy Gilligan, was long gone by the time Jerome and Bernie came into the picture. Of course, Jerome was long gone by the time Bernie came into the picture. But they left a little remembrance for his mom each time.

Right now, Arnie was the flavor of the month, but he couldn't come to the beach today. He repaired roads and had a chance to get extra pay. Bobby knew his mom was mad, but Arnie promised to bring dinner over after he got out of work, so she was happy. Bobby wondered if Arnie would leave his mom with a baby. He knew Arnie would leave. They all did eventually.

He didn't mind any of the men in his mom's life. They never abused the boys or her. They weren't bad guys. They just never stayed long enough or were inclined to marry her. Why would they? What was that saying? Oh yeah, "If you can get the milk for free, why buy a cow?" Not that his mom was a cow, but she liked men. A lot. She also liked money a lot and never wanted to work for it. So, if the man in her life gave her cash and provided somewhat for the kid they fathered, she was happy. Mom liked her massages and facials, her new clothes, her good times, all at the expense of her kids.

But there was never enough money. It was always tight. Bobby knew he needed new sneakers, and the younger boys still wore his hand-me-downs. But they were growing fast and would require new sneakers soon. His brothers never complained about wearing his castoffs or the holes in their shoes. Yeah, they were young, but they were good kids.

If Arnie weren't bringing dinner later, he knew it would be boxed macaroni and cheese again. Their choices were always limited—peanut butter and jelly or bologna sandwiches, mac and cheese, or cereal and milk—if there was milk, otherwise just plain cereal. They were never hungry, but they were never full either. He swore to himself that when he was old enough, he would never be poor again.

Bobby knew mom loved them and did the best she could, but she wasn't mother material. She was high-maintenance, as one of the men described her just before he left.

He needed to earn some money to help, but he wasn't old enough to get an official job. Maybe he could work for ole man Jones. The old man always had jobs for kids to do. You just needed to be fast enough to avoid the "accidental feely." The first time it happened to Bobby, he didn't realize Jones intentionally copped a feel of his junk. He thought the old man was reaching for his book and missed—shame on him. The next time when he tried to grab his ass, Bobby realized the old man was a lech and was quicker to avoid him. The only thing that kept him going back was the money. Jones paid twice as much as anyone else to have chores done and always had a hard time getting kids to help. Go figure.

Robert woke up when Amber moaned and moved her hand just underneath his waistband. His cock got hard and wanted to come out and play. She slyly looked at him and grinned.

Robert looked around, but no one was paying attention to them. "God, Amber. What you do to me."

"Hmm. What say we move this into our room?" She rubbed his cock. Hard.

"Amber?"

Robert and Amber looked up at a dark-haired woman standing a few feet away from them. He had no idea who she was, and Amber seemed not to know either.

"Steph. Stephanie White." Stephanie smiled, waited a minute, then her brows furrowed. "Oh, you don't remember me. We met once when I was with Marlee."

Robert lightly pinched Amber's thigh to warn her not to say anything.

"Um. Hi," said Amber, looking everywhere but at her.

The woman apparently got the message and said, "Well, I've got to run. See you." She turned and walked down the beach.

"You've got to be kidding. Of all days to run into someone Marlee knows. How do you even know her?"

Amber thought for a minute. "I think I met her at one of Marlee's parties."

"I'm not happy about this."

"I know, babe. But she doesn't know you, so I don't think this is anything to worry about." Amber started packing up their blanket and towels. "Come on, we have better things to do."

Oh yes, they did. But Robert couldn't help worrying about

Stephanie reporting back to Marlee that she saw Amber and him together. She could ruin everything.

CHAPTER TWENTY-THREE

Sam sat in the middle of the big conference table in her office. She had fallen in love with the dark walnut, reclaimed wood table the minute she saw it in an antique store. She loved its character and the fact that it was long enough for twelve chairs to fit comfortably around it. It brought back memories of happier times around a similar dining room table that her parents owned before they died. She thought they would be proud of what she had accomplished and wished they were around to share in her success. She shook her head. Enough childhood reminiscing. She had a business to run.

Phil Donovan, her IT guy, was setting up the projection screen and fiddling with his computers. Ben and Marlee were due to arrive any minute so they could go over what Phil had so far on Robert Gilligan. Luke and Joe had just arrived and grabbed some water before they sat down.

"That Marlee is a pistol. I heard Pete was giving her self-defense lessons, and she accidentally gave Hank a nut shot." Luke grimaced.

Groans all around.

Sam looked around the room at her staff, who had become friends. Luke appeared more content working at KnightGuard. She knew he appreciated that there was less shooting, stable working hours, and a better clientele. On the plus side for her, she got to see her best friend Grace more often, especially now that Grace was pregnant.

Joe had a darker past that he didn't talk much about. She knew he had been a SEAL, had worked for the government for a while; his background check confirmed that. She knew he grew up in foster homes. But something happened to him either professionally or personally that made him a loner. Maybe the foster homes? So far, he was an exemplary employee and got along with the others. He wasn't a touchy-feely, let-me-tell-you-my-life-story guy, but that was OK. He was very good at his job, and his co-workers trusted him to watch their back. That was all she could ask for.

Sam had already received Pete's assessment of Marlee's skill. She shook her head. Marlee was a pistol all right. "She's a fast learner. I'll give her that. Now, if she can remember to do that when it's for real."

The door opened, and Ben and Marlee walked in.

"Hey, slugger," teased Luke.

Marlee rolled her eyes and put her hand up. "Stop. Right. There. It was embarrassing enough without you numbnuts making fun of me."

Ooohhs all around.

Ben sat next to Luke and punched him in the arm. Luke pretended to fall over.

Sam yelled, "OK, children, let's settle down."

She turned to Phil. "Phil, why don't we go over what you've found so far."

"Alrighty then." Phil fiddled with his computer. "First, I haven't found a second set of books. Yet."

"Damn," said Ben. "I thought this would be easy, and Marlee could get on with her life. Guess that isn't happening."

Phil pulled up a feed from a neighbor's house. "I've mentioned it already, but the delivery truck was legit. We don't have much on the delivery man. The company confirmed he is their employee. The camera feed came from a couple of doors down and is grainy at best. The police said no one spotted any out-of-place cars." He looked around the table. "I'm sorry I don't have more right now.

"Phil, you're doing fine. Robert will make a mistake sooner or later", said Sam. "What else do you have?"

"So," Phil continued. "I went back and dug into Robert Gilligan's life. I've already told Sam this. He was born to a single mother who has two other sons from two other men. They grew up poor. His dad skipped out early and didn't have any contact with him, although he paid some child support. Robert was smart in school and got scholarships to college. Good grades. Still trying to find some friends from college. Seems to have kept to himself. He doesn't live extravagantly."

He nodded to Marlee. "And he worked at an accounting firm until he bought into your dad's business."

"Where did he get the money from to buy in?" asked Ben.

Phil shook his head. "It appears he had a healthy bank account. I couldn't find any illegal withdrawals."

He turned to the projector. "The IP address from which the money was sent to Marlee's account checks out as coming from the firm but doesn't tell me who authorized it."

Marlee pursed her lips. "Dang, I was hoping for more. Like an arrow pointing to Robert saying, 'He did it. Him.' I guess that's not happening."

The next slide showed the internet café around the time the family pictures were sent to Marlee. "Anyone look familiar?" asked Phil.

Marlee asked him to do a close up. She pointed out one

man. "Maybe?" Then she looked at another and slumped. "Maybe? If he's disguised, I won't recognize him." She wiped her eyes. "I was so hoping this would be easy."

"If it were easy, we would have Robert already," said Sam.

Phil gave Marlee a little smile. "We're not giving up. We know Robert was not in the office when the pictures were sent. We have him on camera earlier, walking out with a woman, probably an employee. I'll check out some other security cameras and see if we can pick him up on one."

"Great." Sam turned to Marlee. "Do you remember how your father found Robert?" she asked.

Marlee thought for a moment. "No, I was in college when Robert started there. I think Dad was sick by then. But I don't know for sure. I can ask him."

"Do that." She turned to Luke. "Luke, why don't you fly up north, find his old firm, and stop at the college to see if anyone remembers Robert or can add anything. Maybe talk to the mom or his brothers."

"Will do. Are you putting someone else on Marlee's detail here?" asked Luke, since he and Joe were spending part of the day guarding Marlee when Ben had to leave.

"I think I'll bring on Pete since he knows Marlee and has some free time."

Ben sat there, listening to all the plans. "What do you want me to do?"

"Marlee is safe with you. Let's keep doing what we're doing." Sam raised a brow and stared at Ben and Marlee. "Are there any issues I need to know about?"

Sam observed them looking guiltily at each other. There were issues all right. Issues more dangerous than being shot at. Relationship issues. Matters of the heart. Sam could only hope that Ben's intentions toward Marlee were good; she'd heard about his reputation with the ladies. She also suspected they were doing the nasty, which was against her better judgment. But there were no hard and fast rules yet at Knight-Guard about falling in love with a client or having sex with them.

THE MEETING WENT ON FAR TOO long with few results. Ben sat and listened to all they didn't have. The only bright spot was when Marlee thought she recognized Robert in the internet café but then wasn't sure. He had to admit Robert was clever and staying under the radar.

Robert still went to work each day. There had been no charges in Jim's murder since the gun was unregistered, and according to the police report, there were no witnesses to Jim's shooting. The police but were still looking for information. Nothing on security cameras in and around the building. Robert claimed the cameras were broken.

They couldn't pin the fishing camp shooting on Robert since Marlee said the man had a mask on, and Ben only saw his ass running down the road. If it was Robert, he hadn't used his own car and the partial came from a different car. There were no security cameras at the camp, something Seth Bowman was fixing.

They couldn't prove Robert set the bomb that blew up Ben's house. Robert was at work and had ten witnesses who corroborated that he was there all day and never left the office.

They had no proof he trashed Marlee's house or that he sent the pictures of her dad and grandma. Phil confirmed the images came from an internet café outside Lakedale. Marlee couldn't pinpoint Robert at the café. Disguised? Maybe.

They hadn't found the second set of books Robert was keeping.

Basically, they had nothing. Robert was smart, that's for

sure. Maybe he was working with someone else? If so, they hadn't found the other person yet.

They had a big fat zero, and Marlee's life was still in danger.

"I'm so disappointed we don't have positive proof that Robert is behind this harassment," said Marlee as they left the meeting.

"I know sprite. I know. It's just a matter of time, though. He can't keep avoiding us."

Ben loved being with and having Marlee around, but she was getting antsy. Her life was in upheaval, and she needed to work. Marlee passed a couple of ideas past him regarding that. She also needed time with her girlfriends or maybe with Sam and her friends. Perhaps he could convince Sam to take Marlee out for that girls' night that she mentioned.

The meeting was over, and Ben sent Marlee out with the guys, promising to meet her upfront. He hung back to talk to Sam.

"What's up?" she asked.

"Well." Ben rubbed his chin. Could this be any more awkward? He was not used to setting up playdates, especially for his woman. But she needed female companionship, so he took the bullet. "Well, I was thinking Marlee needed some time away from me and was wondering if you and the girls could take her out some night."

Sam thought for a minute. "You know, we were going to do that, but everyone got busy. Why don't I make some calls and see what I can do? I'll call Marlee when we get a date."

"Thanks. I appreciate it. I know Marlee will too." Ben gave her a two-finger salute and went off to find Marlee.

THURSDAY NIGHT and Neptune's Navel was hopping. Sam knew the owner, Jake Summers, through Ben and Luke. The girls were sitting outside at the Tiki Bar, enjoying the water, the soft breeze, and Jake's special drink, the Tiki Express. A frozen drink guaranteed to help them forget all their troubles, Jake claimed as he brought over the first round.

The band was hot. The drinks were flowing. Sam realized she hadn't laughed so hard in ages. Marlee was hilariously regaling them with tales of her grandma interfering with her dates. Sam knew Marlee was sassy but put a drink in her. Watch out! She had them all in stitches. They probably consumed far more alcohol then they should, but Grace was their designated driver since she couldn't drink now that she was pregnant.

Occasionally, a couple of them would get up to dance with each other on the small dance floor situated by the bar and band. Sam was glad Ben and Luke weren't there because the women attracted a lot of unwanted attention. She only intervened once and accidentally pushed one ardent admirer of Marlee's into the water because he wouldn't leave her alone.

Jake finally sent a bouncer over to watch over them. Actually, Sam was afraid he sent the bouncer over to protect the men from her—didn't matter.

Marlee was drinking a little too much and told the girls she would be right back. Sam walked with her to the ladies' room. As Marlee was washing her hands, the door to the ladies' room opened, and a tall brunette walked in.

"Marlee," she squealed.

Marlee squinted at the woman. "Oh, my gosh, Steph. What are you doing here?"

"Oh, I'm here with a friend. We've never been here before and heard great things about it."

Stephanie was one of the girls she went out with occasionally. Marlee missed the good times they had, but this wasn't the time to get maudlin. Marlee introduced Steph to Sam. The ladies' room was empty, so they had a couple of minutes to catch up.

"I'm so glad to see you. How have you been?"

Steph shrugged her shoulders. "I'm okay, same ol', same ol.' Hey, I've been trying to call you, but your phone isn't working. Did you get a new number?"

"Oh, I did." Marlee felt in her pocket. No phone. "I'm not sure of the number, but I'll call you with it. What's happening with you?"

"Nothing much. Hey, I saw your friend Amber at Pelican Point Beach the other day. I said hello, but I could tell she didn't remember me, so I didn't say anything else. She was with some guy who looked like your boss. They couldn't keep their hands off each other."

Boss? Jim? If only. But Jim was gone.

"It couldn't be him. He's been dead for a while."

"Well," said Steph. "I'm probably mistaken. I only saw your boss once."

They talked for a few minutes before Steph left to meet her friends.

"Amber is your friend, isn't she?" Sam asked as they were walking out.

"Yes. She's taking care of Jeffrey for me." Marlee wiped away tears. "I miss him so much. But Ben isn't into cats, and I think Jeffrey's happier at Amber's."

Sam patted Marlee's arm. "I'm sure Jeffrey is fine."

Marlee nodded.

Anne and Hailey were waiting for them to return and pulled Marlee back onto the dance floor.

"Oh my gosh, Sam, this is the best night ever," Marlee gushed as she sat down from dancing yet again. She took a long sip of another Tiki Express. "I can't remember when I had such a goood time."

"Oooh, I need to go to the little girl's room. I'll be right back." Marlee got up too fast and held on to the chair back. Sam reached up to catch her, but Marlee caught her balance.

"Hang on, Marlee. I'll come with you." Sam got up and put her arm around Marlee's waist. Oh yeah, Marlee was sloshed. Sam made a note to keep a careful eye on her. Ben wouldn't appreciate anything happening to her.

Marlee saluted her. "Lead on, Admiral Knight."

Damn, Marlee was drunk. They made their way through the crowd, avoiding a couple of touchy-feely hoping-to-cop-a-feel hands and trays of drinks.

"Admiral Knight," Marlee said, rubbing her stomach and belching. "I don't feel so good."

Sam thought Marlee looked a little green and realized it was time to shut off the drinks as she helped Marlee into the restroom.

Marlee took one of the stalls, and a minute later, Sam heard her throwing up. Yuck, taking care of sick drunks was not her favorite thing to do.

"Need some help, Marlee?"

"Nooo, I'm good," said the small voice from the stall.

A few minutes later, Marlee walked out, looking pale, washed her hands, and splashed water into her face. Apologizing profusely, she told Sam she was finished. Finished drinking. Finished dancing. Finished for the evening.

Sam rubbed her shoulder, suggested they get back to the table and get their things.

BEN WAS WATCHING a game when Sam and Marlee walked in. Ben thought Marlee looked a lot worse for wear. They must have had a good time at Jake's.

"Honey, I'm home," she slurred.

"I can see that. How are you feeling, sweet cheeks? Did you have a good time?"

"Ah, yeah. We had a perfect time, didn't we, Sammie Whammie?"

Sam looked over at Marlee, who was now grinning like a Halloween pumpkin. "Yeah, sweetie, we did. But I think you need to go to bed."

"You're right." Marlee licked her lips, reached for Ben's hand and tried to pull him up from the couch. "Benny, we need to go to bed and fuuuck."

Ben jumped up. "What the fuck? Sam, she's drunk."

"No shit, Sherlock. Apparently, our girl can't hold her liquor." Sam backed up to the door and said, "She's all yours. Good luck tonight."

Thanks a lot, Sam.

Ben grunted. Sam left as he was being dragged into the bedroom by Marlee. "Sweetheart. Hold up. Let me get you a glass of water."

"No." She pouted. Ben wanted to kiss that pout away, but she was drunk.

"OK, then." Ben tried to take her clothes off. "Let's get you out of these clothes and into bed."

"No."

"Marlee, you need to go to sleep."

"Bennie, I don't want to sleep," Marlee whined as she slapped at his hands. "I want to fuck your brains out and then do it again. Pleeease."

Ben thought that would be an excellent idea if she wasn't so drunk and didn't hiccup that last word. Of course, his cock got hard at the moment Ben noticed Marlee was already stripping her clothes off.

"Shit." He reached for Marlee. "Baby, just a minute. Let me help you."

Marlee slapped at his hands. "I can do it." She fell back on the bed, laughing hysterically.

Ben sat next to her and started pulling her shoes off. Marlee kept rubbing his head and kissing it. He managed to get her skirt off just as she tried to put her hands down his pants. Oh, Lord, save him. Marlee was stuck in her top, and Ben untangled her from that. She tried to take her bra off but started giggling so hard she had to stop.

He was getting ready to tuck her under the covers when she suddenly sat up and covered her mouth. Damn. He hated it when people got sick. But better sick in the toilet than on him. Ben picked her up and rushed her to the bathroom and held her hair while she puked her guts out.

"I am so embarrassed," she moaned.

"Don't be. We've all been there."

When she finished, he washed her face, made her rinse her mouth, picked her up and brought her to bed. He covered her with a sheet and went to get a glass of water for her. When he got back, she was snoring gently into the pillow.

Ben stared at his sprite. She looked so peaceful and beautiful, even though her hair was half in, half out of the elastic, and her makeup was a little skewed. All in all, she looked like she had a rough night, but Ben thought he'd never seen a more beautiful woman.

Tomorrow, when she felt better, he would show her how much he loved her.

CHAPTER TWENTY-FOUR

"Let me run over and say hello to Amber."

Marlee and Ben had stopped at her house to check on the cleanup. The crew told Ben they completed the cleaning a day ago and that everything worth salvaging was in a box by the front door.

There were no lights on in Amber's house, but her car was in the driveway, so Marlee took a chance that Amber was there, plus she wanted her Jeffrey fix.

She knocked once. Twice. No answer. Marlee rang the doorbell and called Amber's name. She saw movement in the hall, thought she heard a man's voice, and heard Amber call out to wait a second.

A minute later, Amber opened the door. Her hair was askew, and her face flushed.

"Marlee? What are you doing here?"

"I hope I'm not disturbing you." She peered in the kitchen. "Do you have company?"

Amber looked over her shoulder. "No. Why would you think that?"

"Oh, nothing. I thought I heard a man's voice."

Amber hesitated, then stepped out and closed the door. "No man's voice, just me."

"Anyhow, we're checking on my house, and I wanted to say hello and see Jeffrey."

"Jeffrey is roaming around here somewhere. I let him out a while ago."

"Oh, he must be behind the house." She glanced around. "No worries. I'll look for him. Oh, by the way, I ran into my friend Steph the other night, and she told me you and some guy were getting it on hot and heavy at the beach. Do you have a new guy?"

Amber took a moment to answer. "No. I've been on a couple of dates but nothing serious. By the way, your apartment looks great. When are you planning on moving back? I miss you."

"Miss you too. I'm still having a problem at work, and with my house being trashed ... " Just saying that aloud caused tears to form. She wiped her eyes. "Ben still wants to keep an eye on me." Marlee felt bad that she couldn't say more, but Amber could be in danger from Robert if it got back to him somehow.

"Oh, are you still at Ben's house?" asked Amber.

"No, he had a problem at his house; we're staying somewhere else."

"Can I come visit? Or does Ben have you on a tight leash?" Amber's mouth was pinched, and she looked upset.

What? Marlee didn't know how to process that snarky comment. Amber never talked to her like that. *And what was that about a leash?* Ben didn't have her on a leash at all. Was Amber jealous? Could she be unhappy Marlee found Ben? Weird.

"No tight leash. Just trying to stay under the radar." *And alive.* She was not telling anyone where she was staying even though Ben hadn't said not to.

"Marlee," Ben called out. He stood on the path that connected the two houses, waved and said hello to Amber. Then he reached for her hand and told her a box of her things was in the entry if she wanted to go through them.

Hugging Amber, Marlee walked back to her house with Ben.

"Wait a second," she said as she pulled on his arm. "I need to find Jeffrey and give him a hug."

There was a small groan from Ben that she ignored. She called out to the cat, who came running over, a small mouse in his mouth.

"Oh, aren't you a good boy." She bent over to scratch his head while he purred loudly. Amber walked over and bent down to pick him up. "I'll take him in the house," she said. Marlee waved goodbye, took a deep breath, and walked in the front door.

A small cardboard box was in the entry, and she bent down to look in it. No clothes. Junk—a couple of pots, a few dishes, batteries, a hammer, a screwdriver, and a calendar. That's all that remained of her house—junk.

Tears slid down her face. She tried to wipe them away so Ben wouldn't see she was crying. Too late.

"Sweetcheeks, I'm so sorry." He pulled her into his chest and rubbed her back.

Hiccupping, she told him it was all right. There wasn't anything in the box she wanted to bring home with her.

"Wait a second. I'm going to put this in the bedroom closet. No telling when I might need a calendar," she said sarcastically.

"GODDAMN IT, Amber, what the hell did Marlee want, and why was she here?"

Robert was lying naked on her bed, hands behind his head. He couldn't believe Marlee came back. It had been a couple of weeks. He still parked a street over and walked here, so no one knew he was visiting Amber.

He had been fucking Amber hard while she bent over the sofa and was almost ready to come when the doorbell rang. Who knew a doorbell could be as powerful as a cold shower? They stopped; his dick went limp. They could barely see the top of Marlee's head at the back door. Frustration didn't begin to describe how he felt at that moment.

If Amber hadn't told him the bodyguard was with her, he would have had Amber invite Marlee in, and he would have done away with her. But no. No orgasm. No killing Marlee. The mood broken.

"Well, I did find out that she is staying with Ben at another house. Although she wouldn't tell me where. Also, that friend of hers who saw us at the beach mentioned it to Marlee. Thankfully, she didn't recognize you. We need to be more careful until Marlee is taken care of," Amber said. She looked at him and licked her lips.

Robert groaned. Leave it to his woman to know how to please him. Marlee forgotten, he concentrated on Amber's tongue and lips. She loved his cock, and he loved that she did. He pushed her head down to take in the full length of his cock as she moved her mouth in and out. Then blew on the tip, then in and out. He was rock-hard. Ready to explode. Oh yeah, he was definitely going to come.

———

IT WAS early afternoon when Ben and Marlee arrived at her dad's house. Marlee called ahead, and her grandma was already waiting at the front door the minute Marlee walked up the path.

Grandma threw her arms around Marlee and nodded to Ben. They walked into the house. Marlee's dad was watching TV. Grandma said she would make some coffee and hustled into the kitchen.

Marlee kissed her dad on the cheek. "Missed you."

"Hey, pumpkin. What brings you kids up here today?" Mike tilted his head and raised his eyebrows. "Is everything all right?"

"So far. We're still protecting Marlee." Ben shook his head. "Haven't been able to get anything on Robert. He's still going to work acting as if nothing is going on."

Mike took a minute to inhale his oxygen. "Bastard. I should never have brought him in the firm."

Marlee took his hand. "Dad don't get upset. But we did come here to ask you how you found Robert."

"Let me think." Mike stopped to collect his thoughts. "It was about ten years ago that John and I brought Robert into the firm."

"So, you and John Bennett started the firm?" Ben asked.

"Yes, John and I knew each other in college. Always talked about starting our own firm. At the time, we were working at other firms." He looked at Marlee. "Your mother just died. I needed more challenges, wanted to start my own business. John and I got together, decided we would start the business. It kept growing and growing; we needed more cash and a partner to help run it."

"Coffee, anyone?" Grandma brought in coffee and a cake. They all nodded.

"Dad, you were saying?"

"Um, oh, yes. Robert was a rising star in another firm. He graduated top of his class and was looking to buy into a firm. We met him, everything checked out, he had the cash to buy in, and we sold him one-third share." He shook his head.

"What a mistake. When John died, Robert and I inherited an equal share."

"How did John die? He must have been pretty young."

Mike rubbed his cheek. "Yes, he was. He died of a heart attack. Totally unexpected. It was a shock to all of us. John never mentioned a heart problem."

He leaned forward and punched his leg in frustration. "Damn. I feel so helpless. I can't believe all this is happening." He settled back in the chair. "Anyhow, after I got sick, Robert bought out half of my portion of the company, and the agreement was that he would send monthly checks to me until the balance was paid off."

"How did a young guy like that have the money to buy into your firm?" Ben asked.

"Hmm, I'm not sure." Mike fiddled with his oxygen line. Marlee hated that Ben was asking him about the firm. Her dad was clearly uncomfortable, and it was distressing her. But they needed more information. He continued. "Robert had the cash in the bank. His credit was good. We checked him out."

Ben scratched his neck. Marlee knew he was embarrassed by the questioning. "And, if I can ask, how much did he put in?" he asked.

"The business was doing quite well at the time. If I remember correctly, it was a hundred thousand in cash, and Robert would put in another hundred thousand over ten years. Of course, that changed when John died, and I got sick."

"Whoa, that's a shitload of money. Where did he get that kind of cash from?" Ben looked surprised because Phil told them he hadn't found any extravagant spending in Robert's past.

"He told us he inherited some and saved the rest."

"Humpf. Did you ever hear anything negative about Robert?" Ben asked.

"Not really. Robert never talked about his personal life. I gathered he didn't have an easy childhood. Never met a girlfriend although I know he dated. He had a friend or two meet him at the office occasionally, but that was about it. I never suspected anything was wrong."

"Do you remember any of his friends' names?"

"No, that was a while ago."

Marlee was disappointed that he didn't have more information. She could see he was getting tired, however, Ben had one more question.

"Mike, do you remember Jim Matthews?"

Mike looked up at the ceiling and sighed. "Yes. Jim came on after I left. But I didn't really know him. I can't believe he was murdered." His head was starting to droop.

"Ben, I think Dad's had enough," Marlee said. "Do you have enough information?"

Nodding, Ben got up and pulled Marlee up. "Thank you for taking the time to answer our questions, Mike. Good to see you both again."

Marlee hugged her dad and grandma.

The ride back to Black Pointe was quiet. They were both lost in thought. Her dad didn't add much. She hoped Luke would be able to find someone that knew Robert, who might add to what they had. Too bad about Jim's death. She hadn't known him long, but he was a good boss and a nice guy. However, a remnant of a conversation with Jim kept playing around in her head. What did he say to her that night before he was killed? Something about leaving her a present. Was it evidence? *Think, Marlee.*

Nope. Nothing there. It would come to her sooner or later. She hoped.

CHAPTER TWENTY-FIVE

L uke arrived midafternoon at the University of Connecticut and put on a jacket. He'd left Florida during a heatwave, so the cooler weather was a relief.

He struck out with Robert's mom. He found her living in an older section of town in a rundown apartment. Luke wasn't sure what kind of reception he would receive. But he had been surprised when she took one look at him and almost dropped her clothes or ripped his off. He now knew what feeling like a piece of prime beef felt like. The icing on the cake, so to speak, was when she licked her lips, stuck out her boobs and asked with a wink, "What can I do for a good-looking hunk of man?" Good lord, the woman was in her late fifties, at least. She was still a looker, just thirty years too old for him and miles away from Grace. When he asked her about Robert, she'd turned nasty. Told him she had nothing to say, he was a good son and told Luke to go pound sand. OK, then.

He found the youngest brother, Davey, living in the next town over. Davey informed him Robert was a great brother, had supported the family from college and financially helped him through the electrician program. Davey told Luke their other brother was vacationing out west. Disappointing. By all accounts, Robert sounded like a saint.

UCONN's main campus in rural, bucolic eastern Connecticut was a beehive of activity when he arrived. He read on the plane that it began as an agricultural college in the late 1800s. Luke thought he might have time to walk around campus, but parking was impossible. The school was enormous. The many brick buildings were spread too far apart. Thousands of students were walking around, talking, laughing. He asked a dozen students where to find the School of Business. Only a couple knew. And he realized he wasn't even close to the building. Great. He had an appointment with the Dean of the School of Business at two, and he would be late if he couldn't find it.

He waved down a security guard, who gave him directions and offered a ride in a golf cart to the school. So here he was, sitting in the busy office watching students walk in and out laughing and talking, and wondering if he missed all this by not finishing college.

Nah. He was satisfied with his life. He didn't need a four-year degree when he went into the service—wouldn't hurt, wouldn't help. He didn't need it when he joined the force. The Police Academy gave him the education necessary for police work. Then it was work hard, study hard, make detective. Now he was working at KnightGuard Security and more than satisfied with his job and life. Especially being with the love of his life, who was pregnant with his child.

Talking to the Dean was a long shot. He knew the office wouldn't be able to give him any personal information on Robert Gilligan, but he hoped someone might know his friends or have some information that would point him in the right direction.

"Mr. McBride?" Ben looked up at a young woman who stood in front of him. "Dean Silvers will see you now."

After the noise in the outer office, the Dean's office was an oasis of calm in beige and grays. The outside office became just background noise. He shook hands with the Dean and then sank into a comfy chair. Dean Silvers looked about sixty, with gray hair, glasses, and a ready smile.

"So, what can I do for you, Mr. McBride?"

"Well, I'm working on a case for KnightGuard Security in Black Pointe, Florida, and we're looking for information about a Robert Gilligan who graduated from here about fifteen years ago. We have reason to believe he threatened our client and maybe murdered another person."

"Oh, dear. Have you been to the police?"

"Yes, but I was hoping to get more information about his time here or friends he had."

The Dean frowned. "Now, you know I can't give you that information, even if I had it."

"Well, I thought I would give it the old college try." Luke smiled. "Can you at least tell me when he graduated?" Having struck out two times already and since this was his third try, Luke realized he had been too optimistic about this trip. Sam had already given him the date, but he hoped to tease out some information.

"If you ask my administrative assistant, I'm sure she can look up that information, but as for anything else in his file." He shrugged. "I'm sorry."

He stood up. "Is there anything else?"

"No. I'm sorry if I wasted your time."

Dean Silvers walked him out to the office and asked the young woman to look up Robert Gilligan's graduation date.

Luke shook his hand, thanking him. He sat at the woman's desk. Judy Gorman, the nameplate read.

Judy looked up Robert's graduation date and gave it to Luke.

"Did you know him?"

She shook her head. Didn't hurt to ask.

As Luke was walking out, a middle-aged man he noticed walking into the office while he was talking to Judy followed him out.

"Excuse me. You were asking about Robert Gilligan?"

Luke stepped over to the side of the hallway. "Yes, do you know him?"

"Yeah, I know the bastard." The man looked around the crowded hall before focusing on Luke. "Do you have time for a cup of coffee?"

"Sure. Where do you suggest?"

"Coffee shop around the corner. Name is Mason Connors," he said as they shook hands and Luke introduced himself.

They arrived at the small coffee shop and grabbed the last empty table.

"What'll you have?" asked Mason.

Luke told him, and Mason came back with two cups of coffee.

"So, how do you know Robert Gilligan?" Luke asked.

"Well, it's a long story and not one I'm proud of. Robert was in my class and always seemed to be rolling in dough. I'd gotten a girl pregnant and needed a few hundred dollars fast. Couldn't tell my parents. They would have cut me off or worse. I heard Robert was a good source to borrow from, so I asked him for the money. He gave it to me."

Mason took a deep breath, exhaled loudly. "With strings attached, of course. He was charging twenty percent interest for the first sixty days. Then he said the interest would go up after that and to make sure I paid it back on time or else."

Mason fiddled with his cup, finally taking a sip. His hands were trembling.

Oh, Luke knew the ending to this story. Loan sharking, bottom feeders. *Robert, Robert, Robert. You naughty boy.*

"Well, I paid some of it back but couldn't pay the whole amount within the sixty days. Didn't want to ask my parents for it, and the interest on the loan went up to thirty-five percent for the next thirty days."

Luke groaned. Oh, this was not good.

Mason nodded. "Yeah. I know. Well, I managed to pay it off, but it cost me a lot of money. I had to borrow from some friends. But that's not the worst part." He rubbed his chin. A sheen of sweat across his brow threatened to overflow. "A friend of mine also borrowed money, and when he couldn't keep up with the interest amount, Robert had someone pay him a visit."

Luke knew where this was going. He hadn't been a detective for nothing. "What happened?"

"Let's just say it would have been cheaper for my friend to come up with the money. The guy was in the hospital for a week with broken fingers, cracked ribs, and ice packs on his balls for a couple of days. That wasn't the first time I heard a story like that."

"Ouch. Did anyone suspect Robert?"

"Sure, but no one could prove it was him. I heard he had a cousin or someone who was doing his dirty work."

"I'm betting no one went to the police?"

"Right. Everyone was terrified of what would happen."

Mason looked drained. Luke thought if he had to relive a situation like this, he would be too. However, he did get some useful information.

"Do you remember the cousin's name or know where I can find the guy he beat up?"

"Well, I haven't kept in touch with my friend, but I think

the cousin's name was Ray. Ray Bonetti?" Mason tapped his head and thought for a moment. "No. Bilotti." He snapped his fingers. "That's it. Ray Bilotti. Saw him talking with Robert once with another mean-looking dude. The guy is a sleazeball. Actually, they all are."

There wasn't anything else Mason could add. Luke thanked him. He looked at his watch and realized he had just enough time to catch an earlier flight home. Grace would be happy. At six months pregnant, she was still working but starting to get tired quickly. Plus, if she was still awake and not too tired, he could get some loving. And he definitely needed some love after this trip.

At least he had a name, and KnightGuard could go from there.

CHAPTER TWENTY-SIX

Marlee couldn't remember a more perfect day. She and Ben made love all morning. Wild, monkey sex and sweet, gentle sex. They showered together and had more sex. Ben left late afternoon. He had a couple of meetings and needed to catch up on paperwork.

He called her as soon as he got to the office to tell her Luke was still up north, and Joe was off for the night. She would be alone until he got home. Fine by her. It would be nice to have the time to herself without someone always around.

An idea for a business was swirling around her mind for a few days. She passed it by Ben a few days ago, and he liked it.

She needed to make some money. The firm wasn't paying her. Robert told everyone she quit. Sam suggested letting it go so Robert would feel like he was in the clear and, hopefully, make a mistake. Plus, she didn't want to upset her dad any more than necessary. She had the time during the day to do something. Well, sometimes, anyway. Ben kept her busy but in a good way. However, as much as she liked it, she couldn't exist just on sex. Could she? *No, Marlee, you can't*, although the thought did tempt her.

She spent the afternoon setting up a website for an online accounting business. She believed she could take on a couple of small businesses' books, and the few accounts would keep her in the black.

It was late, and she'd promised Ben that she would make his favorite meal of steak, potatoes, and chocolate cake. Checking the cabinets, Marlee realized they were out of chocolate and flour. Darn. She knew Ben was looking forward to that cake. *Hmmm?* Ben never said she couldn't go out. He wouldn't be home for a while, and the store was just down the street, a few miles or so, she thought.

Grabbing her purse and the phone off the counter, she got her car keys to her new, used car and walked into the garage. It felt good not having someone tag along. How long had it been since she went to the store alone? Too long.

Marlee forgot how beautiful the palm tree silhouettes were against a sunset. The sky was streaked with gray with shots of salmon and white clouds. Beautiful. But she needed to pay attention to the road, not the sky.

Having been on the street to the shopping plaza only once before, it took her a few extra turns to find the entrance. Walking inside the grocery store, she marveled at the sights and sounds. She let out a heavy sigh. It had been so long since she felt free. Walking up and down the aisles, she was amazed at the variety of products available. She found the flour and chocolate and a few other items they needed and located the checkout.

"Marlee?"

Marlee turned quickly. A tall, blond woman was smiling. "Emily," she squealed. By gosh, Emily Hatteras. She hadn't seen her friend or called her since this fiasco started.

After they checked out, Emily gave her a big hug. "You

disappeared. I've been calling you, but your number isn't ringing. What's going on?"

"Oh, Em, there's so much going on." Marlee looked at her watch. Yup, she had time. "Hey, do you have time for a cup of coffee?"

Emily nodded. "I think there's a coffee shop around the corner."

They agreed to meet there after they put their groceries in their cars.

Five minutes later, Marlee and Emily were sitting at a table with their coffee. Emily took her hand and said, "Marlee, please tell me what's going on. I've missed you. Steph said she talked to you once, that you got a new phone, but didn't give me any details."

Marlee wasn't sure how much Ben wanted her to divulge, so she told Emily the basics. She had problems at work, someone was stalking her, and Ben was keeping her safe. Emily gasped when she heard what Marlee was going through. But she had lots of questions, especially about Ben. Was he cute? Did Marlee like him? Were they going out? Were they together twenty-four seven?

"What did you think of that picture that Amber took of Jeffrey?"

Jeffrey. Marlee missed him so much. If it weren't for Emily finding him roaming the streets as a kitten and asking if Marlee wanted him, she wouldn't have him.

"I haven't seen it yet." Marlee pulled out her phone. No bars. Nothing. Damn. She picked up the one burner phone that hadn't been charged. Yup, in her mind, she could see her other phone sitting by the nightstand, charging.

"Here." Emily pulled up the picture. He was snuggling on Amber's lap, looking cute as a button.

"He's so cute. Text Amber that the picture is adorable."

Emily texted Amber, and they sat and talked for a while

more. Marlee looked at her watch. It had been a good hour
since they sat down. Damn. Ben would be home soon, and
she hadn't started the cake, let alone finished dinner. He
probably wouldn't get the cake tonight. But it was fun
connecting with her girlfriend. Hugging Emily goodbye,
Marlee promised to keep in touch.

It was much darker now. Marlee was feeling a little guilty
about the time. But the house was only a short distance away,
and she would still be home before Ben.

Rush-hour traffic was heavy this time of night. The street-
lights were on, casting ghostly shadows on the road. Marlee
barely made it through the intersection. She was in a hurry
now. She drove a couple of miles, but nothing looked familiar,
and the houses were spaced farther apart then she
remembered.

At the next stop sign, she thought the street looked familiar, so she took a right. That brought her on an even quieter
road. Now there were fewer cars, only a couple ahead of her.
She noticed a black SUV following a little too close to her but
thought they might be in a hurry to get home. She was
driving a little slower than usual, looking for familiar
landmarks.

She drove a couple more miles, praying she would recognize something. She realized too late that it turned into a
packed dirt road, and the street was not lit. The other cars
turned a way back, but the black SUV was still following her.
For a fleeting moment, she thought Robert found her. *Silly
woman, how would he know you were going to the store?*

The SUV was edging closer to her bumper. Marlee started
to panic. Where the hell was she? There were no houses on
the road that she could see.

The SUV blinked its high beams on and off. Marlee
panicked. What did they want her to do? Pull over? Speed
up? Not taking any chances, she sped up. Her car hit several

potholes, shaking her teeth. Her heart was racing, and her hands were slippery on the steering wheel.

What was going on?

The black car appeared even closer to her bumper. Marlee prepared for impact. She stepped on the gassurged ahead. Whew, that was close.

Suddenly her car was shoved forward. Her head bounced back and forth. What the hell? She glanced in her rearview mirror. The SUV was behind her and coming back fast. She put her foot to the gas and floored it.

Bang.

Rear-ended again.

Bang. She hit her head hard on the steering wheel just as the airbags inflated.

Bang again. But this time, the car stopped. The front of the car was smashed into a tree. Steam was coming from the hood. Marlee moaned and felt blood running down her forehead. She reached for her purse, pulled out her pepper spray. No way was she opening her door. She prayed other cars would come down the road, but it was deserted.

A shadow passed by the side of the car. The next thing Marlee knew, the man was hammering at the side of her window. She screamed and tried to get out of her seatbelt to move to the other side of the car. She had a death grip on the pepper spray and her hands were slippery and sliding off the seat belt. *Where the hell was the connector?*

The window shattered. A hairy hand reached in, opened the door, cut her seatbelt, and pulled Marlee out of the car, throwing her to the road. Marlee kept screaming help, but no one was around to respond.

She tried to crawl away from him, but he roughly pulled her up by her hair. She kicked out, connected with his shin. Oh God, this was not happening.

"Stop fighting, bitch. You're not going anywhere."

He slapped her hard across the face and began dragging her to the SUV. NO. She wouldn't get in there. She was dead if she did. He still had her by the hair. Her head bent at an awkward angle. The pain unbearable. Tears were flowing down her face. Couldn't wipe them.

She managed to get the cap off the pepper spray with her thumb, prayed she wouldn't spray herself, and summoned every ounce of energy that she had left. He still had a firm grasp on her hair. Bringing her hand up, she shot a stream into his face. The surprise on his face was priceless.

"Aaaargh. You bitch." The man let go of her hair and jumped around yelling and furiously rubbing his eyes. Marlee took a moment to kick him in the balls—hard. Then she turned and ran.

BEN GOT HOME a little after 9 p.m., about an hour later than he thought. He had to leave a voice mail earlier for Marlee since she hadn't picked up her phone. His mouth watered at the thought of the dinner she was preparing.

The house was dark. Opening the door, he called for Marlee. No answer. He pulled out his gun.

He carefully checked every room. No Marlee. He went into the kitchen, and it looked like she started dinner, then stopped. She never called to tell him she was going out. Where the hell could she be?

He pulled out his cell phone to call her again. It rang and rang. He got Marlee's voice mail. But the ringing sounded close, like an echo. He dialed again and followed the ring into their bedroom.

Damn, there was Marlee's cell phone on the table, charging. She never went anywhere without it. And she never went anywhere. Did she have the second burner phone with her? He dialed that. No answer. Damn.

He didn't want to panic. But with a murderer gunning for Marlee and a madman blowing up his house, Ben could only imagine the worst.

The hell with not panicking. His heart was racing. His hands were sweating. Damn. Damn. Damn. Why couldn't he keep a woman safe?

He pinched his nose. Luke was still away. Joe was off for the night. He thought about calling Sam. He worried Sam would think that if he couldn't handle a 110-pound dynamo, how the hell could he handle someone else?

The hell with his pride. He needed to find Marlee. He dialed. Sam promised to come right over.

SAM ARRIVED over an hour later and told him Joe was asking around the grocery store and that they should wait at the house in case Marlee called. They sat in the living room, drinking beer. His hands were shaking as he picked up a bottle. He hoped Sam didn't notice. Ben couldn't control his fear for Marlee's safety. He and Sam were discussing plans on how to find her.

The phone rang. Marlee!

No. Joe. "The clerk at the store recognized Marlee. Said she was talking to another woman in line, and they left. I don't see her car in the parking lot."

Damn. Ben closed his eyes. Where was she?

"I'm going to check the routes to your house in case she got a flat or something. I'll call if I find her."

Ben told him Marlee's phone was dead and to call if he found anything.

The phone rang a half-hour later as Ben got up to get

another beer. It had to be Joe. Sam beat him to it and answered it.

Then the front door opened and Marlee stood there, all disheveled, looking like she did when they first met—smudges on her arms and face, leaves sticking out of her hair, and dirty. So beautiful.

"Oh, dear God. Marlee." He went over, hugged her hard, and released her. She was alive!

"What the hell happened? Where have you been? Are you all right?" He patted every inch of her body for injuries.

She fell into his arms, sobbing and trying to talk.

Ben led her over to the sofa and sat down, holding Marlee in his lap.

"That was Joe. He found her car smashed into a tree on old route 610," Sam said. "There appeared to be a scuffle. He called to say he couldn't find Marlee, but here she is. He said he had her purse."

Ben held her tight. It was a good amount of time before she could speak. He had a chance to look at the scrapes on her hands and knees. It looked like she was going to have a shiner, and he wanted a few minutes with whoever hurt her. Then there was what looked like a small bald spot where her hair had been. It had to have hurt. The rage he was holding in threatened to erupt. But he needed to keep himself together for Marlee. However, the urge to punch the wall, hell, punch the bastard who hurt Marlee was simmering below the surface.

"It's OK. It's OK," he murmured into her ear. She hiccupped a couple of times and put her arms around his neck.

"I'm so sorry," she whispered.

He smoothed her hair after removing a couple of twigs. "Why? You have nothing to be sorry for. You're here. That's all that counts."

Sam came over and took her hand. "Marlee, can you tell us what happened?"

"I needed some chocolate for my cake. I was going to call Ben to let him know that I was going out, but my phone was dead." She swiped a tear and sighed. "I thought I would charge it on the way over, but I forgot."

She grimaced. "Sorry."

Sam gave Ben a look. Not a good look. Some bodyguard he was turning out to be. His worst nightmare was coming true. He couldn't protect someone.

Marlee looked at Ben and Sam. "Please don't blame Ben. This was on me." She gave a little shoulder shrug. "I didn't realize I grabbed the old burner phone by mistake. Anyhow, I got to the store, picked up the things I needed. While I was in line, I ran into my friend Emily. We stopped to have coffee, and she asked if I saw the picture of Jeffrey that Amber sent."

Ben could only shake his head. That cat was going to be the death of him.

"I hadn't, so when Emily showed me the picture, I asked her to text Amber that it was adorable. We talked a while more, and I left."

She told them about her trip home, getting lost on the dirt road with no lights or houses and the SUV rear-ending her.

Ben groaned.

She rubbed his chest and continued her story. When she got to the part about spraying her attacker with the pepper spray and then kicking him in the balls, Ben was drained. Her story both frightened and angered him.

"Did you get a look at his face?" asked Sam.

Marlee thought for a moment. "It all happened so fast. He had dark hair, tall but not as tall as Ben. And really red eyes." She started giggling. "And blue balls."

Sam snorted, and after a moment, they were all laughing

themselves silly. By the time Ben caught his breath, he realized the laugh was cathartic for them.

It was a few minutes later when the door opened, and Joe walked in holding Marlee's purse. Marlee was still giggling. Joe cocked a brow, and Ben said, "Don't ask."

"What I would like to know is how they—Robert, I'm guessing—found you? You have a new car. You don't go anywhere. The phone isn't bugged. How?" asked Sam.

"I only met with Emily, and that was a chance meeting. I didn't see anyone watching me."

Ben thought about it for a moment. "But you said Emily texted Amber."

Marlee nodded.

"Maybe one of them has a connection to Robert."

"No way. They're my friends," exclaimed Marlee rather vehemently.

Sam looked at Ben and nodded. Good. Sam would dig into Amber and Emily's backgrounds, and if something was there, they would know.

"Well, that's my cue to leave." She started toward the door. "Joe, are you coming?"

"Yes, ma'am."

Ben closed and locked the door behind them. He walked over to Marlee and hugged her tight.

"Sweetcheeks, is there anything I can get you or do you want to go to bed?"

Bed was her answer. Tomorrow they would have the talk. The talk about security. And hopefully, Sam would have some answers.

BEN OPENED his eyes slowly and yawned. Nothing like a lot of cuddling and sex to make a man satisfied and hungry. He was starving. Wafts of coffee brewing and bacon frying were making his mouth water.

He got up, brushed his teeth, and walked into a sweet domestic scene. Marlee was cooking breakfast. She wore her favorite blue apron that her grandma gave her and nothing else.

"Sweetcakes, if you keep surprising me like this, I'm going to have a heart attack."

Marlee handed him a plate and gave him a knowing smile. "Why don't you eat breakfast and gain back some strength. I have in mind some exercise this morning."

"What kind of exercise?" He hoped it was the one he was thinking of.

She winked at him and sat down with a cup of coffee.

He smiled. Breakfast with benefits was his kind of meal.

After their shower, Ben was satiated but the safety talk was on the table later. He couldn't protect her if she didn't understand she just couldn't leave by herself until Robert was caught.

They spent some time cleaning up, and Ben was anxious to drive over to see where Marlee was almost kidnapped.

When they got to the site, her car had already been removed, and all that was left was some glass swept to the side of the road. Ben looked around at the deserted dirt road, and bile caught in his throat. Thank the Lord, Marlee carried her pepper spray and took the self-defense lessons, or ... He didn't want to think about the "or."

"Let's go home. Nothing to be gained staring at the road," he said, feeling dejected they hadn't found any clues.

It was after dinner before Ben broached the subject of safety with Marlee.

Ben patted the sofa. "Come here, sweetheart. We need to talk."

Marlee sat down and started rubbing her body on his.

He gently pushed her back, or they would never have this talk. "Sweet cheeks, I'm so glad nothing more happened last night, but I'm curious as to why you left the house, especially if no one was here to guard you. And why didn't you call me? I thought you had more common sense than that."

The silence was deafening.

"Common sense?" she said with a tight smile. Marlee cocked her head, glared at him. "Really? I can't believe you just said that."

The talk was not going as well as he hoped. He stared down at the scrappy woman whose eyes were shooting daggers at him. Raising his voice, he said, "Yes, I did say that. What is wrong with you? You know better than to go somewhere without a bodyguard. You were almost kidnapped last night." He was furious. How could she be so lackadaisical about her safety?

"Well, I got away." She shrugged.

"Yes, you got away this time. What about the next time? Goddamn it, Marlee," Ben roared. "People are putting their lives on the line to keep you safe. Sam has gone out of her way to find this safe house for us. What were you thinking?"

Marlee took a deep breath. "What I was thinking is that I'm tired of being babysat."

She stabbed him in the chest with her finger. "I'm tired of reporting to you."

Stabbing him again, her nostrils flaring. "I'm tired of running," she growled.

Stab. Stab. "I'm tired of missing my friends and not working. I'm tired of you bossing me around. I'm. Just. Tired."

She started walking toward the bedrooms. "And now, I'm just plain tired, and I'm going to bed."

Marlee stomped to the guest bedroom and slammed the door. Ben heard the lock click. Damn, the woman was exasperating. Didn't she know they were just trying to protect her? Didn't she realize she scared the shit out of him when he couldn't reach her? But most of all, didn't she know how much he loved her? And how much it would hurt if something happened to her?

The hell with her. Ben walked to the master bedroom and slammed the door.

HOURS LATER, he was still trying to calm himself. Tossing and turning. Thinking of all the things that could have happened to her. If anything happened to Marlee, he would never have forgiven himself. He got out of bed and stomped over to the guest bedroom. He tried the doorknob. Locked. He put his ear to the door and heard sniffling. Should he force his way in or not? Not. Marlee deserved to cry after putting him through this agony.

He got himself a beer, actually several, and sat on the sofa. Turning on the TV, he tried to get into a game, but it was useless. He was keyed up, couldn't follow the score, and was still frightened and angry that she walked home in the dark.

He heard rustling in the kitchen. Opened his eyes slowly. They felt gritty. It was early morning. He must have fallen asleep. The beer was sloshing in his stomach. He felt sick, but he wanted, no needed, to see Marlee. He hoped to talk some sense into her.

Her eyes were red from crying. Marlee turned her back to him and wouldn't say good morning. It infuriated him more.

"Goddamn it, Marlee, look at me."

"No."

"Marlee, look at me," he roared.

She turned around and sniffled.

Finally, he had enough. He enveloped her in his arms and

held her tight until she shivered a couple of times and calmed down.

Kissing the top of her head, he whispered, "I love you. If anything had happened to you, I would have died."

She relaxed against him.

He picked her up. Looked to her for permission. She nodded, and Ben carried her into the bedroom, where he lavished his love on her for hours.

CHAPTER TWENTY-SEVEN

Marlee confided in Ben that she desperately wanted to get back to her normal life. She was sick and tired of waiting for Robert to make a mistake or for Phil to find something.

Although Ben thought life couldn't get any better with his sprite. She was funny, smart, high energy and really into sex—with him. His friends liked her a lot. Her dad and grandma liked him. Life was good. If only they could catch Robert doing something, anything wrong. Robert was keeping a low profile. He was smart; Ben had to give him that.

Joe was at the house with Marlee. Remembering they were low on groceries, Ben promised to bring back lunch. He stopped at his favorite deli to order sandwiches. He had plans for Marlee after they ate and when Joe left. Plans that included dessert—mainly her.

His favorite, Deli Belly, home of the "ginormous" corned beef sandwich, was on his way to the safe house. The popular deli was on a busy corner, so he was forced to park a block away. The scents wafting from the deli hit him as soon as he got out of the car. Following his nose, he groaned when he entered the crowded restaurant. Everyone was on their lunch hour. It would take forever to order and wait for the sandwiches. But the pull of corned beef, pickles, bagels—damn, just food, was too much. He was hungry. The hell with it. He pulled a number and stood in line.

His eyes and ears hurt. The red and white deli was an overload of colors, scents, and voices. He made a note to himself not to come here again during rush hour.

"Ben Green?" A woman's voice hollered out his name.

He looked around the busy restaurant.

A red-haired woman was vigorously waving at him from one of the tables. She didn't look familiar. Had he dated her and had forgotten? Hoped not, but it had happened before.

She waved him over. He looked back at the line, counted fifteen people ahead of him. He had time to say hello and hopefully remember who she was before he got to the table.

"Hey."

Nope. Didn't look familiar, even close up.

"Oh, Ben." The woman pouted. "You don't remember me." She was there with a couple of good-looking women who were eyeballing him.

"Don't you remember me? I was with Harrison at the barbecue."

Oh shit, he remembered her now. She spent the evening clinging to Harrison with her tongue in his ear. Not that Harrison minded. What the hell was her name? Julie? No. Juliette. He remembered her saying Harrison was her Romeo, and she was his Juliette. *Gag me now.*

"Juliette, of course, I remember you." *Am I suave or what?*

She introduced him to her girlfriends. One licked her lips and looked like she wanted to gobble him up. *Good grief save me from man-eaters.*

"Yeah. The barbecue was fun. I remember you saying you just started at KnightGuard Security working with Harrison."

She looked at the other women, smiled, and licked her lips. *Not going there, lady.* "You used to be a cop, right?"

He nodded.

"How is your girlfriend?" She gave him a sly smile. "Marlee, isn't it? She's adorable."

Whoa, this one was way too cozy for him. What did she care about Marlee? She only met her once, and the way she was hanging on to Harrison, Ben wasn't sure she even noticed anyone else.

"Yeah, she is." He glanced around, thankfully heard his number called. Said goodbye and placed his order at the counter.

A COUPLE OF DAYS LATER, Sam called. "Ben, we have a little issue. Can you come in? Don't bring Marlee."

OK, what was that about? Ben hoped Sam had a breakthrough.

Sam asked him to come into her office and closed the door. What the hell was going on? Did he mess up somehow? She never closed the door when he came in before. Was it bad news?

She covered her face with her hands, then looked at him. "I just had a disturbing call."

"OK?"

"Not OK. A woman from Marlee's office called. She's made some serious accusations against Marlee. And damn it all, they throw a wrench into our investigation."

Ben started to protest.

Putting her hand up, Sam said, "Let me finish. I'm not going to believe what anyone says until we talk to Marlee and get her side. But the information is damaging to Marlee's interpretation of what happened."

What the hell was going on? Marlee told them everything, didn't she? "Who is the woman?"

"I understand you met her the other day."

Ben was confused. He didn't meet anyone the other day. Wait. He did. He remembered talking to Juliette and her friends, who kept ogling him.

"I was at the deli and talked to Harrison's date. She was with two other women. Was it one of them?"

"Yes. Her name is Tanya West, and she works at the accounting firm. According to her, Jim Matthews and Marlee were dating."

"Dating?" he sputtered. Why didn't Marlee inform him of that factoid?

"Yes, and because of that, Tanya was passed over for a promotion. Although I'm not taking much stock in that."

"Agreed."

"She also said Jim questioned her about Robert and his accounts, which she didn't know anything about or believed. She claimed that Marlee was making an uncomfortable working environment for everyone there. She seemed to be spying on everyone's work. She always thought Marlee felt empowered because she was the owner's daughter."

"Perfect." Ben closed his eyes and sighed. "So how did Tanya find you?"

Sam looked at her notes. "You told her friend, Juliette, where you were working, and Tanya put two and two together."

What the hell was going on? Juliette? What a pain in his ass. Ben thought Tanya's information could be sour grapes. Why did Tanya feel the need to share this now? And why had he even stopped to say hello to Juliette?

"Why haven't we heard about this before?" Ben's stomach churned. He couldn't go there again with Marlee. It took them a while to make peace with her confession about Jerod.

Was this a pattern of hers? He hoped not, but the old saying, "Fool me once, shame on me, fool me twice, shame on you" popped into his head. Great! Now he was channeling grandma.

"Well, we weren't looking for information from other employees. We trusted Marlee's word. I still do. But we have to talk to Tanya. And Marlee. One thing we never pursued was finding out more about Jim Matthews's life."

Yeah, Sam was right. But damn. This was awkward, and he sure didn't want to tell Marlee about this new information.

Sam sighed. "Listen, I'll get Tanya's story, and anyone else's who will talk to me. Then I can talk to Marlee, or we both can."

"What a clusterfuck. I was hoping we were ahead of the game." He rubbed his face. "Okay. Let's wait to tell Marlee about Tanya until after you speak with her. Let me know what you learn."

SAM COULDN'T BELIEVE what a debacle Marlee's problem was turning out to be. Every step forward, they took turned out to be two steps back. Now, this.

Tanya wanted to meet close to the accounting office. She didn't want to meet at all, but Sam managed to convince her it was important. Sam arrived at the coffee shop fifteen minutes ago mostly to watch for a tail on Tanya. She didn't think Robert would do that, but one couldn't be too careful.

Looking out the floor-to-ceiling window at the sidewalk, Sam saw a short brunette scurrying down toward the coffee shop and continually looking over her shoulder. She wondered if it was Tanya. As the brunette walked in, she looked curiously around, spotted Sam and walked to the table

"What can I get you girls?" a fiftyish server asked as soon as Tanya sat down.

They both ordered coffee. Tanya kept picking at the handle of her purse and gulping.

"I didn't expect I would have to meet you. Everything I know, I told you already. I don't know why you need more information. My boss is expecting me at the office in a half hour, so we need to be quick."

Tanya said that practically in one breath. Oh yeah, harassing Tanya was going to be fun.

"I know what you told me. But those are serious accusations against Marlee, and I just want to be clear.

"Humpf. Whatever."

Okay, Tanya was going to be difficult. Sam tried a different approach. "So how long have you been working at Burns, Barnett, and Gilligan?"

"For about ten years. Robert Gilligan hired me."

"Is he a good boss?"

"Generally. Although why he let Mike Burns hire his daughter is beyond me. Look where that got him."

"What was your relationship with Marlee or Jim Matthews?"

"Marlee and I didn't have one. She was the boss's daughter and thought she was above us all. Jim and I were close friends, or so I thought."

A different server laid the coffee in front of them with the milk and sugar.

Sam took a big chance here. "Did you and Jim date?"

Tanya took a deep breath. "I wanted to, not that it's any of your business, but Jim was hung up on Marlee. I believe they were dating."

Jealous perhaps? "Were they dating, or did you just think so?"

Tanya gave Sam a dirty look. "Look, I wasn't born yesterday. They spent a lot of time together, whispering to each other. He had the hots for her. Sounds like dating to me."

Sounded like jealousy to her, so Sam took another avenue. "Who oversees the office when Robert isn't around? Another partner?"

"Well, it was Jim, but I'm in charge now. There are no other partners. Jim had his sights on becoming one, and Robert promised him it would happen. Now, I'm expecting Robert to bring me on board as a partner any day now."

Sam didn't want to pop Tanya's bubble, but Tanya would be waiting till hell froze over if she thought Robert was going to make her a partner. Hadn't happened yet. It was hard to embezzle if another person was in your personal business.

"Who double-checks the books?"

"Well, that was Jim's area, but now it's mine."

"Have you seen anything strange going on?"

Tanya shrugged her shoulders. "Strange as in how?"

"Oh, I don't know. Strange people hanging around, strange entries into the system, strange behavior. You know, anything out of the ordinary."

Sam waited.

"No, nothing out of the ordinary."

Tanya was lying. She wouldn't look directly at her. Tanya was hiding something, but Sam knew she wasn't going to get anything else from her today.

"Why weren't you curious about Jim's accusations?" Sam watched Tanya wrestle with the question. If this wasn't a case of jealousy, she needed to get out of the protection business.

Tanya looked around the coffee shop. Stared at the ceiling. Looked at the floor, the door, the windows. Everywhere but at Sam. Sam figured she could hold out not saying anything a lot longer than Tanya.

Finally, Tanya looked at Sam and said, "I didn't want to create any more embarrassment for the office and for Robert.

Jim is dead. Marlee is a troublemaker. Plus, I heard rumors she has ruined more than one person's reputation."

So much for only the partners knowing about Marlee's mistake. Sam wondered who mentioned it. Her money was on Robert.

"So, from where I stand, Marlee is out, Jim is dead, and the office is moving on."

Tanya finished her coffee and pulled out her wallet. Sam put her hand up and told her she would take care of the bill. As Tanya rushed off, Sam went over their conversation. She didn't get anything new out of Tanya.

Tanya was lying. Plus, Sam suspected she was jealous that Jim wanted to date Marlee but not her. Interesting that Robert promised to make her a partner when he hadn't in all the years he owned the business. Maybe it was time to check Tanya's bank account.

PHIL CHECKED Tanya's bank account. No outstanding deposits. She made a decent salary, owned a moderately priced condo, a used car, didn't buy lavish items, just lived comfortably and within her means.

Sam was confused as to why Tanya came forward. What did Tanya get out of this? Three reasons stood out in her mind. One, Tanya didn't like Marlee and was more than happy to stick a knife in her back. She'd already mentioned she didn't like the fact that Mike Burns hired his daughter.

Two, Robert had something on Tanya or vice versa. Although Tanya didn't seem smart enough to fall into that trap. That couldn't be it. Maybe Tanya was hoping to snag Robert. He was single and wealthy. Not with his own money, but some women didn't care about that.

Three, Tanya was jealous of Jim and Marlee. Perhaps she

wanted to date Jim, and he didn't want her. That was more plausible.

Whatever. Sam put in a call to Marlee and was hoping to hear from her soon. She was frustrated this case was taking so long. Marlee needed to get her life in order. Although Marlee's online accounting business was starting to take off, it wouldn't provide enough money for her to live on in the short run. And Marlee already told her that she didn't want to live off Ben, even though he was more than happy to provide for her.

Sam shook her head. That Marlee was a pistol. High-spirited, fearless, funny as hell, especially when she drank. The girls really liked her, and she seemed to fit right in with the group.

The fact that Robert was evading them bothered her. The one thing going in her favor besides her company was that she was tenacious. Sam was sure that Robert would mess up eventually. Plus, Robert hurt her new friend, and for that, he would pay.

IT TURNED out Jim Matthews had a sister. Marlee volunteered she'd spoken to her a couple of times on the phone in the past. She, Sam, and Ben were on their way to meet Sue at her house in Middleburg, about one hour from Black Pointe.

They arrived at Sue's condo, mid-morning. She lived in a small community of two-story condos just a few blocks from the small downtown. The street was typical for a small town. Marlee didn't see any stores, and only a few people were walking about. It was too quiet for her.

Whoever Marlee was expecting, Sue wasn't it. She wore a long purple caftan and was taller than Jim's six feet. She looked just like her brother. Marlee held back a sob. Jim had been a friend and a nice guy.

"Welcome. Come in. Sit down." Sue waved her hand toward the living room.

After making introductions and offering drinks, Sue asked what she could do for them.

"Sue, I'm so sorry about Jim's death," said Marlee. "He was a really nice man."

"Thank you." Sue wiped a tear from her eye. "I miss him so much. We were the only family we had. So, there's a big, empty hole in my heart."

Silence. Marlee wasn't sure what to say next, but Sam broke in. "Sue, we're so sorry for your loss. But we have a problem that we hope you can help us with. Jim and Marlee were investigating embezzlement at the accounting firm. Do you know anything about that?"

Sue fiddled with her hands, clenching and unclenching her caftan. The grief still strong. "I don't know too much. Jim told me a little about what he suspected. He was keeping records of what he found on his computer. He said he had a thumb drive for evidence."

"A thumb drive. Do you have it?" Marlee got excited. This was what they were looking for. Proof that Robert was embezzling.

Sue shook her head. "No, Jim told me he was going to keep it someplace safe. He didn't want me involved in case things got bad at work."

Damn. Sam asked if it could be in his apartment.

"No, his apartment was cleaned out just after his death. I believe it's been rented already."

Sam rubbed the back of her head. Things just weren't going their way. "Sue, have you spoken to the police?"

Sue's eyes shifted around the condo. She pursed her lips and drew a deep breath and shook her head. "I should have, but I didn't. Jim once told me Robert Gilligan was in tight with the police in Lakedale. When they came to tell me that Jim was dead, they didn't ask too many questions, and I didn't volunteer anything. Felt it was best at the time."

"Probably best," said Sam. "Did Jim tell you anything else about what was going on in the office? Did he ever mention a Tanya?"

Sue looked up in shock. "That bitch. What's she done now?"

"Sam, you never mentioned you spoke to Tanya," Marlee said. "We were friends at the firm. What's going on?"

"Hmmm, I'm sorry I didn't mention it sooner, but Tanya had some not so nice things to say about you." She proceeded to repeat what Tanya told her.

Marlee gasped. "I can't believe this. She was so nice to my face, and all the time she was backstabbing me. I feel like going down to the office and calling her out." She punched her fist in her hand. "That bitch." Glaring at Sam, she asked, "Did you believe her?"

"No. I didn't believe anything she told me. But I would like to understand why she felt she needed to defend Robert or Jim," said Sam.

"I think I know," said Sue as she got up from the sofa. "I have Jim's computer in the other room. If I remember right, Tanya sent him some interesting emails."

Sue walked into a small room and brought out a laptop and placed it on the table.

"This is the only thing I took from his apartment." She pressed the power button. "Damn, it's dead. I need to get the cord."

She came back, plugged it in, and they waited for it to boot up. Sue put in the password and opened Jim's email account.

"Jim told me he was being harassed by a woman at work

who kept sending him emails. She kept asking him out and telling him Marlee wasn't right for him."

Ben spoke up. "Marlee, were you dating Jim?"

"Ah. Not exactly," she mumbled.

"WHAT THE HELL does that mean? Not exactly. Did you, or didn't you?" Ben demanded. The little green monster called envy was annoying him. Marlee never said she dated Jim. Why not?

"Ah, Ben?" Sam broke in, cut her hand through the air. "Now's not the time."

Tough. He stared at Marlee.

She hemmed and hawed. "Well, we had coffee once but decided we were better friends than a couple. Besides, nothing came of it except a kiss on my forehead at the end of the night. We got along great at work and decided we didn't want to spoil that relationship."

Hearing that, Ben sat back in the chair. When they got home, he thought they might have another discussion about who she dated.

Whoa. No. That was not going to happen. It wasn't any of his business. Marlee was a grown-up who didn't have to report to him. Besides, even if she did date Jim, that was before Ben met her. He certainly didn't feel he needed to tell Marlee about all the women he dated before her. Well, except for Patty, but she came to the house. And that was a different circumstance.

Sue jumped into the conversation. "Jim had a major crush on Marlee, but he told me after their one meetup that they had fun, but Marlee wasn't into him, so that was that. Tanya, however, wanted to date Jim badly. She sent him quite a few emails, as you can see." Sue turned the computer around to show them.

Tanya must have written every week, sometimes brazenly asking Jim if he was going to be around for the weekend, sometimes asking him to go out for a drink. Jim's responses were either that he was busy or tired.

One mystery solved, Ben thought. Tanya was jealous of Marlee and Jim. But the mysterious thumb drive was still nowhere to be found. Jim's computer didn't have any files on it that said: "secret, don't read."

"Sue, would you mind if I took Jim's computer for our IT guy to look at?"

Sue thought for a minute. "No, but I would like it back when you're finished. It's silly and of no use to me, but it's all I have left of Jim."

There was nothing else to be gained from Sue. They picked up the computer and left.

Marlee was incensed all the way home, lambasting Tanya and all the ways she was going to hurt her. Ben mentally laughed but was relieved he wasn't the subject of her torture. What an imagination! He was glad to be on her good side.

However, they were no closer to finding out what Robert was doing than before. What was it going to take to catch him in the act?

CHAPTER TWENTY-EIGHT

Ben gave Marlee a long, passionate kiss and blew a big one at Joe as he walked out the door. Joe pretended to gag.

What a way to start a morning. A beautiful, warm, bright morning. Ben promised to take her to the beach in the afternoon. Marlee couldn't remember the last time she was at the beach. Working the hours she did, at least when she had been working, there was never enough time to go.

Dang. She remembered she didn't have a bathing suit. The last time she and Ben decided to go to the beach, Ben's house blew up. *Ugh. Not a good memory.* Ben asked her to model bikinis for him, but she never got the chance. Today she would go to that chichi swimwear store downtown and buy a bikini especially for him.

"Joe, come on. We're going shopping," she called out.

A groan and a heavy sigh came from the living room. "Do I have to?" Joe sounded like a little kid who had to go to the doctor with his mom.

"Oh, come on. It won't be that bad, and you can stare at all the women coming in to try on bathing suits," Marlee said.

Joe walked into the kitchen, grumpy written all over his face. "Fine. Let's get it over with. This is over and above. I'm asking Sam for combat pay."

The tony shopping center of Black Pointe was filled with every imaginable high-end shop. There were lots of people laughing, talking, shopping, and stopping for a bite. Marlee dragged Joe down a little side alley. They passed a gurgling fountain and entrances to more small shops. Incense wafted from one store, and staircases to second-story apartments were covered with planters filled with colorful flowers. *Everything for the Beach* was located at the end. The windows showcased bikinis, tankinis, one-piece suits, and cover-ups in all the latest colors. Marlee had made a little extra money with her online business, and she knew she was going to blow it all here.

"Maybe you'll model some for me." Joe's eyes lit up.

"Not on your life," Marlee said, and added, "or mine."

She pushed him toward the outdoor coffee shop. "Have a cup of coffee; I won't be long."

"So says every woman on the planet," he grumbled. But he walked over and ordered a coffee.

There was only one young girl in the beach shop. She helped Marlee pick out a couple of styles of bikinis. Marlee thought about getting the one-piece or tankini but decided, since Ben had already explored every inch of her body, there was no good reason to cover it up.

She chose one of the open dressing rooms, closed the curtain, and promised the salesgirl she would call out if she needed help. The first bikini she tried on was navy blue, a color she liked, but it was little more than a thong and barely-there top. She knew Ben would love it on her, but only if she wore it in the house. Even then, Marlee doubted she would have it on very long. She tried on a turquoise bikini with a more modest top and a bottom that had loop side ties. A little racy, but both pieces covered more than the first. This was the one.

She took it off and put her clothes on. Bending over to reach her purse, she felt a rush of air.

"Whaaat ... ?" She never got the words out.

A hand covered her mouth. Turning her head, she saw Robert, a smirk on his face. She tried to scream, but he wasn't letting up on her mouth. She tried to bite him, but the pressure of his hand on her mouth was too intense. *This couldn't be happening.* Her heart was racing.

Struggling out of his arms, she lashed out at his balls, trying to remember everything Pete taught her. But she hit a blank. Nothing stuck.

Screaming a pitiful "help," she picked up her purse and swung it at him again and again. Didn't seem to bother him. The contents were flying out, making it unlikely it was hurting him. Her hands were slick with sweat.

Robert pulled back the curtain and started to drag her out of the changing room. She kicked at him again. He grabbed her around the waist and pulled her in close. "You can scream all you want, bitch, but no one is coming."

She squirmed, but he was too strong. He got a good grip on her hair and tugged hard. Pain. Marlee thought he pulled a chunk out. *Great, another chunk gone.* Her eyes watered. She couldn't move, and Robert wasn't letting go.

"Oh, bitch, you're not getting away from me now."

Marlee was immobilized except for her feet, which she tried to kick backward. She felt Robert pull something out of his pocket. *Oh, dear lord. What was he doing?* She struggled, squirmed, and finally got loose from his grip. She tried to run past him.

Too late. She didn't see his fist stretch out but felt the gut-wrenching pain in her stomach. Oomph. Her breath caught. She couldn't inhale. She couldn't double over. The pain was intense. She could only stand there, her lungs screaming as she tried to suck in air with her body protesting the action.

He smirked as he took the cover off a needle. Marlee could only watch in the mirror as he inserted it into her arm, and she felt a prick. Then he picked her up like a rag doll and threw her over his shoulder. Her last thought was that she would never see Ben again. Then, darkness.

———

ROBERT COULDN'T REMEMBER why he was even downtown. But call it a fluke, serendipity—Christ, call it anything you want. It was the break he needed.

He saw Marlee and the other bodyguard walking down a side street. He knew there was a small alley behind the shop. No one was around, so he was able to park in the alley. Lucky for him, his cousin gave some propofol just in case. He got out of his car and was walking toward the store. A clerk was opened the back door. He went in.

It was so easy to overpower the little stick of a thing. The young woman barely batted an eyelid when he back-handed her and knocked her out. He glanced out front and saw the bodyguard drinking coffee—some bodyguard. There was nobody else in the shop now except him and Marlee. She wasn't hard to find. There were only three dressing rooms.

Marlee was picking up her purse when he pulled back the dressing room curtain. The shock on her face when she finally realized it was him was priceless.

He had no problem punching Marlee in the gut—*that had to hurt*—then sticking her with a needle and hauling her into his car. Thankfully the clerk was still out of it as he stepped over her prone body to get Marlee into his car.

He couldn't just drive around with Marlee in the car.

Where to go? Amber's. Not the best scenario but better than nothing.

Robert had a euphoric high going. He was really going to up Ray's bonus. Robert didn't want to think about how Ray got so many drugs. So many of everything, whenever he needed it. Drugs, bomb-making materials, fake passports and licenses, collection services that served him well in college. And his cousin always came through for him. He was happy to give him a cut of the profits.

It was a straight drive to Amber's house.

He needed to get rid of Marlee and make it look like an accident. But how?

JOE FINISHED DRINKING his coffee and went back for another. He wasn't sure how long it took for a woman to try on bathing suits, but Marlee had been in the shop a while. He sighed, remembering another woman. A beautiful, kind young woman. It always seemed like hours waiting for her to shop, even though she never had money to buy anything. But he loved every minute of it. Not going there. He shook his head and concentrated on the time.

He'd give Marlee another fifteen minutes before he went looking for her.

A long fifteen minutes later, Joe sauntered into the shop. Rows of bathing suits and bikinis in every color assaulted his eyes. How could anyone choose? Give him black trunks, and he was a happy camper.

He glimpsed around the shop. Empty. *What the hell?* Where was Marlee? He called her name. No answer. Maybe she was in the dressing room and couldn't hear him.

Shit, he did not want to go back to the dressing rooms. Ben would kill him if he saw Marlee naked, even if it was by accident. And where were the salespeople? The store was so quiet. Too quiet. The hairs on the back of his neck prickled.

He walked toward the back of the store and saw a lump of red on the floor. Was it Marlee? He ran over. No. It was a young woman moaning, holding the side of her face, and trying to sit up. He started to help her up but stopped. Marlee was his charge. He would deal with the woman later. Propping the young woman up against a wall, he told her to hang tight. He would get help.

Joe raced toward the dressing rooms while pulling out his gun. He pushed aside the beach-themed curtain covering the first changing room. Looked in. Empty. Creeping along, he repeated the action on the second room. Empty.

He pulled the curtain back on the third changing room, which looked like a war zone. The wall had several holes in it. It looked like Marlee had struggled. She was gone. How? Where? Why didn't he hear her scream for help? Oh, yeah. Because he was outside having coffee.

He yelled her name again. Nothing. Looking down, he saw her purse contents lying all over the floor as well as the bathing suits she was trying on. Shit, Shit, Shit. Not good. Ben was going to kill him.

He whipped out his phone and dialed Ben. "Marlee's gone."

BEN WAS IN A PANIC. When he got Joe's call, the one thing he didn't expect to hear was Joe telling him Marlee was missing. Sam was driving him and Luke over to the shop. He was glad Sam was driving. The way his hands were shaking, he didn't think he would be able to.

As Sam parked, Ben raced into the shop to find two police officers dealing with a sobbing young woman.

Joe was standing to one side and motioned to Ben.

"Where the hell is she?" Ben roared. He pushed Joe into the wall.

Joe pushed back and stepped into Ben's personal space. "Calm down, man. Getting angry isn't going to help."

Ben took a deep breath. He needed—no, wanted to punch something, someone, but he needed to find Marlee first. Luke and Sam walked into the shop and were now talking to the cops and the woman.

"Come with me." Joe led Ben to the side of the store and pointed to a dressing room. "This is where Marlee was abducted."

Ben took in the contents strewn around the floor. The bathing suits Marlee tried on, the contents of her purse—innocent items—and felt sick. His woman put up a fight, but she would be no match for a strong man. He was confident Robert was behind this.

"Where the hell were you?" He couldn't contain his anger. One job. One job was all that they had to do. Protect Marlee. Now she was gone. They failed. He failed.

"Marlee wanted to go in alone to try on bathing suits. I was sitting outside having a cup of coffee waiting for her. I didn't notice anyone following or watching her. No one went into the shop, at least not using the front door. When it seemed like she was taking too long, I came in." He opened his arms. "This is what I found. I'm sorry, man."

Joe was distraught. Pissed. But at this point, Ben didn't care. Marlee was missing, and Joe was supposed to be guarding her.

He felt a hand on his arm. Sam was standing next to him.

"Ben, we talked to the clerk. She said a man came in through the back door. She asked him to leave. But he punched her in the face, knocked her out. She doesn't remember what he looked like, only that he was tall with dark hair.

"Has to be Robert." Sam pointed to the back door. "That's how he took her out. It leads to an alley. He must have parked his car there."

"Goddamn it, Sam," Ben yelled as he rubbed his hands through his hair. "How could this happen? Why now? We took every precaution. And how did he know she would be here?"

"I don't know, Ben, but we'll find out. Hopefully, we can tap into the surrounding security cameras, and they might tell us something."

Ben bent down to pick up the contents of Marlee's purse. He knew he shouldn't. He had been a cop, after all. But there might be something in this mess to help them find her. He picked up her wallet, a brush, some makeup, her phone. Oh God, she didn't even have her phone to call for help.

He swiped at an errant tear. *Stay safe, sprite. I'll find you.* He looked around again, saw a small clump of hair—Marlee's hair. He clenched his fist. *Goddamn son of a bitch.* He was going to kill Robert. He picked up a piggy keychain and some loose credit cards. Put the items in her purse and gave it to Joe and told him to put it in the car. Joe raised his brow but didn't question him. There might be something in it to help Marlee, and he wanted KnightGuard on it, not the police.

There wasn't much more they could do. They spoke to the officers, hoping to get more details, but the cops didn't have any information to add. The clerk was still sobbing and couldn't tell them anything.

They walked out. Joe and Luke promised to meet Ben at home. Home. Ben wasn't sure he wanted to go back to the house. Without Marlee in it, it was just a house, not a home.

Sam drove back to the office with Ben so he could get his

car. Neither spoke. The ride was painfully quiet—each lost in thought.

When they arrived at the office, Sam promised to get Phil looking at the shop's security tapes before the cops asked the owner for them.

Ben got in his car. Numb. His mind was numb. His thoughts were going a million miles an hour, sending brave thoughts to Marlee. Would she feel he was close? Was she afraid? Did she know he would move mountains to get to her? A tear slid down his face. He didn't bother wiping it away. Too many others would soon join it.

As he approached his house, he spotted Joe's car coming in the opposite direction. Ben prayed he wouldn't beat the shit out of Joe. Although this could have happened to any one of them, it happened on his watch to his woman. His woman. The woman he loved. The woman he promised to protect. He failed. Who knew bathing-suit shopping could be so dangerous?

MARLEE WAS COMING around when Robert drove into Amber's carport. He couldn't leave it here. Thankfully he had one of Ray's extra cars but still would move it to the next block shortly. She moaned a little and tried to open her eyes. He hoped she would be out longer. But it would be easier and less conspicuous if she could walk into the house on her own instead of him throwing her over his shoulder.

Amber met him at the door. "Whaaat?"

"Amber, open the damn door. I need to get her inside."

She opened the door wide, and Robert walked a woozy Marlee into a guest bedroom. He took a needle out of his pocket and injected Marlee again. *Thank you, cousin Ray.* She tried to lift her arms to punch him but missed. He tied her arms to the bed frame and covered her.

Robert had sleeping pills to put in Marlee's water later, but right now, he needed her out of it. He also needed to come up with a plan.

"Bobby, what are we going to do with Marlee? Why did you bring her here?" Amber sounded worried.

"Spur of the moment opportunity. I had nowhere else to bring her." Robert put his arms around her shoulders and drew her close. "Relax, babe. This is the beginning of the end. I'll take care of Marlee soon, and then we'll be sitting on the beach sipping margaritas and having sex every hour."

Kissing her gently on the lips, Amber pulled him close. "Oh, you say the sweetest things." She rubbed her breasts against his chest, and his cock got hard. It always got hard around her.

Marlee was forgotten. His cock needed attention now. Finally, capturing Marlee put him in a fine mood.

"So, tell me again. How did you find Marlee?"

It was an hour later, and they were at the kitchen table. Robert took a sip of coffee. "Sheer luck. I was driving downtown, and who did I see get out of a car but Marlee? She wasn't with the boyfriend." He told her the whole story.

CHAPTER TWENTY-NINE

One hour missing.

Marlee had been missing for one excruciating hour. No calls from her. No one had seen her. No one had seen Robert. Not at work, not at home. There was no ransom note—not that Ben expected one. The police were called in and checking out Robert's condo, speaking with Amber and Marlee's friends. Nothing.

Ben was regretting his decision to stay at the safe house in case she called. He studied the house that Marlee made into a little home for them, even if it was temporary. He recalled her laughing at his dismay when she bought the colorful pillows for the couch. Pillows, for Christ's sake. Real men didn't do pillows, is what he told her. *It's just a couple of pillows, Ben. Not the end of the world. I'm not redecorating.* If she were only here, he would buy her a shitload of pillows. They would be drowning in pillows. Ben picked one up and pressed it to his face. Coconut and lavender. Marlee. His soul was crying.

Joe came in a few minutes later with Luke right behind him. He put Marlee's purse down on the table and put his palms out. "Man, I'm so sorry."

Ben saw red. He stomped over to Joe and let one rip. Caught Joe right on the jaw. Joe was knocked back by the blow. Joe shook his head, rubbed his jaw, and stepped into Ben's space. "Again, I'm sorry. I'll give you that one, but if you ever punch me again, all bets are off."

Luke was watching the action and shook his head. "Ben, you okay now? If not, go into the other room until you calm down. We are not turning on each other. This could have happened to any one of us."

Ben was shaking with anger and frustration. But Luke was right. It could have—it had— happened to them. To him. They weren't gods who could control evil. Just men. He had to accept that.

He eyed Joe and figured he would be sporting a nice bruise on his cheek later. "I apologize. Not for punching you but for blaming you."

Joe nodded. "Fair enough." He put out his hand.

The hour passed slowly as a sloth crossing the road and still no word from Marlee or about Marlee. Sam had every available body out looking for her. Checking Robert's company, his condo, every known address, restaurant, any place he had been. No Robert. Phil was checking security feeds surrounding the store and Robert's condo.

Ben debated whether to tell her dad and grandma she was missing. He thought it best to wait a few more hours and prayed she would be found before he confessed to them that he lost her. He didn't relish passing on the fact he hadn't protected her. He wandered around the safe house, going from room to room, not knowing what to do with himself. Joe was drinking a beer and trying to keep him calm. It wasn't working.

Ben banged his hands down on the kitchen counter. "Goddamn, where is she?"

Joe shrugged. It was a rhetorical question.

Joe's cell phone rang. A few grunts later, he turned to Ben and Luke.

"Ok, Sam asked that we come to the office. Phil has the video feed to go over."

"I'll meet you there," said Luke, who had driven his own car.

The ride over was quiet. Joe drove Ben's truck since he was in no condition to concentrate on the road. Joe was a quiet sort of guy, and Ben was surprised when Joe turned the engine off and told him to get out. They were already at the office.

Sam had pulled in every spare person. The cubicles were full. Multiple voices were questioning, cajoling people, begging for information. But Ben walked past them all into Sam's office. The place he considered his second home now felt alien. He prayed Phil had something for them.

"What do you have?"

Sam looked up from her desk. "Good, you're here. Let's go into the projection room."

Harrison and Pete were already sitting down at the gray, U-shaped table. A computer was set up, its screen mirrored on a big monitor on the wall. Sam, Ben, and Joe took the remaining seats.

"Phil will be here in a minute to show us what he has," Sam said, opening a notebook.

Ben noticed a whiteboard in the corner with Marlee's name on it, and he wanted to tear it apart. His woman, the woman who trusted him to protect her, was gone. Failure. Now she was just a name on a piece of cardboard.

He could only pray they got her back alive. Any mental stress she suffered, a professional could help with. Robert, *that bastard,* he would deal with personally. He looked up to the heavens and swore to God that he would never let her out of sight again if they could only find her and have her be safe. He swore he would love her for the rest of his life.

"Hey everyone, let me set this down, and we'll start." Phil walked in with his computer and looked over at Ben. "I'm sorry to hear about Marlee. Hopefully, someone will recognize something we can use."

Ben nodded.

Phil started by telling them he was still having problems with the financials. While he found a couple of accounts buried deep, they were small. There were probably others with significant amounts of money in them.

Then he showed them a feed from a neighbor's house the day Ben's house blew up. They watched a delivery man hand Marlee the package. She glanced at the package, surprised and happy. The package Marlee said was from her dad. Ben sighed. How had this case gotten so messy?

"Damn, Phil, we already know this."

Phil held up his hand. "Wait, there's more."

He went to a street over and pointed out a telephone truck that had been sitting there for over an hour. No one ever got out of it. Phil called the telephone company, but they didn't have anyone scheduled to be on that street that day.

They had to assume the person sitting in it set off the bomb by cellphone.

Ben groaned as he watched he and Marlee rushing over to his burning home. The anguish in his face and the distress on Marlee's face only added to the drama. He watched as they hugged each other and then were turned away by the firefighters.

Phil pulled up pictures of Ray Bilotti.

"So, Luke gave me information on Robert's cousin. Here's Bilotti, a local crime figure. I checked his background, and he is Robert Gilligan's mother's cousin. Bilotti is into fake IDs, drugs, bombs, runs a local whorehouse; you name it, he does it. An across-the-board despicable guy. And I bet he was behind the bomb that destroyed Ben's house."

He pulled up a couple more pictures. He pointed to a short, rotund man. "This is Tony Tomasco, aka 'Double T,' Bilotti's enforcer and all-around handyman."

Sam looked at the picture of Tony and shook her head. "Amazing. He looks so ordinary, like someone's uncle."

"Right." Phil snorted. "If their uncle is into pain and suffering. The man is a pig. Word on the street is that he loves to hurt people."

"Yeah, he was involved in Robert's loan enforcement at UCONN," chimed in Luke.

They looked at more footage of the accounting firm—nothing out of the ordinary. People were going about their business as if nothing were wrong.

Phil went through the rest of the information he had. Nothing there that would point to where Marlee was. Ben felt despair on a major scale. Nothing. They weren't any closer to finding her. Failure.

"Ben, I just remembered you said that you found Marlee's phone. I don't have it. Do you?" asked Phil.

"Shit, yes." He stood up. "I forgot I have her purse in the car. Do you want it now or later?"

Phil took a moment. "Well, since we're going over everything now, why don't we take a break, and you can get it?"

Ben wasn't sure if Marlee's phone would have any answers. But while everyone took a coffee break, he went to his truck and brought back her purse.

Emptying it on the table, he picked up the phone and handed it to Phil.

Phil poked through the spilled contents and picked up the pink pig keyring. "Haven't seen one of these in a while."

"A pink pig keyring?" asked Ben. Ben felt sure Phil was losing it.

"No, a pink pig keyring thumb drive. They make all kinds of shapes." He put his hand in his pocket and pulled out a bullet to show them. "Thumb drive. I also gave a Power Ranger one to my niece."

"Holy shit, was it in Marlee's purse all along?" asked Ben.

Settling down, they continued to look at the pictures. When Phil got to the bathing suit shop's feed, Ben watched as Marlee happily picked out bathing suits, including a couple of bikinis to try on. He wanted to reach out and kiss her.

Then the black moment when Robert come in the back door, approached the clerk and clocked her. Groans came from around the table. They followed Robert as he peeked out the front windows and then walked back to the dressing rooms. The cameras only caught the hallway, not inside the dressing rooms.

They observed him opening the curtains to the other dressing rooms. Then saw him smile as he realized Marlee was in the last dressing room. He stalked toward it.

Ben's heart was racing. He didn't want to look. He knew what was coming but was still unprepared when he saw the surprise in Marlee's eyes as Robert tried to drag her into the hall.

They watched as Marlee kicked out. Her tiny, bare feet tried to kick Robert in the balls and but bounced off his thigh instead. Robert smirked. Bile was backing up Ben's throat.

They watched her trying to defend herself with her purse, the contents spilling everywhere.

As they watched, Robert put his arm around her waist and yanked her hair so hard, her mouth opened in a wide "O." There was a chorus of groans when Robert pulled back and punched her in the stomach so hard, she doubled over. Ben couldn't watch anymore. He looked down at the table but looked up again. He needed to be here for Marlee. He moaned as Robert took out a needle and jabbed Marlee until she collapsed in his arms.

Ben was itching to punch someone, something. He couldn't sit still anymore. He got up and punched the wall. Was preparing to punch it again when Luke and Joe restrained his arms.

"Goddamn motherfucking ass. I'm going to kill him. How dare he hurt a small, delicate woman like Marlee?"

Luke snorted. "Small, yes, but delicate, no way. She's a goddamn spitfire. Did you see her put up a fight?"

They led Ben over to a chair. "Can we let you go now, killer?" asked Luke.

Ben nodded. Luke let go of his arms. He winced when he looked at Sam, the hole in the wall and his bloodied knuckles.

"The answer to your question is yes. I will be taking that out of your pay. Sit down." Sam turned to Luke. "There's a whiskey bottle in my bottom drawer. Can you get it and a glass?"

Luke left to get the bottle, and Phil started the slideshow again.

The next group of pictures was more of the same but of an earlier date. Random photos of Robert going to the office like nothing was wrong. Robert going to his condo. Robert going about his everyday life while Marlee was being stalked. Ben was getting agitated again. Why should Robert have a life when Marlee was missing?

Robert here, there and everywhere. Robert seemed to like staying at hotels by the beach. They had shots of him spending weekends there. He always appeared alone, although there were lots of people walking in and out.

"Whoa," yelled Joe.

"What? Do you see something?" Ben asked. His mind was a blur, and he was still angry. What had he missed? No one stood out in the pictures. Men, women, kids, they all looked the same.

"Phil, get in tighter on the last couple of pictures."

Phil enhanced the pictures.

"Dude. Look at the brunette. Recognize her?" Joe asked Ben.

Ben squinted at the picture. It was a little blurry. The brunette? Where the hell had he seen her? "Holy shit. That's Amber Logan."

"Amber? As in Marlee's landlord and friend?" Sam asked

"Yeah. What the hell is she doing with Robert? What am I missing? Is he fucking her?"

Phil looked up the name of the hotel and pulled up its records. No one asked how.

"It looks like the room was under her name, and reservation was for two people. I bet she's his girlfriend. Maybe she knows something about Marlee's disappearance?" Phil said.

"And I bet Amber was the one who told Robert about Marlee and Emily having coffee. And had his cousin send the goon after Marlee," said Sam as she slammed her fist on the table.

Ben noticed the coldness in her eyes. He was glad Sam was on Marlee's side because shit was going to fall. But he wasn't waiting around for Sam and KnightGuard or the police to get Marlee.

He got up and gathered his things.

"Where are you going?" Sam asked as she turned from her whiteboard.

"I'm going over to Amber's and force her to tell me the truth."

Sam put her hands up, "Ah, just wait up. You can't go over half-cocked." She turned to the crew. "Ten minutes. Ten minutes people to come up with a game plan."

Ben started walking toward the door. He would do this

alone. He didn't need help. His woman was waiting. He failed once with Kimmie. He wasn't failing again.

"Stop. Ben, I know you're anxious to get Marlee, but running off willy-nilly won't help her. I need you to stay until we have all the information we need. If Amber is involved and we scare her, we may never find Marlee. Sit down." Sam wasn't asking.

The desire to confront Amber about Marlee and wanting people having his back warred with his mind. Ben knew Sam would fire him if he walked out. Although at this point, he didn't need the job. But he did need her help, and Sam was right. He couldn't do this alone. If Amber wasn't at her house or with Robert, and they disappeared, they might never find Marlee.

Ben sat down.

"Holy shit," exclaimed Phil. He was quietly fiddling in the corner with the thumb drive on his laptop. "It's all here—Robert's second set of books. Marlee had the information the whole time. Did she know it?"

"I don't think so. She would have said something already or given it to us," Ben said. "It was only luck that I picked up her purse."

Sam was jotting down items on the whiteboard. "Okay, let's write down what we know, then go get our girl."

MARLEE'S STOMACH WAS ROILING. She couldn't see. Something covered her eyes. She struggled to remove it, but she couldn't move her hands. She was groggy. Where the hell was she? Not home for sure.

She moaned and heard a voice whispering. "She's awake. What are we going to do?"

"We're going to do exactly what we discussed. Get a glass of water."

She heard footsteps walking away. Marlee turned her face in that direction and was blinded by light when someone pulled the blindfold off. Squinting, she looked up into the face of a man. A man she recognized. Robert. Oh, shit. He was smirking.

"Well, Miss Nosy, here we are. Finally."

Marlee struggled with the ties, but she couldn't loosen them. "You bastard. Let me loose."

"Not on your life." He grinned. "Actually, the ties are the least of your problems. I wouldn't bet on your life anytime soon. I just haven't decided how to end it yet." He opened his arms. "Enjoy this little respite while you can."

A brunette woman came in. "Bobby, here's the water."

A familiar voice. No. Couldn't be.

"Amber?"

"Hello, Marlee. Long time no see." Amber moved closer to her, her hair tousled, a small smile on her face.

"What the hell are you doing here?"

Amber looked like she didn't want to answer but finally made up her mind and shrugged. "Bobby and I have plans. You ruined them. I'm a little upset with you."

"You're upset with me? Are you crazy? I'm the one tied up here. I lost my home. I lost my job. Jim was murdered. And for what?" Marlee asked, looking at Robert. "Him?"

She had been betrayed by a woman she considered a friend. It hurt, but not as much as death would.

"And why? Why me? I thought we were friends."

"Not hardly. You were a means to an end." Amber handed Robert the glass and walked out.

"Well, Jim was murdered because he was an idiot and nosy, and you're going to die for the same reasons," Robert said.

"You're not going to get away with this. You're both crazy.

Ben and KnightGuard will find you," she yelled, mentally praying it was true.

Robert shook his head. "I don't think so. Most definitely not in time to save you. Amber and I have been very careful. The money is hidden well. No one knows about Amber and me. The only loose end is the thumb drive. And you. So, where is it?"

Marlee was confused. *A thumb drive?* That's what crazy one and crazy two wanted? A thumb drive?

"I don't know what you're talking about. I don't have a thumb drive."

"You do. Jim wouldn't lie. He told me he gave it to you as he was begging for his life. I should have killed you in the office that night and been done with all this nonsense. Amber and I could be lounging on the beach drinking margaritas right now."

"I don't have it. I don't know where it could be." Hoping for a little reprieve, she said, "Maybe it was lost when my house was trashed or in the fire."

"Nah, we checked your house carefully. Nothing." Robert shrugged. "Doesn't matter now."

He dumped the contents of a pill in the water and approached her, holding the glass. "Not taking a chance you'll spit out a pill. Open up. You must be thirsty."

"Uh, I don't think so." She turned her head.

"I think so." Robert forced Marlee's head around. She tried hitting him with her elbows but had no power with her hands tied. She tried biting his fingers—no luck. She squirmed away from him best she could. But she was too weak and not able to fend him off.

"Amber, get the hell in here," he yelled.

When Amber came back in, he asked her to hold Marlee down, and he put the glass to her lips. Marlee kept her lips pressed tight, but Robert pinched her nose until she opened her mouth. He poured the water down her throat. Swallowing and gulping for air, she managed to spit some at him but missed.

"Night, night, little Marlee. Sweet dreams." Robert put the blindfold back on and walked out.

Seeing Amber with Robert was shocking. Marlee knew Ben would be searching for her, but they never figured on Amber. She hoped he would find her before it was too late but wasn't optimistic. God, she loved him. She never imagined answering a client's phone call would lead to murder, Jim's, or hers. Or to love, for that matter. *Ben, please hurry.*

A faint memory kissed her thoughts. Jim had been trying to tell her something that night he was killed. What? Something about a present he gave her. Something about proof of Robert's embezzling. What did Robert say? She was so tired, thinking hurt. Marlee had no idea what Jim was talking about then or now. But it seemed important. Could it have been about the thumb drive? Too late now.

Ben's kiss was the last thing she thought of before she drifted off into darkness.

CHAPTER THIRTY

F our hours missing

Four hours of not finding Marlee. They were coordinating with the police, who were looking for Robert.

Four hours of sheer hell, wondering if she was OK. Where she was, and did she know Ben was doing everything possible to find her?

Luke had Amber's house under surveillance, but he reported there was no unusual activity. Robert wasn't hanging around. Luke had knocked once, and Amber had opened the door. He asked about Marlee and Robert. After a graphic description about where he could put his questions, she told him in no uncertain terms she hadn't seen Marlee. And it was none of his business who she dated. She also didn't know anything about Robert embezzling or a Jim Matthews. She slammed the door in his face. The police were waiting on a warrant to search her house.

Joe had Robert's condo in his sights. Robert hadn't been there in a week, according to the doorman, and Phil couldn't find any payments to hotels under his name. So, where the hell was he? Phil checked again under Amber's name, but there were only a couple of reservations weeks ago. They figured Robert was paying cash or using a fake ID.

Four hours of knocking on doors, following up with people. Four hours of agony.

The thumb drive proved Robert was embezzling. Jim had managed to find Robert's hidden books and put them on a thumb drive. They would probably never know how. If Robert agreed to pay the money back, he still likely wouldn't serve much time. The gun that killed Jim wasn't registered. The police hadn't changed their minds that Jim's murder was a robbery gone bad, so they couldn't pin his murder on Robert. Amber didn't have any money in a hidden account, Phil found she did have a property in her name in the Caymans.

Where the hell was Marlee?

Ben and Sam were going to take another crack at Amber. They were less than ten minutes away when Luke called to tell them Amber just left pulling a suitcase and did they want him to follow her?

"Is she alone?" Sam asked.

"Yep, but she's planning on taking off for sure."

"Follow her. We're not far away. Call when you find out where she's going."

"Will do."

Having Amber leave was making things a little easier. Sam said she had no problem breaking into Amber's house for clues, especially since Amber wasn't there.

They were discussing what to look for and hopefully clues as to Marlee's location when the phone rang. She put it on speaker.

"Sam, it's Phil. Isn't Marlee's address 6208 Seagull?"

She looked at Ben, who nodded.

"Why?"

"Just monitored a call from the fire department. There's a reported house fire, and they're on their way there."

"Jesus, what does that mean? Could Marlee be in the house?" Ben was frantic. "Drive faster."

"Ben, I'm driving as fast as I can on these narrow side streets. We'll be there in a minute."

They heard the sirens screeching before they saw the fire truck passing by them, racing toward Marlee's house. By the time they reached the beginning of Marlee's street, the road was blocked off. Sam parked near a neighbor's house, and they ran toward her home.

Two more fire trucks, an ambulance, and multiple police cars were in front of Amber's house. Firefighters were getting hoses out. Police were keeping people away. Several first responders were there with their equipment. People were yelling. Flashing lights. Sirens. It was chaos.

The smoke. The heat. The flames. Ben was frantic. Was Marlee in the house?

Sam knew the fire chief. She went over to tell him that they suspected a woman was in the house. He yelled the information to his men.

They were spraying water on the flames.

A boom. A small explosion, but it took more of the house with it.

Ben ran toward Marlee's house, but two firefighters grabbed him. He was pulled back.

"You sons of bitches, my girl is in there," Ben shouted. He got a good punch into someone's gut before they hauled him off the firefighter.

The flames were spitting embers on the ground. Hot, red flames were angrily reaching toward the sky, crackling, dancing, leaping. No one was getting in or out.

He tried to run in again but was restrained by Sam and two cops.

"Stop," Sam yelled. "There's nothing we can do."

They stared at the fire's flames beckoning to them—it was an invitation to hell.

"Ben, the fire is too hot. We don't even know if Marlee is in there." Sam and the cops had a death grip on him.

"Get your fucking hands off me. My woman is in there." Ben struggled but couldn't get out of their grasp.

Suddenly, another explosion. Whatever was left of the house blew up and crumbled on itself.

Ben roared. *No. Please, God, please tell me Marlee isn't in it.*

He shook off the hands holding him back and stomped over to Amber's house. Kicking in the door, he yelled, "Marlee!"

No answer. He was on a rampage. Sam followed him.

The house was too quiet—no one was there. Ben raced into each room, yelling Marlee's name.

In the guest bedroom, he spotted a rag and sleeping pills. There were restraints on the bed. He bent down and smelled the pillow. It smelled like Marlee—coconut, and lavender.

"Oh, dear God, she was here." Ben moaned into the pillow. "Oh, my God."

He flung the pillow down and raced outside, screaming again that there was someone in the house.

Too late.

The house was destroyed. Burned to a crisp. Just a charred skeleton. Smoldering ash and smoke permeated the air. As small flames ignited, they were put out. The firefighters aimed their hoses at it, trying to keep it contained.

"Marlee," Ben screamed. Then he dropped to his knees, hands over his face. His tears flowed like rain.

Sam rubbed his back and tried to help him up. "Ben, there's nothing more we can do here. We need to leave."

"I can't. I can't leave. I need to find Marlee."

"Marlee's dead. There isn't anything you can do now." Sam hugged him tightly.

Leading him back to the car, Sam told Ben she wanted to talk to the fire chief one more time.

Ben got into the car. Marlee. His brave, sassy sprite had been burned alive in that house. Big sobs surfaced from deep in his gut. How could he go on without her? What would he tell her dad and grandma, who thought he was protecting her? He failed again. How could he ever look at himself in the mirror?

He was going to kill Robert and Amber when they were found. Where did they go? Didn't matter. Until the end of his days, he would search for them.

It was a good hour before the firefighters got the fire under control. Sam came back to check on him a couple of times. Several employees from KnightGuard had driven over and were murmuring among themselves just outside his window, letting him mourn in private.

Suddenly a cheer went up. What the fuck? Who was cheering? There was nothing to cheer about.

Sam screamed, "Ben! Ben. Come quick."

Ben looked over at her and saw a fireman carrying a woman's limp body.

Could it be?

Marlee?

Was she alive?

He got out of the car and raced over.

Yes.

It was Marlee. Beaten, bruised, burned. But she was alive.

"We were clearing bushes behind the house when I heard a cat howling and went to investigate. The damn cat was sitting on her chest, hissing and growling at us. Wouldn't let us near her until one of our female firefighters, came over. I bet Marlee crawled out a window and then passed out over there," said the fireman, pointing to the back of the house.

Ben looked toward heaven and said, "*Thank you.*" This was his Marlee. His sprite. His ninja warrior. She was small and fierce. A fighter. More importantly, she was alive.

The medics rushed over and placed Marlee on a gurney and started oxygen. He didn't want to leave her, but the medics wouldn't let him in the ambulance. Neither would the damn, wonderful cat who was keeping guard of Marlee.

Sam and Ben hugged each other, tears in all their eyes. She bent down to pat Jeffrey, who was slithering around her legs and then jumped into her arms. "Oh, you sweet thing. Let's get you into my car." Stupid cat was purring in her ear.

It was a day of miracles, Ben thought. First, Marlee being found and then the damn cat protecting Marlee and taking a liking to Sam. He only hoped it would let him in the car.

Sam touched his arm. Sam and Ben hugged each other, the damn brave cat between them, tears in all their eyes.

"Let's get to the hospital and see our girl," Sam said.

Robert gleefully watched the fiasco unfolding from an empty lot a half block down. The lot was filled with brush, and he didn't think anyone would notice him. He couldn't see everything going on, but he cheered as the flames shot into the sky, and Marlee's house went boom. His job here was done. He turned and walked a block over to get his car.

What a disaster this almost turned into. He had sent Amber ahead to the motel room they rented. She didn't need to see what he was going to do. Their flight was scheduled to leave in the morning. When that nosy security guy knocked on Amber's door to ask about Marlee, Robert knew he had to push everything up. It would have been nice to have the house burn down at night when people were sleeping, and the response would have been slower. But he always had a plan B.

Luckily, Amber's back door faced away from the street. He wrapped Marlee's inert form in a sheet. She was sleeping soundly, and while he didn't care if she died or not, he preferred that she sleep through the fire. After thoroughly researching how to start a gas leak fire, he decided to have cousin Ray give him another phone bomb.

One problem solved. Now on to the next. His cock was hard. His woman was waiting. And he was going to satisfy her every need before they left the country and began their next big adventure.

CHAPTER THIRTY-ONE

Ben held Marlee's limp, bandaged hand, and stared at the small woman lying so still in the hospital bed. Her hands and feet were bound. He knew they bandaged the side of her body as well. Her face was smudged, and her long auburn hair was singed at the edges and full of branches and leaves, reminding him of the first time he met Marlee. His sprite. How could he have known at the time how important she would become to him? How much he loved her.

Taking a deep breath, Ben thanked God she was alive. The doctor didn't think she inhaled too much smoke. How she got out of that room, especially being drugged, was a miracle and a story for another day.

Marlee sighed and opened her eyes. Sleepy blue eyes. "Ben," she whispered.

"I'm here, sweetcheeks. How are you feeling?"

"Better, now that you're here." She swallowed hard, hoarse from the smoke. "Can I go home?"

Marlee tried to sit up, but her bandaged hands threw her off. "Ouch. What happened?"

Ben lifted her up and put a pillow behind her head. "All I know is somehow you climbed out the bedroom window and passed out in the bushes behind your house."

Marlee gave a little smile. "That seems to be my life. Traipsing through the flora and fauna of Florida." She closed her eyes.

ROBERT CAME in with another glass of water. She didn't want to drink it. He was putting something in it that was making her sleepy. She heard them talking and making plans to kill her. Oh, Ben. Could you speed up the rescue? I don't know how long I can last. Please. Determined this time not to swallow as much or to throw it up, she fought Robert when he tried to get her to drink. She could smell gas on his hands and wanted to gag. He slapped her face this time. "Bitch, you can drink this or be awake when you're burned to a crisp."

She drank. When Robert left, she turned on her side. Her hands were tied in front of her. She brought them up and tried to get her finger in her mouth. If she could vomit, she would be awake and maybe have a chance to save herself. Her hands wouldn't fit in her mouth. She tried just her thumbs. Gagging. Pushing down her tongue again. Gagging. Then the water gushed out as she turned on her side. Drained, she lay back down and fell asleep.

Marlee was groggy and thought an hour or so passed when Robert came back again. She fought to stay awake, but she was so sleepy. He wrapped her in a sheet and slung her over his shoulder, mumbling about dead weight. "Amber, open that back door so that I can get out."

She didn't dare open her eyes. He still smelled like gas and sweat. She prayed she wouldn't vomit on him. He would know she wasn't sleeping soundly. She heard him open another door and walk into her house. At least that's what it sounded like. He threw her on the bed.

"Bobby, this is insane. I hate what you're doing."

"Amber, this is the only way. They'll never know we put her body here. Besides, we'll be long gone before anyone finds her. Look, why don't you get your suitcase and meet me at the motel. I'll take care of this."

Amber protested, but Robert insisted. "Go, baby. I've got this."

Marlee heard Amber leave. Robert was outside her door doing whatever to kill her. She heard him close the door. Marlee forced her eyes open. She must have swallowed more than she vomited because her arms were limp. She was still groggy.

What had Robert said? Start a fire? Blow up the house? ? Oh, dear God. Ben would never find her in time. She loved him so much. So, this was how her life was going to end? Going out in a big bang? She always wished more from life but dying early wasn't what she wished for. She felt a tear slide down her face.

She tried to lift her arms. So heavy. How much time did she have? How does one even blow up a house? And why was she even wasting time thinking about that? She was going to die if she didn't stop pitying herself and get out of here.

Rolling over to her side, she managed to get off the bed. More like falling out of it, but who cared. She felt like a sloth. Pulling herself up to the window, she tried to open it. No strength. She needed both hands free. But how? Time was running out. At least she thought it was. She was still here, right?

She pushed at the window with all her might. Nothing.

She heard a pop outside the door. Oh God, this was it.

She remembered she put her box of belongings in the closet. Hammer. There was a hammer in it. She crawled over. She could smell smoke now.

She reached into the box and felt around. Where the hell was the hammer? She pulled out the calendar, some knickknacks. Finally, she got it out of the box only to drop it. She was choking on smoke. Couldn't stop the coughing. The air was acrid. She pulled the hammer between her hands, creeping backward until she reached the window.

Forcing herself up, she held on to the sill. It was now or never. Smoke was snaking its way under the door.

The first strike bounced off the glass. The second shattered the glass. She was thankful Amber never installed hurricane-resistant glass.

Smoke was filling the room.

Not much time. The fire was close.

She gagged. It was hard to breathe.

Marlee struck the window again and made a bigger hole. There were so many jagged pieces of glass. She frantically hit them with the hammer. The smoke curled under the door and around the ceiling like a gray snake beckoning to her.

Pulling herself up the sill, her tied hands hindered her. She fell back. She tried again and managed to push out the screen. She forced her body over the sill, the shards of grass catching her side, gouging her. She plunged to the ground. Jesus, it was hard and full of little branches. Amber really ought to rake up around here. Why would she care about Amber raking? She was delusional, that was the only answer.

Her hands took the brunt of the fall. Sharp branches punctured her skin. Pain. Using her elbows, she snaked to some bushes about a million miles away. Tired. She was so tired.

She closed her eyes for a moment. She heard Jeffrey purring. Was she in heaven? Then peace.

She never heard the firefighters coming. Or the sirens. Or Ben calling her.

Waking up in the hospital and seeing Ben's sweet face was the best gift ever.

IT WAS a couple of hours later that Marlee opened her eyes again. Ben thought they looked more focused and clearer. Their friends kept vigil in the waiting room. Her family was anxious to see her; they'd stopped in for a few minutes earlier but allowed him to stay with Marlee. His parents were on their way.

"Hey, sweetcheeks, you're back."

"Hmmm." His angel. His sprite. She had a little smile on her face, and he bent over to kiss her.

Marlee looked around the hospital room. "Ben. How long have I been here?" she whispered. The smoke still clogged her throat.

"Just a little while. Sam has some pull here, and they found a private room for you."

"My dad? Grandma?"

"Out in the waiting room with everyone else. I'll go get them."

He walked out to give everyone the news she was awake. A big cheer went out. Ben let her dad and grandma go in first. Then everyone piled in to say hello.

Marlee was overwhelmed by the gesture and started to cry. Ben wiped the tears from her eyes.

After everyone left for the day, Ben sat next to her. "When you're up for it, I want to hear how you got out of that house. I'm sorry to say there's nothing left."

Marlee thought about that for a moment. "I'll tell you later. But as for my house, I don't care what's in it. I only care that I'm here with you."

Ben leaned over and kissed her forehead. "Me too. But sweet cheeks, we are definitely going to have a talk about personal safety. Mainly yours."

She smiled and licked her lips. "Sounds like a plan. Can we do it in bed?"

Ben shook his head. This woman was going to be the death of him.

EPILOGUE

B en watched Marlee helping her grandma set the dining room table. It was a peaceful scene compared to Ben and Joe finding Robert.

Sam handed Ben a slip of paper indicating where Robert was hiding out. He didn't ask her where she got it from. He doubted she would have told him. She had secrets and connections he didn't want to know about. Sam also didn't ask what he was going to do when he got there.

Joe volunteered to come with him. Ben couldn't have asked for a better partner. They left early the next morning and knocked on a nondescript motel room by the airport. When Robert didn't answer, Ben looked around, didn't see anyone. One kick, two kicks, they were in.

Robert was coming out of the bathroom wiping his hands. His eyes narrowed and he slowly slid his hand around back of his shirt.

"Get the hell out of here," he yelled.

"Not happening, asswipe. You have a date with the cops," said Ben.

Robert sneered, reached behind his back and pulled out a gun. "The only date I have is with a flight out of this shithole."

Ben looked at Robert. Could this guy get any more stupid?

Ben and Joe separated slowly. Robert moved the gun from one to another. "I will kill you both if you don't get out of my way."

"You may kill one of us but not both. If you don't want to die, put the gun down," Joe said softly. They slowly moved back and forth in front of Robert.

"Not happening." Robert's eyes were wide. His body stiff. His hands never shook.

Bam.

Joe yelped and went down. Ben took a quick look, Joe was shot in the thigh, blood oozing onto the carpet. Joe struggled to get up while reaching for his gun.

Too late.

Another shot echoed in the small room. Ben felt a hot bullet whiz by his left arm. "Damn," he shouted.

Ben's arm was burning, but he thought it was just grazed.

Robert aimed again, but before he had a chance to pull the trigger, Ben saw red. He charged Robert, knocking the gun from Robert's hand.

Then he pulled back and punched Robert in the gut. Robert doubled over but quickly came up with a right punch and hit Ben on his injured arm.

Damn that hurt.

Ben grabbed Robert and rammed his head into the wall. Robert turned quickly and whipped out his hand, knocking Ben down and pressing on the bullet wound.

"You son of a bitch," yelled Ben. He managed to get control of Robert who was still pressing his thumb in the wound.

Ben kicked out and got direct hit into Robert's groin.

"Oouff." Robert yelled out and fell to the floor.

Ben looked for the gun just as Robert managed to pick himself up from the floor and charged. Ben kicked him again. Jesus, was this guy superhuman? A kick in the groin should have incapacitated him.

Robert spit blood from his mouth, then jumped on Ben. They both went down, with Robert on top punching Ben in the face. With a superhuman push, Ben managed to get Robert off him. Then they were both on their feet, swaying.

Ben threw a left hook and punched him in the gut. Robert grunted.

Time to end this. Ben drew back again, curled his hand into a fist and punched him again. Robert staggered backward through the sliding glass door, his arms wind milling over the balcony rail and landed on the ground.

Ben looked over the rail. Knocked out cold. His chest moving, blood flowing from the many cuts on his face from the shards of glass. The balcony was littered with bloody glass. Sirens were going off.

Joe limped over and looked at Robert's prone body. "A little overkill, but he deserved it."

EVEN THOUGH THE bandages came off a while ago, Marlee was still sore. Ben spent the afternoon helping her dad around the house with projects he couldn't do easily anymore.

Handing Marlee a dish, Grandma said, "That young man of yours is a hard worker and quite handsome."

Marlee nodded. "Yes, he is on both counts." She was watching Ben, and her dad wash up outside. Ben's shirt was off; his wound had healed and she could see his muscles rippling in his arms and chest. *Oh my.* He was handsome. Ben looked up to catch her looking and winked.

"Now if I were only twenty years younger," Grandma started.

"Grandma, if you were twenty years younger, you'd still be twenty years too old for Ben. Now leave my man alone." Marlee loved teasing her. She didn't know that Marlee knew their neighbor, Ron Brown, was sweet on her and that they went out occasionally. Marlee suspected they had sleepovers.

She shook her head. *Nope, not going there*. Grandma wasn't that old and still very attractive. What she did in her spare time was none of Marlee's business.

The men walked into the kitchen as her dad was thanking Ben again for helping.

"My pleasure, Mike. I don't get to do outside work enough."

Marlee knew Ben was still upset that renovations weren't finished at his house. Thankfully, Ben's next-door renters had moved out, and they were able to move into there.

Ben walked over to Marlee and gave her a huge kiss.

"Beeennn."

"Sweetcheeks, I think your family knows we kiss," he teased.

The conversation was lively around the dining-room table. Dinner was almost over, and Marlee thought Ben was looking squirrelly. He kept staring at her dad and then at her. All the while, smiling to himself. Squirrelly for sure.

Grandma suddenly stood up and asked Marlee to bring the dishes into the kitchen. Her favorite lemon cake was sitting on the counter, and Marlee brought it to the living room while coffee was brewing.

"Ben, I don't think we can ever thank you and Knight-Guard Security for getting back the money Robert embezzled from the company," said her dad.

"That was all Phil Harkin, IT guy extraordinaire," said Ben. "He was able to find it with help from a pink pig." He winked at Marlee.

"He didn't do anything illegal, did he?"

"Nah. We kept it legal and passed all the information on to the FBI. They were able to trace all the money back to Robert and transferred what Robert owed you back into your account. The rest of the money went back to the company. Marlee is in the clear."

Marlee sure didn't want them to worry about that. Ben had told her Phil didn't leave any fingerprints on the accounts. It was all the FBI. Her father was given total control of the company and was going to have Marlee run it.

Robert was going to prison for a long time and Marlee got the impression from Sam that she put a bug in a friend's ear and Robert would be very popular with the other inmates. Amber was arrested as she walked into the motel and was singing like a canary. She was going to be spending a good amount time in jail for her role.

Marlee served the cake and coffee and sat back on the couch next to Ben. She snuggled into his arms. This whole disaster somehow ended well. Her family had their retirement restored. Ben's house was being rebuilt. Ben's job at KnightGuard was going well, and she and Ben were in love. What else could she ask for?

"Hmmm, Marlee." His breath was hot on her shoulder. *Mmmmm.* Marlee's thoughts went south to private parts that wanted him, all sweaty two hundred pounds of hunk, thrusting into her folds.

"Yes, Ben." Sex would have to wait. *Could they leave now?* Dang. Marlee didn't think so.

Ben smirked. Could he read her thoughts? *Oh, God.* What if her dad and grandma could too? *No.* They were looking elsewhere.

"The house is going to be ready soon, and I'm hoping that when we move back into it, you'll have said yes." Ben could feel his face getting red. Sweat was dripping down his chin, his stomach flipping like a pancake. He wanted to be suave about this, but his body was ruining his plan. Mike gave him permission to ask Marlee to marry him. Now it was up to her.

"Yes, to what?" Marlee was confused. "Yes, to moving into the house? Yes, to the dress? What?"

Ben got down on one knee. "Yes, to becoming my wife. I love you, sprite. I love your sassiness and your courage. I love the way you stand up for me. I even love the way you love that da— darn cat of yours." He pulled out a small black box and opened it.

Marlee exhaled and stared at the cushion-cut diamond ring surrounded by several smaller diamonds. "Ben, it's beautiful."

"Please say yes."

"Yes, yes, yes." She jumped off the sofa, almost knocking Ben over.

He put the ring on her finger. "Your dad and grandma gave me their blessing. The center diamond was your mom's. I had the jeweler surround it with the smaller diamonds. If you don't like it, you can choose anything else you want."

Marlee wriggled her fingers, gazing at the sparkling ring. "It's beautiful. And the fact I'm wearing my mother's diamond makes it even more special." Hot tears ran down her face.

"Ben, I love the ring, and I love you."

Wrapping his arms around her, he kissed her. "Marlee, I love you, and you have just made me the happiest man alive."

Marlee turned to her dad. "Thanks, Dad. I had forgotten about Mom's ring. Now I feel blessed that I have a part of her sharing in my marriage."

"Oh honey, one of the last things your mom asked of me was to give this ring to you when you got engaged. Grandma and I are so happy for you both."

Ben couldn't believe all that happened to get them to this point. From dating a different woman every week, to getting shot on the job, to Marlee tasering him at the fish camp, to strengthening their relationship, to her almost getting killed, things had gone from bad to worse to perfect.

Robert was behind bars, hopefully enjoying the welcome committee. Amber had turned on Robert. Her dad got his retirement back. Joe was recovering well from getting shot. Marlee was running the accounting firm, and most importantly, the love of Ben's life said yes.

Life was very good, indeed.

Look for Book 3 of KnightGuard Security, *Evidence of Lies,* Pete and Julie's story. Turn the page for a preview.

As always, reviews are nice. If you enjoyed the book, please leave a review.

Follow me on:
Twitter: @lsferrariwrites
Facebook: @lilaferrariauthor
Instagram: @lsferrariwrites
Pinterest: @lsferrariwrites
Goodreads: @lilaferrariwrites
BookBub: @lilaferrariwrites

For more information on books by Lila Ferrari, visit her website at www.lilaferrariwrites.com, where you can subscribe to her newsletter to get updates on releases, fun facts and enter giveaways.

EVIDENCE OF LIES

One year ago—Georgia

Ginger Rose's body undulated to the heavy bass, the movements designed to show off her nearly naked body. She'd shed the outfit she came out in tonight—the policewoman costume with extra bells and whistles—two songs ago. She placed her cop hat temporarily on a regular's head while she worked the baton between her legs, making love to it in front of him. The men went wild—extra tips.

She strutted around, teasing the crowd with the handcuffs, and men were begging to be handcuffed to her—more extra tips.

Now, she was down to her thong and bra. The jeers, cheers, and whistles provided just so much background noise. Strobe lights lit up the stage. The heavy bass invaded her mind, helping her to move seductively across it.

Her hips swayed as she simulated making love to the pole. She bent over, swishing her hair, gyrating her butt, caressing her breasts, all moves designed to get better tips. They worked. She was one of the highest-tipped dancers at the Strip Away Club, Live Girls. *Live girls? That's a laugh. Who would want to see dead girls?* The thought made her smile as she stepped away from the pole and bent over to give one of the regulars a clear view of her privates covered only by a G-string. She stuck out her butt and shook it but side-stepped one exuberant customer who got a little too close to the goods. She was so not going there. *Look, but don't touch.*

Ginger Rose knew she wasn't big-breasted but bending and swaying like this made her breasts appear larger. Even the stilettos made her legs look longer, although she was of average height.

A Britney song was pulsating in the background, the strobe lights keeping the beat as she danced. She looked out at the tables watching men and, yes, some women eating, drinking and paying little attention to her, unlike the men in the front row, who were whistling and staring at her breasts as if they never saw breasts before. Most were drinking, salivating while she danced. Most harmless.

She took her bra off and then she was clad in her G-string and pasties—the silver police stars covering her nipples tonight. Nevertheless, her work wasn't over after this last dance. She still had two regulars who booked a lap dance from her. Both big tippers, so they would get the full treatment. No real sex but lots of pretend, and they paid highly for it.

Ginger Rose rubbed her hands sensuously up and down her breasts and then over her hips. The men groaned. She knew she was in great shape despite having a baby almost a year ago She worked hard to get back into shape, and it paid off. The ballet lessons she'd taken growing up kept her limber. The hours were good, and the tips and extra lap dances provided milk and diapers for Axl as well as food and a roof over their heads. Only the basics, nothing left over for any small pleasures or treats. But it was way better than worrying about the bill collectors and her landlord camping out at her doorstep. Some might look down at stripping, but she didn't care. A woman had to do what was necessary for her family.

"Sweetheart, bend over again. Give papa a great view of those titties."

Ginger Rose stared at the man nursing a beer in the front row. Decent-looking, dark hair, middle-aged, not sloppy drunk. He had been here before a few times but wasn't a regular. If she remembered right, he was a good tipper, so she sauntered over in front of him and bent over slowly, rubbing and shaking her star-covered breasts in front of him.

Leering at her, he groaned, "Girl, you're looking outstanding tonight. Turn around and give daddy a nice view of that very fine ass."

Ginger Rose raised an eyebrow and snapped her G-string.

"Oooh," shouted his friend as he elbowed the man. "You gotta pay for that."

Taking the hint, the man laughed and put the twenty that he had been flashing in her G-string, all the while trying to grab an extra feel. She shook her finger at him—no. Then she smiled and turned around, bent over with her ass swaying, breasts undulating back and forth to the music. Standing up, she slowly rubbed her hands over her breasts and thighs. The men went wild. She sashayed around the stage, then danced back to the man, squatted, and shook her breasts in front of him as he placed another twenty in her G-string.

She did a long stretch on the floor, seducing the audience, giving them a great view of her barely covered pussy, stretching left, then right, standing, squatting and doing the hair shake, all the while praying her brunette wig wouldn't fly off her head. Then back to the pole. Ginger Rose twirled and bucked around it another few minutes, then walked once more around the stage, shaking her tits whenever someone tucked money in her G-string.

The last song ended. She blew a kiss to the audience as she sauntered down the runway through the lighted string curtain to the dressing room. She had a half hour to change, fix her makeup and get to the private dance room. She spent a few minutes exchanging pleasantries with some of the other dancers. They were a mixed bag of full-time strippers, students and single moms trying to stay one step ahead of the bill collectors. That was her.

Makeup fixed, she pulled up the thigh-high boots and adjusted the straps of her uniform as she quickly walked to the private rooms. Her first lap dance was with a new client who requested she dress up like a nurse.

"Good night for you?" asked one of the burly guards. He didn't look familiar, but management was always hiring new bouncers. Many of them had families to support like her. His name tag read Manny. Thankfully, she worked in a decent club, and there was no hanky-panky going on in the club or drugs that she knew of. The club's owner, Henry, made sure the girls working there were safe and protected. What the girls did in their spare time outside the club was no one's business. Inside, the men behaved, or they were "escorted" out and not in a nice way.

"Great tips tonight," she answered. The guard smiled. The strippers had to share tips with the bouncers and management, so a good night for her was a good night for everyone. He saluted her and started down the hallway.

"Manny?"

The bouncer stopped and turned. "Yeah?"

"I have another dance after this one, and that guy"—she hesitated—"is a little weird."

"Weird, how?" He made a fist. "Do I need to toss him out on his ass?"

"No. Nothing like that. I'm just uncomfortable sometimes because he's always asking me to run away with him or marry him. You know, making a joke of it. But he tried to follow me once. I ... " She fiddled with the uniform strap again. "Just check on me occasionally. Okay?"

She didn't want to lose a good customer, but she also

didn't want someone creepy following her, learning where she lived. She was glad Manny would look out for her.

"Yeah, I'll keep an eye out. Give a shout out if he bothers you."

"Thanks."

Pushing open the scratched, cheap wooden door to the private room, she saw her new client was already comfortable in the armless chair. The smell of sweat and sex covered up by the overpowering vanilla scent of their cleaning liquid nauseated her. She exhaled deeply. The client stopped rubbing himself and gave her a big, toothy grin as she glided in, the background music already playing.

An hour later, Ginger Rose was on her way to her last lap dance of the evening with the other regular. He usually had no special request for her and kept his hands to himself. He was easy to please, albeit a bit creepy. He was also talker, always trying to get personal information about her, always asking her to run away with him, always making it a joke. She always smiled and shook her head.

Ginger Rose knew he had a crush on her, but he never went any further except for that one night when he had hung around outside hoping to talk to her. She got concerned and had to set him straight. He apologized, left, and it hadn't happened again.

He came to the club almost every night she danced and sat in the front row, staring at her. Definitely weird but not the only one, though. Besides, he was a good tipper. He didn't look rich, and she wondered how he could afford the drinks, tips and lap dance. She shrugged. Not her concern.

The only concern she had at this moment was performing, cleaning up, and going home to sleep. She would pick Axl up from Trish's tomorrow morning and then watch Trish's daughter while Trish worked her shift at the club. That saved her thousands of dollars she didn't have and benefitted both of them.

Stripping was not how she planned this part of her life. She always assumed she would be married to Jim and they would raise their son together. She never planned on Jim's dying. She always believed that she would finish college and establish her own business, preferably a quaint bookstore with a coffee bar. But that dream was put on hold when her mother, who was babysitting and helping her financially with Axl, died. Then Axl got so sick, she couldn't pay for doctors. So here she was. Stripping and dancing for men, making good money for part-time work. Putting her dreams on hold—for a while.

Sighing after her last lap dance, Ginger Rose changed into her street clothes, waved good night to others leaving, checked the parking lot, then walked to her car. Life was as good as it was going to get until Axl went to daycare full time and she could get a day job.

Aaron Oakman watched from the shadows as Ginger Rose and another girl walked out of the Strip Away Club. They called good night to each other, and she got in her little red car and drove off. He wanted to follow her, to see where she lived, to finally bring her to his home. But his mama's car had died a couple of months ago, and with no extra money, he was forced to walk, hitch or take the bus. He shrugged. None of those were conducive to following a person.

Although it was late at night, the air was still humid. He swiped at the drops of sweat running down his neck. He stopped to adjust himself, his cock limp, but, damn, his underwear was damp because he shot his load again while

Ginger Rose was rubbing against him. He wondered if she knew how she affected him. He'd learned to wear dark pants.

He walked around the corner to catch his bus. He was grateful they ran all hours of the night, but he would still have to walk a mile to get home. He strolled past the club, which was always busy and would be until the wee hours of the morning. Music blasted from the various bars lining the street. A few drunks who couldn't hold their alcohol shuffled around the alleys. Smells of liquor, unwashed bodies, and vomit permeated the street. People were laughing and walking around to different bars, but the Strip Away was his favorite. It's where he met Layla, God rest her soul, and now Ginger Rose.

He sat at the empty bus bench, figuring he had about a half hour to wait. Plenty of time to rehash his latest visit with Ginger Rose. His pants were getting tight again. His cock got hard every time he thought of the green-eyed, brunette beauty, how she danced just for him, rubbed her delectable breasts against him, smiled just for him. Soon he would be able to touch and fuck her as much as he wanted, and she would love it.

Learn more at lilaferrariwrites.com.

BOOKS BY LILA FERRARI

KNIGHTGUARD SECURITY SERIES

Each book in the series is a stand-alone and can be read in any order. Reviews are greatly appreciated.

Evidence of Betrayal — Book 1 (Luke and Grace's story)

Evidence of Murder — Book 2 (Ben and Marlee's story)

Evidence of Lies — Book 3 (Pete and Julie's story)

Evidence of Deceit — Book 4 (Joe and Claire's story)

Evidence of Revenge — Book 5 (Sam and Mark's story)

Evidence of Secrets — Book 6 (Hank and Laura's story) - available soon

Evidence of Evil — Book 7 (Logan and Maddie's story) — available in 2022

NEW SERIES

SEALs of Distinction – Book 1 available in 2022

Haywood Lake Mysteries — Book 1 available in 2022

ABOUT THE AUTHOR

I've been writing forever. Poems, plays, short stories, cookbooks, grants, newsletters, newspaper articles and now full-length novels.

Growing up in New England where summers are sweet but winters are long and cold has given me lots of opportunity to expand my creativity.

I have enjoyed: basket weaving, spinning wool, quilting, canning, teaching cooking and traveling.

I have been a recipe tester, sailor, farmer, shepherd, cattlewoman, chick herder and Master Gardener.

Like many women, I have worked full-time, raised two children, and helped my husband's career. Finally, I get to make my dream come true. After all, dreams never die, and new doors open every day.

Today, I live in sunny Florida with my husband enjoying paradise. In addition to writing novels, I recently took up birding and photography. My photos have done well in local contests.

My stories are about courage, redemption and second chances. Everyone deserves them, don't you agree?

Made in the USA
Columbia, SC
07 May 2024

35364845R00188